MUSEUM
PIECE

Also from Metaphorosis

Metaphorosis Magazine

Metaphorosis: Best of 20xx
Metaphorosis 20xx: The Complete Stories
annual issues, from 2016

Monthly issues

Plant Based Press

Best Vegan Science Fiction & Fantasy
annual issues, 2016-2020

from B. Morris Allen:
Chambers of the Heart: speculative stories
Susurrus
Allenthology: Volume I
Tocsin: and other stories
Start with Stones: collected stories
Metaphorosis: a collection of stories

Verdage

Reading 5X5 x3: Changes
Reading 5X5 x2: Duets
Score – an SFF symphony
Reading 5X5: Readers' Edition
Reading 5X5: Writers' Edition

Vestige

The Nocturnals, by Mariah Montoya

MUSEUM
PIECE

an unusual collection

edited by
B. Morris Allen

ISBN: 978-1-64076-360-9 (e-book)
ISBN: 978-1-64076-361-6 (paperback)
ISBN: 978-1-64076-362-3 (hardcover)

JH
Joyful Heave

from
Metaphorosis Publishing

Neskowin

CONTENTS

From the Editor

Museums are, by nature, places of mystery and curiosity. Even the dustiest, driest exhibits are there to help visitors place themselves in the past, to try to envision what life was like, why decisions were made, how people thought. It's imagination that makes museums work.

It's a theme that struck me one day when I happened to read a few museum stories in a row — including some of the ones in this book. Good museums are fascinating, curious places. And good museum stories are ones that take you places you'd never even considered going. That train of thought led directly to this anthology — a collection of great stories about weird and wonderful museums.

The museums that follow are as varied as they are unusual, from tangible to evanescent, from personal to conceptual, localized to global. Whatever their nature, all these museums are packed full of color and character. So, slide your ticket stub into a pocket, and step into our gallery of exhibits for the visit of a lifetime.

B. Morris Allen

EXHIBITS

THE MUSEUM OF LOST DREAMS

Arlen Feldman

The museum had a visitor. That happened sometimes, but not often. The museum didn't advertise. Hell, it didn't even show up on Google. But every now and then, somebody wandered in. Usually when it was raining, like now.

I took the guy's ten dollars, handed him a badly photocopied museum map, and pretended to not notice him staring down my cleavage.

"So, what sort of stuff do you have here?" he asked.

He'd given me ten dollars without even knowing what museum he was in. Well, the storm outside was getting pretty intense, with rumbles of thunder every few minutes.

"This is the Museum of Lost Dreams."

"Dreams? That's stupid."

I shrugged but didn't disagree. I was here because it paid a buck over minimum wage. This joker had actually shelled out ten bucks for the privilege.

He glared at me, then turned and wandered into the museum. I watched him for a bit, then returned to my book, only to be interrupted by a crash of thunder and all the lights going out.

I heard muffled curses and thuds from the exhibit area.

"Sorry, sir," I called out. "I'll get the lights back on in a minute."

Using the flashlight on my phone, I made my way into the back room. It was a maze of old props and pieces of exhibits, all filthy. It looked like nothing had been cleaned in a decade. Well, not my job to clean it.

I paused at the rusty cover to the fuse box, wondering if I was paid enough to risk my life doing this. But then I thought about having to find another job if this place closed down. I grabbed the handle and pulled the cover open.

The fuse box was old-school, with a series of round fuses with little glass windows. One of them had a black smear on the glass, which told me it was the one that was blown. I unscrewed it gingerly, then screwed in a replacement from the box of fuses sitting nearby — on the head of an Egyptian bust.

The lights flickered back on, then off, then back on again. A jolt of electricity shot through me, throwing me backwards and making my teeth clack together. I tripped on something and went ass-over-teakettle, thumping my head on the concrete floor.

For a second, I genuinely saw stars, like in a cartoon. There was a horrible electric-metallic taste in my mouth. I pulled myself unsteadily to my feet. The thing I'd tripped on was some sort of plaque. I picked it up and headed back to the front desk, cursing silently.

At least the lights were back on.

When I got back to the desk, it was just in time to see the joker leaving. He'd not bothered to make sure I was okay. Chivalry was obviously still dead.

I shut off the flashlight on my phone and took a deep drink from my Coke can. My hands were still shaking, and I realized with annoyance that I'd ripped my blouse when I'd fallen.

The plaque must have been silver, because it was tarnished black. It was round and there were holes in it where I assumed it had once been attached to something. I poured a little bit of my Coke onto the plaque and rubbed at it with a paper towel until a little bit of silver showed through. Finally, I got it cleaned up enough to make out the words:

The Dreams You Follow Today are the Memories of Tomorrow

I snorted. It sounded like an ad for a cruise company. I could see funhouse reflections of myself in the silver, my face distorted and wrinkled. No doubt how I'd look in fifty years. Something to look forward to.

I shoved the plaque into a drawer in the desk, where it immediately got stuck, stopping the drawer from either opening or closing. It was that sort of a day. Well, it wasn't like I used that drawer for anything, anyway. I decided that ignoring it was the best policy.

I picked up my book, but before I could start reading, the main door opened again. *Another* visitor. For the museum, this was rush hour. I'd worked here for four months, and I don't think there'd ever been more than one visitor in a week, let alone on the same day.

The second visitor was a well-dressed woman, perhaps in her sixties or seventies, looking slightly confused. Then she saw the sign over my head — *Welcome to the Museum of Lost Dreams. $10 entrance fee.* Her expression cleared and she reached into her purse.

"Where would I find Happiness?" she asked as she handed me her entrance fee.

Not here, I thought. "Second floor, between Fortune and Love."

She smiled at me briefly, which made her look thirty years younger, then turned and headed for the stairs. She struggled slightly going up, leaning heavily on the railing. I considered offering to help her, but by the time I'd convinced myself that I ought to, she was already most of the way up.

I felt vaguely guilty about it, which reminded me that I hadn't called my mother in a long time. Not that I intended to break the streak. She'd just ask me if I was seeing any nice boys/was going back to college/had lost any weight/had cured cancer. I'd stick with the guilt, thank you very much.

I'd gotten bored with my book and was doomscrolling my way through Twitter when my phone dinged to let me know that it was time to close up. It was only then that I realized the woman hadn't left. She'd been up there for more than an hour.

Sighing, I figured I'd better check on her. Make sure she hadn't fallen or had a heart attack. I jogged up the stairs and squeezed past Fame and World Travel — my nose wrinkling automatically at the pervasive, musty smell given off by the exhibits. Happiness was a diorama. A sunset over a papier-mâché ocean. Two crude cloth dolls sat hand-in-hand on the beach, staring out to sea.

There was no sign of her.

The museum wasn't particularly large, but there were a few odd nooks and crannies. I checked them all, then checked downstairs just to be sure.

She must have left without me noticing. My desk was by the only door, but I *had* been reading. Oh well, not like there was anything in here worth stealing. I set the alarm and locked the door. There was a little nagging worry at the back of my mind, but I ignored it.

🏛

The woman came back a week later. I had mostly forgotten about her, but I still felt a little bit of relief when I saw her. She smiled at me as if we were old friends, and I smiled back.

"Back for Happiness?" I asked.

"Absolutely. It's amazing, isn't it?"

"Uh—" Amazing that anyone actually paid to see it, maybe. "It is definitely interesting. You know, I think you may be our first repeat customer."

"That's a shame." She read my name badge. "Emma, is it?"

I nodded.

"Nice to meet you, Emma. Do you like working here?"

Another question I didn't want to answer.

"It pays the bills."

"Can't argue with that. I used to work in a place like this, too. A long time ago."

"A girl's got to eat."

That got me another one of her year-shedding smiles.

"Well, I'm sure you'll see me again." She gave a little wave and then started up the stairs.

This time I was a lot more vigilant waiting for her to leave. I kept an eye on the stairs the entire time, even if I was still reading and playing games on my phone. There was no way she could have made it past me, but when closing time came, she was gone.

I set the alarm, locked the door, then unlocked it, disarmed the alarm, and went upstairs.

Since that was where she said she was heading, I went over to Happiness first. The dolls didn't seem happy to me. If I were being honest, the whole thing seemed a little bit sad.

Some of the displays, like Fortune, which was piled high with fake gold coins and gems, were pretty straightforward, if kind of stupid. Others, like Happiness, were just weird. I guess happiness is in the eye of the beholder.

I stared at the display, trying to see what the woman was seeing, my eyes crossing in the attempt. For a second I could almost feel the warmth of the fake sun on my face. My mother always said that I had an overactive imagination. I shook my head and then sneezed from the dust. I needed to get out of there while I could still breathe without sounding like Darth Vader.

🏛

"Emma?"

I opened my eyes blearily. For a second, I thought it was my mother telling me I was going to be late to school. Then I managed to focus. It was the Happiness lady standing at the desk, looking embarrassed.

"Sorry, I must have dozed off."

"Well, I hope you are recovering from a hangover after a wild night partying."

I snorted with laughter. "Definitely. I was hanging from the chandeliers."

She laughed back. "Reminds me of when I was your age. I can't tell you how many chandeliers I completely ruined."

"They just don't make them like they used to."

"No. No they don't." She suddenly seemed sad, although she was still smiling. She held out her ten dollars, which I took. For a moment I stared right into her eyes and had one of those weird 'world is backwards' moments.

"I don't suppose we've met anywhere before?" I asked.

She laughed. "I'm the old one who's supposed to be losing her marbles. We met right here at this museum. Don't you remember?"

I snorted.

"Do you need any help up the stairs?"

"No. I'm slow, but I'll get there in the end." She winked at me.

I watched her laboriously climb the stairs. For all I remembered, there might have been some chandelier-hanging last night. I'd gone on a blind date and been stood-up. I'd drunk three or four — or five — sticky cocktails to make up for it. I didn't quite remember going home. Or showing up to work, for that matter. I had a horrible feeling that I might have slept here last night.

A few minutes in the nasty little bathroom in the back made me look presentable, albeit slightly wrinkled. A cup of coffee brought me up to about fifty-percent human. After that, I decided to go check on the visitor. It was just as well she was already up there, or I'd probably have asked for *her* help climbing the stairs.

Except she wasn't. Upstairs, that is. I told myself that she must have slipped out while I was in the bathroom. But I didn't believe it.

It was probably possible to hide in Knowledge — there were stacks of dust-streaked books. It was silly, but I checked anyway. As expected, she wasn't there. I did notice several books from my literature course that I hadn't quite managed to get around to reading. I had the time now, but, alas, these were glued down. I thought that there also might have been something nesting back there, so I backed out hurriedly, sneezing all the way.

And there was nowhere to hide around Happiness — unless there was an opening below the fake waves, which seemed unlikely. I stared at them for a while, fruitlessly looking for a trapdoor or something. The waves were surprisingly realistic.

I turned to leave, sneezed again, then took a deep breath, which was always a mistake in the museum. Except... instead of rot and mildew, there was a salty ocean breeze. I took in another deep breath, feeling it clear my sinuses. I felt sand crunch under my feet.

But when I turned back, everything was paint and papier-mâché, and the smell was the normal, cloying, musty odor I had learned to hate. I went back downstairs.

🏛

Several weeks had passed since the woman had last been in. I wouldn't say that I'd forgotten about her — we didn't have enough visitors to make it easy to forget any of them, let alone ones that managed to regularly disappear — but I was still surprised when she finally came back.

"Hello, Emma. Did you miss me?"

"I did. Been to any wild parties?"

"Every night. All those millionaires and movie stars can't get enough of me."

"I've been busy myself, learning to skydive over jungles."

"Well, if you see Tarzan, tell him to write. I've missed him."

We grinned at each other, and I handed her a ticket.

It occurred to me that my silly chats with this lady were the longest I'd had in months. Pretty damn sad. I was starting to think that I wasn't just working at this place, but was one of the exhibits. I should be sitting on a plinth labeled 'Future'. As in not-having-one.

I watched the lady make her way up the stairs. Instead of waiting for her to disappear, this time I was going to see exactly where she went. As soon as she was out of sight, I got up and raced up the stairs behind her.

She was gone.

"Ma'am?" I called out. "Are you here?"

Yeah, like she was crouching behind the dude riding a camel in Adventure.

Okay, so I checked — just in case. I hadn't realized until then that the camel was completely flat on the hidden side. Someone had helpfully written 'camel' on the wood in thick Sharpie. Kind of took the mystery out of the adventure.

I wandered back over to Happiness. I had a genuine mystery. Two, really. First, where the hell had she disappeared to? Second, why on earth would she keep coming to visit *this* display?

It was slightly better made than the other exhibits, or at least better painted. The ocean was very believable, the waves merging seamlessly into the background. I hadn't noticed before, but there was a boat painted on the background, far in the distance. Probably had the word 'boat' painted on the backside.

Whoever had built this — or ordered it built — had obviously associated the beach with happiness. I couldn't really judge. I'd never been to a beach, at least not that I remembered.

Although — there was the very vaguest memory tugging at me. Soft sand under my legs. The sound of waves. That wonderful salty-ocean smell again, and someone holding my hand.

Maybe I'd been to the beach as a kid. If I ever accidentally talked to my mother again, I'd have to ask her.

Far away, over the soft crash of the surf, I heard a man laugh.

I spun around, but there was no one there. Or no one I could see. I had mace in my purse, but my purse was downstairs. I looked around desperately for a weapon, spotted a broom leaning up in a corner, and grabbed it. The solid wood in my hand made me feel slightly better.

But whoever had laughed was completely silent now. I turned back to Happiness. It was weird, but now that I thought about it, I had a feeling that the laugh had come from that direction. The museum's clutter made figuring out its geography difficult, but I was pretty sure that there was a concrete wall behind the diorama, and empty warehouses beyond that. The sound must have come from there.

I relaxed ever-so-slightly, and backed my way to the stairs, still holding the broom, then raced down the stairs. I decided that today would be a good day to close early.

🏛

I finally called my mother. Well, I actually picked up when she called me, instead of letting it go to voicemail, but basically the same thing. I let her talk for a while, but interrupted her before she really got going on my many, *many* faults. The trick was to not let her build up a full head of steam.

"Hey, when I was a kid, did we ever go to the beach?"

Silence. That was a first.

"Mom?"

"Your father used to take you. When he had custody. I didn't like it, didn't think it was safe."

My father. I only dimly remembered him. He and Mom divorced right after I was born, and then he'd died a few years after that. I hadn't thought about him in years.

"Why did you and Dad get divorced?"

"Oh, well, you know how it is." Mom's voice was strained. "We got married too young and realized we were different people. I wanted to settle down and be safe. He was always daydreaming about adventures. That's what killed him in the end — that stupid sailboat of his."

My mother was still talking, but my ears were suddenly ringing, and I couldn't hear her properly.

Sailing. Dad and me, sitting on the beach watching the boats. He had told me that we were going to sail around the world together.

"I've got to go." I hung up on my mother, then raced up the stairs. There was the boat painted onto the back of Happiness. I needed to get closer, but I didn't want to damage the papier-mâché ocean. Instead, I shoved my way through Fortune, not caring as I knocked over a stack of fake gold bars.

Leaning over as far as I could, I was still a few feet away from the sailboat. I could just barely read the tiny name painted on the front. *Amelia.*

Amelia was my full name — Mum had just started calling me Emma for short. This was my father's boat.

"It's a pretty dream, isn't it?"

My heart just about leapt out of my chest. I tried to turn around, slipped, and brought down a cascade of fake jewels on my head.

"Oh dear. Are you all right?" It was the woman. She sounded concerned, but she also sounded like she was trying not to laugh.

"Well, at least I'm going to die rich," I said, holding up an emerald the size of my head.

That did make her laugh. She pushed her way into Fortune and held out her hand. I was half-worried that I'd pull her down rather than her pulling me up, but she was surprisingly strong.

Once outside of the Fortune display, I dusted myself off, sneezed, then looked at the woman.

"How do you do it?" I asked.

"Do what?"

"Disappear?"

"Oh, that." She looked embarrassed. "Well, I'm not really here, am I? Or, well, I suppose I am." She gestured at me, then looked at my hand. "But not really."

"Well, that clears everything up."

She snorted, then put her hand in front of her mouth. "Sorry." She turned and stared at the diorama of Happiness for a while. I stood next to her, also staring. I knew I should be completely freaked out, but I think I'd gone beyond that.

"What do you dream of doing with your life?" she asked suddenly. It was the sort of question that my mother — and my teachers, counselors, landlady — perpetually asked me. But from this woman, it didn't seem so awful.

"I don't know. That's the problem."

She nodded. "And sailing the world — that was *his* dream, not mine. Not yours, I mean."

Something clicked in my brain. The reason I always thought of my mother when I saw this woman. The way she talked and acted and, well, *connected* with me. When I looked closely, I saw that she had the same nose as me, the same mole over her right eye. It was impossible, surely? But the alternative was that I was cracking up.

"So, you're me, then?"

She shrugged. In exactly the same way I always shrugged.

We stared at the water for a while. I could smell the fresh ocean breeze again.

"It would be nice, though. Maybe not the *whole* world, but to travel. Breathe clean air, see other countries, other people. Get away from this city for a while."

She nodded. "I'm up for it if you are."

"First, I think I need to quit this job. Find something better. I bet sailing is quite expensive."

"Well, you do have that emerald."

"Funny," I said, tossing the fake, and now slightly crushed, emerald back into the Fortune display.

"I hope you do it," the woman — the older me — said. "I'd like to have something like sailing the world to look back on."

I headed for the stairs, the woman not far behind me, but by the time I got to the bottom, she had gone.

🏛

It was the first day of my new job working at the Museum of Lost Dreams. It was pretty damn corny, but it would earn me enough to pay the rent. Thankfully there was no uniform, but I did have to put on a nametag with 'Calvin' printed in gold-on-black plastic. Classy.

I examined my domain — an old desk covered in stains, with one drawer sticking out. I tried pushing it in. It wouldn't go, but a strong yank got it to come out with a squeal. There was something stuck in there — a blackened metal plate with some words on it. Bits of the plate were silver — someone who didn't know what they were doing had tried to clean it. For a moment I considered taking it home to my auntie, who would be able to polish it up beautifully. But I'd probably get accused of stealing the thing. Pity, though. I could see little reflections of myself in the areas that had been cleaned, but with all the dirt, it made me look like I was a hundred.

By moving a few things around, I got the plate back in and the drawer closed without getting stuck. It wasn't much, but I'd improved my world a little.

The guy on the phone had said not to expect too many visitors, but a few moments later, someone showed up. It was an old guy, as black as me and bald as an egg. He looked vaguely familiar. He spent a few minutes looking around, then read the welcome sign above my head.

"Who the hell builds a Museum of Lost Dreams?"

"Honestly, when I spoke to the guy who hired me, he didn't seem to even remember the place existed."

"Serious?"

"Yeah, he said that he wished he'd thought of it. That he'd always wanted to run a museum."

"And you took the job anyway?"

"Not easy finding a job these days."

That got a nod.

"Besides, it's a museum of lost dreams, so if he lost the memory of the museum, seems to fit."

That got me a glare. "Don't be laughing at people's dreams, boy."

"Sorry, sir," I said, although I hadn't been joking.

"Where's Adventure?"

"What?"

"Adventure. It's one of the displays."

"Oh, yeah, right. Sorry." I tried to read the badly photocopied map. "I think it's upstairs. I'll go with you and see. And, uh, I think you have to pay me ten bucks first."

He shook his head, but pulled out his wallet and separated ten crumpled dollar bills. I shoved them in the cashbox, then led him up the stairs. Despite being old, he was in good shape, and practically ran up.

The map showed Fortune, which was fully of tacky fake jewels and gold. It also looked like an elephant had trampled through it. Next to that was the display for Happiness, which was a cheesy display of a beach scene. Finally, we got to Adventure.

"Doesn't look like Adventure to me," I said. It was a diorama of a theater with little chairs facing towards a stage. On the stage was a doll holding a microphone. "More like Fame."

"Guess anything can be an adventure if you put your mind to it."

"Can't argue with that. I'm heading back down. Spend as much time as you like."

He nodded.

Funny, when I went to close up, I didn't see the old guy. He must have slipped out without my noticing.

THE MUSEUM OF THE EVOLUCALYPSE

(AUDIO TOUR)

Dominick Cancilla

Welcome to the Smithsonian Museum of the Evolucalypse, dedicated to the cultural, scientific, technological, and political development of the United States since 2026. We appreciate your renting this audio tour and hope that it will inform, enliven, and enhance your experience.

As you walk through the museum, you will notice that every exhibit is accompanied by a sign with a picture of an audio device and a three-digit number. To listen to the audio for a particular exhibit, enter its number and press the 'Play' button.

We hope you enjoy your visit.

101 Rededication Speech: The original, handwritten speech delivered by President Jiggle'nuf for the museum's grand reopening on August 25, 2028. Additional artifacts commemorating the country's first post-Evolucalypse president can be found in the second-floor Executive Branch gallery, including his Modern Mime bachelor's degree from the revitalized Ringling Brothers and Barnum and Bailey Clown College, pie tins from the exciting climax to his only presidential debate, and his official unicycle, Wheel Force One.

102 Photo of the former Smithsonian National Museum of American History: This historic photo shows the museum building before remodeling and rededication.

The 47 exhibits in the next room are the most important artifacts from the museum's previous incarnation, and are essential viewing for anyone interested in a deeper look at American history.

150 Horse Miniatures: Like many of the artifacts in this gallery, these hand-carved miniature animals are signposts for the creativity and philosophical depth humanity was blessed with after the Evolucalypse. Because the subject of these artworks is miniature horses, these miniatures were carved at a one-to-one scale.

151 The Expressions of Snails: If you are interested in both snails and exercising your powers of interspecies communication, then these flash cards are for you. Available in the museum gift shop.

152 Possible Video of the Arrival of Untua Ship One: 2025 footage from a trail camera on the edge of the property of Swifty Mariner in Plane Pointe, Montana, may be the first evidence of the alien invasion that preceded the evolution of humanity. The grainy film shows dirt in an uncultivated portion of the farm blown about in a manner consistent with either the landing of a large, invisible, extraterrestrial spacecraft or a localized weather event. Whether this is indeed a record of the arrival of the Untua ship has been left by disinterested experts as an exercise for the viewer. To preserve the uniqueness of the event, this video was played once at the time of the museum's opening and will not be played again.

153 Lodestone in the Shape of Margaret Thatcher: Discovered in Gibber, New South Wales, this lodestone naturally has a resemblance to Margaret Thatcher when viewed from a certain angle, as indicated by the red arrow in the display. The artifact was obtained by museum curators in exchange for a lap desk that was uninteresting other than having been owned and used by former politician Thomas Jefferson.

154 War Cube: This approximately three-foot by two-foot by two-foot cube was created by putting all of the former American History Museum's war- and military-related books and artifacts into an industrial 'car crusher' baling press. The action was deemed necessary after the Permanent Peace, to prevent the screaming of enlightened visitors. Should you feel the need for hysterics at even the thought of these materials, we have provided a sound-dampening screaming hood and fainting couch for your use.

156 Doctor Lona Burk's Notes on the Study of Sancerebral Parvacomedere: More than fifteen hard drives of data and one hundred handwritten notebooks contain the complete study of sancerebral parvacomedere, as carried out by Doctor Lona Burk of the UCLA Institute for Biological Science. Although this condition does not and cannot exist, Doctor Burk spent almost a year documenting how it caused both subtle and extreme perturbations of human thought patterns and logic processing, all of which would be completely transparent to others with the condition. Dr. Burk contended that the condition's spread had reached an effective one-hundred-percent global infection rate, which explained why nobody would recognize its existence. She proposed no cure.

157 First Edition of *The SP Conundrum*: Printed only in limited quantities, this brochure was heavily quoted from and rapidly disseminated online. It sparked the still-ongoing debate over whether an imaginary disease should be considered uncurable if a cure cannot be imagined. Also in the display case is a copy of the companion brochure *The SP Continuation*, which examines whether a medical condition can be listed as having been eradicated simply because no current cases can be identified.

158 Interactive Exhibit, *Do I Have Sancerebral Parvacomedere?*: This electronic counting machine consists of a digital readout and a button marked 'No'. Press the button to include yourself in the tally.

160 Transcript and Video Excerpt from the May 15, 2025 *Farming Hour*: *Farming Hour* was a Montana public-access television show on which events of the day relevant to the local community were discussed. On this episode, Swifty Mariner presents show host Pamela Corning with a piece of metal he and his son cut from an invisible spaceship he discovered on the edge of his property. The audio of the video is not played to maintain the museum's air of respectful neutrality, but here is the most relevant portion of Mr. Mariner's presentation: "I only found it because I ran into it with my pickup. Nobody knows how long it had been there, but there was definitely something inside. I know because when I touched it, there was this loud siren and I got a nasty electric shock. I had to get work gloves and earplugs just to cut this piece off. We're going to go back later with my backhoe to get the rest of it. They don't have permission to be on my property, and if they have that many alarms and things to stop me from taking the stuff, you know it's gotta be good."

161 'It's Gotta be Good' T-shirt: Custom silk-screened shirts with the 'It's Gotta be Good' slogan and a caricature of Swifty Mariner were popular for several days after his appearance on *Farming Hour* went viral. Replicas of this shirt are available in the museum gift shop.

162 Invisible Strip of Metal: This piece of metal, first displayed by Swifty Mariner on *Farming Hour*, is the only one in existence. Mr. Mariner sold this strip to the host of *Farming Hour* for a tidy sum and had intended to retrieve additional metal from the ship on his property in Plane Pointe, Montana. No such sale of additional scrap metal took place, as Mariner's attempt to wrest more metal from the Untua ship famously did not have the desired outcome.

163 *Swifty Mariner and his Backhoe*: A picture book, made with the kind permission of the Virginia Lee Burton estate, was created to educate children on the potential dangers of unauthorized use of excavation equipment. The ending, in which Swifty and his backhoe are shown living happily ever after in Heaven, was criticized for possibly misrepresenting the backhoe's feelings about being obliterated along with some 150,000 square miles of Montana (and parts of Canada).

164 Photograph from Space: A satellite photograph shows the crater where Montana had been. The image was taken mere months before all operable Earth-orbiting satellites were decommissioned by unanimous international agreement in the wake of the Evolucalypse.

165 Replica of an Untua Artifact: The explosion of the first Untua ship reduced it to atoms, the dust of which settled across the continent. Though it has been argued that nothing could have survived that explosion intact, this object came to light soon after and was claimed to be of Untua origin. It is believed to be authentic due to the impossibility of something of its shape and form being created using human technology.

166 Signed First Edition, *Artification of Art* by Sigourney Birching: The first and most influential post-Evolucalypse work of art criticism, Birching proposes that the modern artist must not only stand upon the shoulders of giants, but also disassemble those giants and build more original giants out of them. Her influence can be seen in the repainting of the Statue of Liberty, the repurposing of Mount Rushmore, and the hobby of purchasing multiple jigsaw puzzles created using the same pattern and assembling them with the pieces scrambled. (See interactive station #167 if you'd like to try your hand at puzzle rescrambling.)

168 Modified Works of H.P. Lovecraft: These volumes of the complete works of Howard Phillips 'H.P.' Lovecraft were modified by William Atlas of Providence, Rhode Island. Mr. Atlas, with the use of a razor blade, meticulously excised all adjectives from the books, leaving rectangular holes behind to indicate their former presence. For this work and for his suggestion that blank phonebooks be printed for the use of those without phones, President Jingle'nuff presented Mr. Atlas with a 2029 Presidential Medal of Freedom and a can of 'peanut brittle'.

170 Satellite Betting Slips: During the satellite decommissioning, placing wagers on where a given satellite would strike the planet was a popular pastime. One of the few winning tickets — the $1 wager that GSAT-72A would strike a barn in Idaho — is among those collected here.

173 *What Are My Bees Thinking?*: Journals of Oregon amateur apiculturist Duane Franklin, who found that after the Evolucalypse he was able to understand the language of bees. He also discovered that bees didn't have much of interest to say.

174 *What Are Her Bees Thinking?*: Additional journals of Oregon amateur apiculturist Duane Franklin, this time documenting the thoughts of bees on the property of his neighbor Cecily Monroe.

175 *A Rebuttal to Duane's and My Bees*: Journals of Oregon professional horticulturist Cecily Monroe who wanted amateur apiculturist Duane Franklin to stay off her property. Included is an appendix dictated by her cat Rotundo, who thought bees made too much noise.

176 *We're Not Your Damned Bees*: Protest literature, transcribed from the dancing of bees on the Oregon properties of Duane Franklin and Cecily Monroe.

181 Portrait of an Untua: Although the inhabitants of the two Untua spaceships were never seen by humans, artist Willamina Wagner was able to create this stunning portrait. Painted in great detail using a brush with a single bristle and based entirely on visions experienced during oxygen-deprived hallucinations, it has been said that even a glimpse of this image is enough to cause permanent insanity. Postcards are available in the gift shop.

182 *Couplets upon the Consideration of Elemental Hydrogen*: Handbound chapbooks of the poetry of Mavis Gerard who pioneered communing with the microscopic. Each chapbook is sealed in a transparent bag in which the atmosphere has been replaced entirely with the featured element. No smoking in this area, please.

183 *This is a Painting*: The oil painting *This Is a Painting* by artist Monica Whitbeard is an exact copy of René Magritte's *The Treachery of Images*. It serves as a marker for the museum's restrooms, which philosophers note are both at rest and rooms.

184 Lovely Flower (Deceased): Flower from the United Nations building garden near where the second ship from Untua landed in 2026. It is reported that the Untua ship blared out a message in terrible English and frankly amateurish Chinese. As near as anyone could tell, it was a declaration of apology, a noninterference policy statement, and some science-sounding stuff about 'rapidly self-replicating nanites'. There was also a statement that subsequent to the explosion of the first Untua ship humans should not inhale. The young woman who picked and pressed this flower to preserve its memories of the moment was eventually located, tried by a jury of her victim's peers, and sentenced to life imprisonment without the possibility of parole.

185 Vial of Ashes: Permanently sealed in a thick-walled vial for the safety of our guests, these ashes are what remains of the Probably a Weapon brought by the Untua in their second ship and left at the United Nations building. The device was reported to have the ability to 'correct' human minds, which, when combined with the Untua statement about human suffocation, was recognized as threatening in the extreme. Destroyed on the advice of a particularly lovely flower (see exhibit #184).

186 Box of Origami: Seventeen hundred origami frogs handcrafted by the Secretary-General of the United Nations. They were found in a semi-melted safety-deposit box along with two hand-drawn baseball cards and half a sandwich.

187 Ethereal Calculations: The first validated mathematical proof that there are nine times as many cats in Heaven as dogs, and the first scientific work blessed by Pope Whiskers I.

190 Stereopticon and Slides: An antique stereopticon is paired with modern slides commemorating the destruction of the second Untua ship, two days after its arrival at the United Nations building. The endless loop of bad English and Chinese coming from the ship, coupled with the threat of the so-called 'gift' (see exhibit #185) delivered by its robotic attendant, eventually inspired a growing crowd to take defensive action. Images broadcast from the event were transferred to film by photography enthusiast Montgomery Lubland and used to create these slides. For visual clarity, the left and right images on the slides are identical.

191 Statue The Tumbler: Artist Sadie Hakiko created this sculpture to commemorate the moment the second Untua ship began to topple under the weight of the crowd. The iron for this sculpture was obtained by melting down a neighbor's blasphemous bathtub.

192 Elaine Manual Memorial: Elaine Manual's reporting from outside the United Nations building on the day of the toppling of the second Untua ship has become iconic. This bronze plaque is laser cut with a scene from the famed broadcast and inscribed with her immortal final words, "It's falling! Are you getting this? It's —"

193 Simulated Space Photograph: An artist's impression of a satellite photograph showing the water-filled crater that once was Manhattan and surrounding areas.

195 Band Battle One, "Spread on the Wind to Melt Your Mind": A rare vinyl pressing of the one Kicks Gibson single to never break the top 100 on country music charts. Some fans blamed the song's unpopularity on Gibson being traumatized after his wife was vaporized in the explosion outside the United Nations building. Others lamented his canceling of public appearances and refusal to leave his bunker in West Texas for fear of 'micro-robots from alien ship dust that are eating our minds'. Still others suggested he should just go back to singing about trucks and survivalism.

196 Band Battle Two, "You Say It's Rapid Evolution": Vinyl, cassette, CD, electronic, sheet-music, music-video, and music-box versions of the Deap Faek Beatles song "You Say It's Rapid Evolution". The song, which reached number one on all charts — including those for spoken word and classical music — celebrates humanity's spontaneous intellectual mega-response to what was effectively a pair of unprovoked nuclear attacks from Untua. What they termed 'rapid evolution' came to be known colloquially as the Evolucalypse.

201 Drawing of a Penis: A napkin with a crayon drawing of a penis on it.

202 Psychic Testing Cards: These custom-made cards have the standard ESP testing symbols printed on both sides. They result in significantly increased PSI scores among all test subjects, helping to demonstrate humanity's incredible leap forward after the Evolucalypse.

206 Vintage Monsanto House of the Future postcard: This 1950's-era Disneyland postcard sat unused in Santa Monica, California resident Estella Pia's junk drawer until 2027. At that time, Pia wrote on the card, 'With my first breath of air this morning, it felt as if the world had opened to my mind. Everything is so clear. We must never waste another day.' The card was addressed to 'The Mittens' in Monument Valley, Utah and stamped with a Hello Kitty sticker.

210 Vintage copy of *Jane Eyre*: It has been recognized in recent years that Charlotte Brontë's famed novel explains everything from the Evolucalypse to the Permanent Peace. Professor of English Literature Mayna St.

Lawrence explains, 'The passages about expanding your mind to experience the world as an insider are revelatory once you allow yourself to see them. If you're reading the words as written, you're trying too hard. Charlotte never intended that.'

211 Interactive Station — Copies of *Jane Eyre* and *The Old Man and the Sea*: Sit in the chair provided and take a few hours to see for yourself how Brontë uses subtext to describe our world while Hemingway just whines about fish.

218 Tank of air from the *USS Jim Carrey*: In 2026, violence broke out among the crew of the recently renamed destroyer *USS Jim Carrey*, which was the first to arrive in the newly created Manhattan Bay in the wake of the second Untua ship explosion. The conflict reached a stalemate when Navy personnel who believed paint should have a flavor barricaded themselves in the fore of the ship, and those who maintained that the only good corpse was a dead corpse barricaded themselves in the aft. A group of Marines agnostic to the conflict filled as many oxygen tanks as were available with atmosphere from around the ship. They advanced their unit to shore via tactical launches mere moments before the *Carrey* was self-scuttled. These tanks and the 'precious knowledge' they contained were delivered to and opened in countries around the world as part of Operation Open Tanks of *Carrey* Air in Countries Around the World.

224 ESPie Award: Trophy presented to the Incomprehensible Wendy by the International Association of Psychic Professionals at their 2029 annual meeting. It was awarded to commemorate Incomprehensible Wendy's explosive post-facto prediction that in January 2028 all people about to do violence would begin screaming bloody murder and then collapse in a faint, effectively ending the vast majority of violent encounters worldwide.

225 Bears and Vikings Game Helmets: Quarterback helmets from the last game in NFL history. The game famously ended after the first play, during which the ball was snapped to the quarterback and all frontline players from both teams began screaming bloody murder and collapsed in a faint.

228 Experimental Birth Film: The first film of the birth of a human baby from the baby's perspective.

229 GoPro Camera with Headgear: This miniature camera has been specially modified so it can be worn on the head of an unborn child. It was developed soon after many post-Evolucalypse parents discovered that they were able to hear the voices of their unborn children in their head as early as six weeks before the child's due date, similar to how they could often hear the voices of pets, plants, and household objects.

240 Video of a Picture of a Photocopy of a Screen Capture of a Computer Screen with a Report from Professor Luther Farthing: Safely processed documentation of Professor Farthing's annoying and globally disdained theory related to a supposed genetically recombinant adaptive nanovirus that permeated the atmosphere within Untua spaceships in order to allow their inhabitants to survive extended near-lightspeed travel. In the Professor's endless blathering, he implies that even a single unit of such a self-replicating nanovirus might affect human biology, particularly brain function. The report is unreliable both because its author refused to leave the clean room in which he had been locked for several years, and because the results could not be substantiated by any relevant flora (see exhibit #184). Words such as 'dire' and 'immediate action' can be seen on the report in this exhibit, hinting at Farthing's arrogance and documenting his bloated self-importance. That he frequently quotes the work of Doctor Lona Burk does nothing to support his case.

241 Professor Luther Farthing's Formula for Disabling Extraterrestrial Nanoviruses: We apologize that this exhibit is currently offline for editorial review. In its place, please enjoy this 'Sounds Like Farting' pin on loan from the Mocking Farthing website and available in the museum gift shop.

243 Clean Room Live Video Feed: The live-feed video from Professor Luther Farthing's clean room is presented for the entertainment of those interested in the behavior of the disturbed. If you are lucky, you may catch the Professor running about, gesturing wildly to the camera, or holding up one of his entertaining signs. Unfortunately, the feed has no audio component. Also unfortunately, the Professor has not been seen to move since October 2029.

246 Better Better Better Bill Signing Pen: The BBBB Congressional act of 2029 provided for universal health care to all within the country's borders, codified clean food and water as a basic human right, began construction of the nationwide system of public restroom and bathing facilities, created a minimum income for all adults, and made it illegal to be an asshole. It was authored by the annoying Professor Luther Farthing and considered to be clean-room addled, but was passed by Congress and signed by President Jiggle'nuf in the hope that doing so might get Farthing to finally shut up. It did not.

249 Snack Foods: These shelves of snack foods are arranged in order of intelligence, from Ding Dong to Vienna Fingers.

250 Chatty Coffee: You have reached the museum coffee shop, which marks the midpoint of your tour. This room is a replica of the Audio Tour Rental Kiosk you encountered earlier. Refer to audio tour item 101 if you would like a refresher on the kiosk and its function. After you have had a coffee and perhaps taken a moment to check in with one of the ferns, your tour continues up the Swifty Mariner Memorial Invisible Staircase with the Cabinet of Solipsistic Rag Dolls.

251 Return to the Audio Tour Rental Kiosk: To pause for now and continue your tour on a subsequent visit, use this door to return to the kiosk where you rented this audio program. If you have enjoyed your visit, we invite you to experience other Smithsonian museums, including the National Air Museum, the American Art Museum (Revised), and the National Zoo, which remains a lovely spot even after all the animals were returned to the wild to stop their complaining. Have an evolved day!

THE MUSEUM OF SMELLS

John Joseph Ryan

Curator Tony Hidalgo sniffled as he looked out through the glass front door and up at the surrounding warehouses, some converted to lofts. It was noon, and he always canvassed the street at the lunch hour, occasionally stepping out onto the sidewalk when he saw the rare families or groups of kids that he might entice for a visit to his unusual museum. He took out his handkerchief as though that, too, were part of the ritual, shook it out, large as it was, and blew into it in a practiced way. His wife, Agnes, had always marveled that he blew both nostrils at once, sonorously, and didn't pop his eardrums ever. He would just smile at her, tap his large nose, and then pull his suspenders out in mock pride. By then, though, she would usually have turned to oversee the installation of some new display or hurried over to slide a knife under the skin of a just-delivered box. Her custom-blended perfume would be the only trace left of her attention to him. Even small encounters with Agnes during a busy day caused Tony's smile to linger, his nose tickling.

Now, he scratched his back, tugging slightly at the tension of his red suspenders as he returned to his post behind the museum's front desk. Once, when he had been taking tickets after another worker had failed to show up, an excited four-year-old with his mother had pointed at him and exclaimed, "Mommy! What's that?" The mother, young and intelligent-looking, gazed deliberately past Tony to a poster of a giant flower on the wall and said, "Why, that's a rose. See?" Impatient with his mother's error, the boy said,

"No, no. That!" and pointed directly at Tony. Flustered and embarrassed, the mother smiled at the boy and fumbled for words, but Tony saved her. "I'm a clown," he said. "See?" And he grinned broadly at the young boy, stretching out his red suspenders, kicking up his big feet a little, and then blowing his nose loudly into his handkerchief. His face had reddened with the effort, emphasizing the eczema across his cheeks. Satisfied with Tony's answer, the boy tugged at his mother's arm to press onward. She bent to Tony and mouthed an exaggerated "Thank you," followed by an equally silent "Sorry," as her son pulled her into one of the giant nostrils marked 'Entrance'. Tony gazed out the glass door after they were out of sight. *Sorry for what exactly?* he wondered. *The boy or me?*

The front lobby comprised a small area of the old shoe warehouse, perhaps only ten by fifteen feet, but it soared up two stories. That height and the resonating terrazzo tile beneath seemed to expand the space, cause it to hum when only a few people were talking within it. Tony glanced towards the interior of the museum, its first chamber mostly obscured by the massive fiberglass nose that reached up to the mezzanine. The 'Entrance' nostril showed signs of wear. All around its rim, the peach-colored paint had been rubbed off by grasping hands to reveal a clear-green base, while the 'Exit' nostril, to its left, was relatively unmarred. As Tony contemplated applying some touchup paint later on, he heard young voices on the sidewalk. Before he could move from behind the desk to see who was there, the glass front door thrust open, and four teenagers, dressed in various shabby clothes selected to provoke a reaction, loudly entered. Tony greeted them gently, having seen worse. Ignoring him, they disparaged the nose immediately.

"Look, a giant nose," a girl with hair dyed gray-green remarked jadedly.

"Yeah, it's got a booger!" a boy with multiple face piercings exclaimed. They all laughed, and the same girl even rushed over to wipe her hand across the rim of the 'Entrance' nostril and then lick her fingers. This provoked more laughter and some 'eew's, but Tony simply waited until their attention returned to him behind the museum's front desk.

"How much are tickets?" a different boy asked him. Tony could see, behind the boy's mop of dyed-black hair, that he had sensitive eyes. For a moment he thought he saw into the boy — perhaps too eager to be part of a group, but afraid of the reprisals of acting against it.

"Two-fifty for children twelve and under. Four for adults. Now, where do you guys fit?" He grinned, then felt a little creepy as they merely studied him in response. He had always felt most successful with young children, less so with adults, and utterly out of touch with teenagers. Agnes had seemed effortless with the public, no matter the age. Two short girls stepped toward the desk. One had bright red hair, and the other, who had touched the big nostril, had the gray-green hair.

"We're twelve," the redhead said, without blinking.

Tony regarded her. She had already developed amply — and wasn't bashful about displaying that fact. A cheap, spicy version of patchouli, like the one the hippies used to wear, wafted from her. He felt his nose twitch. Twelve? Still, her face was round, heavily made-up. Perhaps she was.

"Okay, then," Tony said good-naturedly. "Two-fifty for you two and four for the gentlemen." The pierced-face boy prodded the one with sensitive eyes, who thrust his hand into his front pocket. Tony collected the thirteen dollars from him and gestured toward the 'Entrance' nostril. He could barely check his grimace, though, as they laughed and passed under it, slapping the rim, joking about 'snot' and 'boogers'.

After their voices diminished, he reluctantly slid open the panel on the hutch above the front entrance desk. Inside were six small monitors, all connected to the museum's surveillance cameras. On principle, Tony hated spying on people. Perhaps because he valued his own privacy so much, he would just as soon not know what people did unsupervised. But the cameras had been a concession to Agnes in the late '80s. The Museum of Smells had experienced the effects of recession, and fewer families were willing to risk their scant entertainment dollars on an unknown quantity. By the early '90s, the museum had become a kind of make-out palace instead, as its most frequent visitors were teenage couples more eager for the feel of each other's bodies than the museum's olfactory exhibits. While Agnes fretted over their receipts and their declining reputation, Tony calmly insisted to her that kids needed a place to go. She was partially placated, but the next day had been too much for them both. When a lone young woman burst out of the 'Exit' nostril sobbing, they eventually got from her that a middle-class-looking, well-dressed man had exposed himself to her in the 'Gallery of Non-Sense'. Despite the tough times, Tony had seen the necessity of the cameras.

He followed the progress of the teenagers from room to room on the monitors. There were five galleries in all, each linked by short, canal-like passageways. The first gallery, a round chamber, had begun as an homage to scratch-n-sniff stickers. It had been Tony and Agnes' first collaboration, back when they stunned friends and family during the high-inflation '70s by leaving their day jobs to pursue the dream of opening their own museum. They had nearly blown their first month's budget on the stickers and the design and construction costs for the room. Late at night before their opening day, they were exhausted, sweaty, their stores of adrenaline draining, and more than a little buzzed from the bottle of red wine they passed back and forth when they realized they had not conceived of a name for this first gallery. Agnes, in a surprising burst of spontaneity, set up a stepladder, grabbed a can of pink spray paint, grinned over her shoulder at Tony, and began spraying the black wall above the lintel. Tony could only lean back on his elbows and watch as a name in loopy letters materialized: *Scratch-n-Sniffaganza!* It had remained there ever since.

Years before the installation of the surveillance cameras, black lights had illuminated the gallery's various stickers. Children ran around, delighted at the purplish transformation of their socks, sneakers, and teeth. They would scratch vigorously at the stickers glued to sturdy, colorful boards at their level, push their noses right to them, and beckon each other excitedly to smell grape, chocolate, pickle, lollipop, ice cream, rose, and lemonade. The youngest children balked at old shoe, sour milk, and rancid cheese, but for elementary school-aged boys, these became a test of bravery and defiance. At the adult level were the scents of various colognes, perfumes, aftershave lotions, flowers, and home-baked goods. If, instead, the adults wanted to sit and observe the mad movement of the children, over-upholstered leatherette couches took up the middle of the space. First-time visitors would be startled at the flatulent sounds of the cushions, then appalled or tickled at the waft of foul air that vented lightly from the floor at the same time. Tony got more positive comments from the adults about those old couches than anything else, and he found that telling.

At the monitor, Tony watched the teenagers disappointedly scan the walls of the Scratch-n-Sniff room, now brightly lit over concerns its prior black-light darkness would lead to more incidents. Fewer than one-quarter of the original stickers were still there, the rest having been overused or peeled off. The ones that remained had lost much of their scent, and most visitors who weren't curious children gave up after scratching and sniffing only a few. He had dutifully tried to replace the lost ones, but scratch-n-sniff stickers were faddish and hard to acquire anymore in large quantities. He had considered putting them behind perforated plexiglass, but then their function, both tactile and olfactory, would have been defeated. Lacking manpower and, increasingly, resources to overhaul the room, he had let it languish.

Bad smells were still easy to come by, though, and the over-upholstered couches continued to fart. It was no surprise to Tony to see the teenagers hopping up and down on the couches and taking flying leaps onto them. He could see their mouths open with laughter, though he couldn't hear them. Reduced to tiny black-and-white images on a screen, they really did seem like children. Minutes later, they moved on.

The next gallery was the 'Chamber of Scents Past'. Largely adult-oriented, Tony had thought it somewhat cruel to make the second gallery a place where adults would want to linger and children would be immediately bored and antsy. Agnes had insisted upon it, though. She didn't want the museum to be just a playground. She would often say,

"School groups are not our only bread and butter," and boop Tony's big nose. So children stomped their way past the Olive Oil and Garlic in Ancient Greece vent, the Stable at the Old Firehouse diorama, the City at the Height of Coal Use's grimy window, the Kerosene-lit Iowa Farmhouse mock-up, and the Adobe Kiln of the Anasazi, which bore the earthy scent of corn tortillas. Tony, with some satisfaction, saw the teenagers glance around, mouth some words to each other, and then continue to the next room. The boy with sensitive eyes and the supposedly twelve-year-old red-haired girl clasped hands.

They entered the next gallery. The sign above its entrance said, 'This Way to the Brain!' Tony was still proud of the detail inside this room. It was the only room he had designed and constructed himself; he and Agnes had been the lucky recipients of a cash grant thanks to another of the city's short-lived efforts at urban renewal. In the center was a cutaway view of a human head, not at all grotesque. (Tony had seen to that.) Its purpose was to show and explain the function of smell, confirming at the bottom that the olfactory was the most powerful sense for evoking memories. Arranged around the perimeter of the room were small, lacquered boxes mounted on podiums. Ledgers accompanied each box and served as the guestbooks for the museum. In this chamber, visitors could inhale whatever aroma a box contained, from shoe polish to Play-Doh to the cordite of fireworks. They could then write down any memories or associations with the smell and their names in the ledger.

Tony and Agnes had never ceased to be amused and even touched at the comments left behind. Surprisingly, there were very few acts of vandalism or vulgar writing here. Every Sunday, after Tony cooked a large breakfast, they would take the old freight elevator down from their loft apartment to the ground floor to clean and tidy the museum. They saved reading the comments in the ledgers for last. Often, they would interlace their fingers as they moved from ledger to ledger. Often, too, they would stop to kiss. Once, they had made love atop the flatulent cushions of the couch in the scratch-n-sniff gallery, laughing and moaning. Tony had been amazed at Agnes' spontaneity that day, back when she had been in robust health.

Tony rubbed his eyes, then watched on the monitors as the teenagers split off to stick their noses in the various boxes. The boy with the sensitive eyes and the girl with the red hair stayed more or less together, while the pierced boy and the girl with gray-green hair made exaggerated hops and strolls around the room. It was unclear to Tony whether the latter were 'together'. If anything, he could sense a kind of one-upmanship between them, one trying to outdo or outgross the other. There was little doubt that the former were a couple, though. He could see that they took their time at each podium, talking excitedly to each other, their faces close. They even lingered to write in the ledgers. Tony found himself looking forward to reading their comments later, even as he fought down the sense that the words might be vulgar.

Eventually, the four drew themselves back together and stepped from one shadowy monitor screen to the next, entering the second-to-last room. The Gallery of Non-Sense had been Tony's idea, and though Agnes had been reluctant to embrace its concept at first, she had later admitted it was a hit. On first inspection, it looked like an ordinary living room, complete with a couch, easy chair, end tables, a TV, stereo, lamps, books, and other everyday items. The lamps were lit, the TV featured a video loop of a scene from *The Wizard of Oz*, the stereo played quiet classical music, and the furniture looked comfortable enough to sit in. What made the Gallery of Non-Sense unique was that nothing was as it seemed — or at least, nothing *smelled* as it seemed. For example, the lamps gave off the scent of peppermint. The music drifting from the stereo seemed to carry the odor of sweetened almonds. The very rays from the TV screen, where the horses of a different color marched around and around endlessly, bore smells so strong you could almost taste them: red was raspberry, green was lime, pink was strawberry. Each object in the room exploded in odor. The two more boisterous teenagers, perhaps hoping for more sound effects, wasted no time in plopping down on the couches. The other two, still holding hands, looked at the sign above the entrance to the final gallery, glanced at each other with a smile, and then went on, out of sight. This last gallery's surveillance monitor was on the fritz; all Tony could see were cascading horizontal lines.

The last gallery had once been set up for changing exhibits, which Agnes had overseen. She had had difficulty keeping employees long enough to assist her in her various visions for new exhibits. Sometimes it was simple economics, but other times, such as when they had the grant, employees left because Agnes was often hard to work for. Her vision and independence, so dear to the more passive Tony, made her a demanding boss. Toward the end of her life, she had spent most of her time in the last gallery by herself, working long into the night. The space had become her workshop, where she would conceive visions for the museum's expansion that she would not live to see. Tony would assist occasionally, as though nothing had changed despite the terminal state of her cancer. More often, he would gently cajole her to rest. But privately, he had felt that their hopes to expand the museum beyond its five galleries would end with Agnes' life. He had never dared articulate that feeling to her. Instead, until Agnes was too debilitated to work, they had pressed on together with her distorted, shifting visions for the space. Before she entered hospice, the gallery had almost nightly become a mess of discarded foamboard models, wadded-up sketches, and empty Enfamil cans, all of which Tony would clean up after an exhausted Agnes had gone up to bed. Now the space was clear of any clutter. Except for occasional dust, it hadn't changed in the three years since Tony reconstructed it as a tribute to Agnes.

Over their lives, they had each amassed a modest amount of life insurance. Tony, ashamed to be Agnes' beneficiary instead of her benefactor, had poured most of the proceeds into the realization of the room's present design. Low, recessed lights threw glowing cones up the curved walls. The walls themselves were thin, velvety to the touch, translucent. Behind them, bands of red and blue lights pulsed at intervals like arteries. Soft flutes and low strings played through hidden speakers. Everything about the room seemed to curve, dip, undulate. Tony kept the temperature there warmer than any of the other galleries, though never hot. In the center of the gallery, two knockoff Eames-style chairs were attached to the floor, one across from the other. Between them, right at the level of one's knees, a small, heart-shaped fountain bubbled up a scented pink liquid. The aroma was unusual, unlike anything else manufactured, exotic yet familiar, and not at all cloying: Agnes' custom blended perfume. In the bowl of the fountain, set in mosaic tiles, was the word *LOVE*. For Tony, that word could not be improved upon, and he had arranged it in light bulbs above the room's entrance as well.

Tony gambled that the quiet couple would not cause any trouble — though mistrust of teenaged visitors seeped into his consciousness. Instead, he kept his eyes on the other two in the Gallery of Non-Sense. The girl, whose gray-green hair looked a uniform gray on the black-and-white monitor, had draped one arm casually over the couch. The pierced boy was intent upon something in his lap. For a horrified minute, Tony thought the boy might unzip his pants, but as he looked more closely at the screen, he could see there was something almost gleaming in the boy's hands. The object was cylindrical, with a rounded end. The boy looked quickly behind him, then brought the object to his lips. Tony saw an eerie gray flash of flame on the monitor. Abruptly, the flame appeared to dart toward the boy, as though seeking refuge. He took the cylinder from his lips, leaned back to cover his mouth, and then passed the object to the girl. She, too, brought the cylinder to her lips, paused with it there for a moment, then bent forward and coughed, smoke billowing out and up. The boy pointed at her and seemed to laugh, smoke pouring from his own mouth at the same time. The screen of the monitor was a wash of gray and white, with two darkish figures at the center. Tony went into a rage.

Do they have no sense? He jumped up, running his hands down the sides of his pants as though smoothing them out. *The smoke alarm! The odor! The room could be ruined!* He considered the quickest way to get to them. Rounding the front desk, he hastened through the 'Exit' nostril. That would put only the museum's last gallery between him and them.

In that gallery, the boy with sensitive eyes and the girl with red hair were seated across from each other. They were holding hands above the scented fountain, smiling blissfully, almost vacantly, looking each other right in the eye. When Tony burst in, they jumped and looked around at him, startled, while he stopped, startled himself by their sudden movement in the room.

"You," he rounded on the couple, halting just a few feet away, unsure why he was uncorking his indignation on them. Their eyes appeared moist or glassy. *So, they weren't so innocent after all!* His misplaced rage surged forth. "How dare you! In this room of all rooms!"

The two looked at each other, confused. Unconsciously, both sat back down like chastised schoolchildren.

"I see it — in your eyes!" He was having trouble with the confrontation already, the words coming out jerkily, his heart racing. As the aroma of the fountain reached his nose, it began to tickle.

"What do you mean?" the boy asked, sounding scared, inclining his head.

"You — your friends. S-smoking — smoking in the m-museum!" Tony sputtered, now feeling his hands shake. His voice had drawn the attention of the other two, who now appeared in the doorway to the gallery. The pierced boy laughed a little, the girl with gray-green hair leaning into him.

"S-s-smoking, in the m-m-museum! Yeah, s-s-smoking ma-ma-marijuana!" the pierced boy parroted, the girl with gray-green hair opening her mouth and laughing without a sound.

Tony turned to face them. "You have to leave. You — you can't *do* that in here!"

"Oh?" the boy asked, at once all belligerence. "What, is that one smell you can't stand?"

"Not in here!" Tony responded dumbly. Unlike Agnes, he had no ready rejoinders in an argument. He only wanted it to end as quickly as possible.

"Fine," the boy responded, shrugging, much to Tony's relief. "We're outta here." He considered Tony for a moment. "Your museum's a piece of shit anyway." At that, the girl with gray-green hair burst into audible laughter, slapping her knee slowly and exaggeratedly. The pierced boy turned to the seated couple. "Let's go. Leave this shithouse circus to the clown." The girl continued to laugh, snorting accidentally, which seemed to provoke more spasms of laughter.

The boy with sensitive eyes and the girl with red hair glanced from Tony to their friends. They looked bewildered.

"But we didn't do anything," the girl said, breaking her own silence. "Why should we have to go?"

"Please. Just leave," Tony said, his hands on his hips. *Because you're a part of them and now I don't know what to do, please just...*

"Yeah. J-just leave," the pierced boy mocked. "C'mon." He tagged the knee of the other boy, who was still seated. "What's that stink?" he continued, leaning near the fountain. "Smells like dog piss. Smells like donkey cum." In his indignation, Tony now felt shock at how quickly the boy had become so vulgar.

"No, it doesn't," the seated boy said softly, not meeting the other's eye.

"It sure as hell does. What's the matter with you?" The pierced boy reached his hand suddenly into the pink liquid and splashed it at the other boy. "There. You like that? Let's *go.*"

The boy with sensitive eyes wiped his hand quickly across his face but kept his head down. The girl with red hair stood up.

"Okay, fine. Knock it off! We'll go!" she yelled at the pierced boy. "Why do you always have to do this shit?"

"Because I like to," the pierced boy said. He reached for the hand of the giggling girl with gray-green hair. They walked toward the last passage that led to the 'Exit' nostril. When they were a safe distance away, the boy with sensitive eyes finally stood to go join the red-haired girl.

"I'm sorry," he mumbled to Tony, at first not looking at him.

"You must go," Tony responded, abashed at his misdirected outburst, but feeling he had to stay resolute no matter what. He found himself wishing Agnes were here.

She would have handled this better. She wouldn't have let the situation escalate.

The boy looked at him. His eyes were moist, old. His face was still wet from the splash of perfumed liquid. He looked Tony right in the eye.

"It doesn't smell like dog piss. The sign is right," he said gesturing to the mosaic of letters spelling the word *LOVE* at the bottom of the fountain. He took the red-haired girl's hand, hung his head again, and proceeded to follow the others through the last passage.

Tony didn't say anything. He followed the course of the four to the museum's front door, just in case the obnoxious pair decided to try anything else. By the time he ducked his head down beneath the 'Exit' nostril, the pierced boy and the girl with gray-green hair were already outside on the sidewalk. The girl was still laughing, the boy talking and gesturing toward the museum, his eyes alive with the pleasure of small power. Without another word, the boy with sensitive eyes and the girl with red hair pushed open the door and stepped out to join the other two. The pierced boy punched the other boy on the arm and began to lead the whole group away, kicking a glass bottle as he did. Tony heard the muffled shatter from inside.

He approached the front door, pressed his forehead to the glass, and looked in both directions. No one was in sight. He locked the door, blew his nose, and considered just what he would do.

He decided to walk back through the 'Exit' nostril and into the LOVE gallery. He skirted the fountain, sniffing the air as he did, but detecting nothing other than a strong whiff of the perfumed water. His nose twitched and his eyes watered some, but he continued to the next gallery.

Here, in the Gallery of Non-Sense, he inhaled more deeply. The fallout from the two bursts of marijuana smoke was still palpable, but not damaging. He moved about the room, sniffing in various spots like a hound, his nose twitching. At one point, he sneezed loudly by the couch. Occasionally, he put his hands to his hips and stared in the direction of the exit, muttering, angry. He looked for signs of physical damage to any of the room's furnishings, but everything appeared to be fine. Just to be certain, he decided he would look through each of the galleries to see that nothing had been harmed. Perhaps he had missed something on the monitors.

He stepped into This Way to the Brain! As he made a circuit around the room, he matched the room as he saw it with the way it had appeared on the monitor. If he remembered correctly, all of the kids had been in view the entire time. As indiscreet as the two more obnoxious members had been smoking, what could they have done in here? He paused, taking stock. His breathing was normal, the adrenaline of confrontation locked away again in its dusty chamber. After taking a deep breath, he recalled that the seemingly innocent couple had written in the ledgers next to the lacquered boxes. *Aha!* There he would find sketched pot leaves and scribbled vulgarities! For a moment, fresh certainty of their guilt beat down his budding shame over possibly misdirecting accusations against them. This detective's satisfaction lasted as long as it took him to examine the first ledger, placed next to a box bearing the aroma of fresh bread:

This makes me feel normal.

Hmm? He flipped the pages, certain that somewhere there had to be proof of villainy. But that was all. He shambled over to the next ledger, alongside a box exuding the smell of Play-Doh:

This makes me feel happy.

Again, Tony flipped through the remaining blank pages but saw nothing. He shuffled over to the next ledger, a sour feeling developing in his stomach. The box alongside it bore the smell of damp cut grass:

This one stinks. Antonio Esposito

Na-ah! Angela Ramos

Tony didn't bother to look through the rest of the pages for hints of vandalism. He knew he wouldn't find any. He checked a few more ledgers just to be sure, but then he chided himself as he discovered yet more innocuous comments left by the boy with sensitive eyes and the girl with gray-green hair. When there was only one ledger left to examine, Tony stood over it, beginning to tremble. The box next to it was a kind of olfactory preview of the museum's final gallery. It predated the pulsing lights and percolating fountain by some years, but the source of its aroma was the same. As he bent over to peer at the ledger, that familiar tickle reached his nose. His eyes grew moist as he sniffled, reaching instinctively for his handkerchief. He read:

This smells like love.

Tony dropped the ledger. He hustled through the Chamber of Scents Past, then the Scratch-n-Sniff Gallery. There still might be time.

He ducked down through the 'Entrance' nostril and came into the foyer. The ring of keys practically jumped into his hands. He fumbled for the correct key to unlock the glass door to the outside. He dropped the whole ring, knowing he would, unable to prevent himself from doing so, cursing himself nonetheless.

By the time he got the door open and had lunged breathlessly out to the sidewalk, the kids were long gone. He looked up and down the littered street, the freshly broken beer bottle a few concrete slabs away. The sun, long sunk behind the neighboring warehouses, plunged the street into a desolate twilight.

Tony's shoulders slumped. He looked up at the museum's faded sign, feeling that last dose of Agnes' perfume firmly lodged in his nostrils, propelling a sneeze that he knew would build and build and never release.

THE MUSEUM OF SPACE EXPLORATION

Marilee Dahlman

MISSION & HOURS

The purpose of the Las Vegas Museum of Space Exploration is to preserve and display extraterrestrial art and material of incredible cultural importance: the Mars Frescoes and Earth's largest collection of MarsBlood.

Monday-Saturday except holidays

10am-5pm (security considerations may change hours)

Timed Entry Only; Self-Guided Tours No Longer Permitted

Gift shop closed until further notice.

GUIDE TO THE MUSEUM

Welcome! Rest assured that your safety is our top priority. Thank you for visiting the finest museum in Las Vegas. Our innovative architecture has won international acclaim, and our exhibits are out of this world! A little history:

The Man. Businessman, philanthropist and explorer Rupert A. Hammer III built this world-class museum. Mr. Hammer famously said, "I bet on red and I won." The red he was referring to was, of course, the planet Mars.

After trumped-up human trafficking allegations cut short a promising political career, Mr. Hammer turned his attention to legitimate off-planet business endeavors. The year was 2060. An international coalition was colonizing the asteroid Ceres to serve as a steppingstone to Jupiter's moon

Europa. Mars was not considered a desirable target for new discoveries or exploitation.

Enter Mr. Hammer. He uniquely saw financial potential in the red planet. He built the fastest freight spacecraft ever made, and responsible government officials awarded him a contract to ship equipment and workers to the growing colony on Ceres. Hammer predicted that his interplanetary shipping venture would break even after his first delivery and become profitable thereafter. Plus, he had another plan to generate revenue: on each return trip, he would stop at Mars and fill his empty cargo holds with something — anything — that might sell on Earth. Ever the perceptive businessman, he reasoned, "If people will pay thousands for a gram of moon dust, what would they pay for a pound of Mars rock?" Scientists had already studied the planet's geology and warned that there was nothing worth the expense of hauling to Earth in great quantities. Hammer ignored the naysayers.

Using discarded mining equipment that had functioned sub-optimally on asteroid rock, Mr. Hammer blasted out a quarry on the softer surface of Mars. They say that fortune favors the bold, and that certainly happened here. Hammer discovered a strange material that would, quite conveniently, be highly economical to ship: an extraordinarily light, iron- and magnesium-rich mineral that possessed a sponge-like molecular structure less than one percent the density of steel but twenty times as strong. It was pink and malleable, much like Earth-based clay. Manufacturing conglomerates, scientific research organizations, and various governments subsidized Hammer's subsequent journeys in exchange for mineral samples. Hammer hired an army of attorneys to maintain a monopoly in the ore, which was justified, given the risk and expense of his efforts. The potential applications for the new mineral ran the spectrum from spacecraft design to dental fillings.

Experts disagreed on the origin of the material and even its existing composition and structure. Some theorized that its molecular structure shouldn't be considered rock at all, and was, in fact, akin to the complex fibers of Earth-based natural spider silk.

At a plant near the Nevada Commercial Craft landing zone, Hammer fired the Mars clay into uniform-sized bricks. Each brick retained an incredible strength-to-weight ratio and gleamed a lustrous red without need for any paint. Hammer marketed them as 'MarsBlocks' for use in urban construction. Public demand was insatiable for such rare, beautiful, and practical extraterrestrial building material. Hammer focused sales in Las Vegas and set premium prices. This city had an ideal mix of wealthy and tasteful consumers, proximity to the brick factory, and flexible building ordinances.

The Discovery. In 2072, on Mr. Hammer's third trip to Mars, he made the greatest discovery of all time: the Mars Frescoes. Beneath the surface of the planet, Hammer discovered a cave with hieroglyphics on the smooth pink walls. The images depicted nude women bathing in a vivid red stream. They were humanoid women, with bodies similar to ours, each with a head, limbs, eyes, nose, and mouth. But they were alien, too. Their eyes and ears were significantly larger than ours. They had seven-fingered hands and long, fluid limbs. Their facial expressions were pleasant. Hammer personally funded the preservation of this glorious art and has made it accessible to all on Earth.

At first, many questioned the authenticity of Mr. Hammer's find. Subsequent events erased all doubt that this explorer had discovered true evidence of alien life. Some suggested that Hammer stop MarsBlock production until his discovery could be fully investigated. He boldly continued and proclaimed, "Development is our destiny." Mr. Hammer spent the next fifteen years excavating the Mars Frescoes, delivering them safely to Las Vegas, and producing MarsBlocks in ever-increasing quantities. He built a futuristic castle-home in the desert constructed almost entirely of MarsBlocks. He began construction of the Hammer Interstellar Hotel & Casino on the Strip, also using MarsBlocks.

Demand stayed high. MarsBlocks became a common feature of Las Vegas residential and commercial construction, including many space-themed restaurants, casinos, bars and nightclubs. Hammer donated MarsBlocks for a new professional soccer stadium. Las Vegas was affectionately nicknamed Mars City.

The Aftermath. To this day, no one knows why the oozing began. The phenomenon gained widespread attention when Hammer did a live online tour of his new MarsBlock three-story pool cabana. A red drop splattered on his bare shoulder. He calmly transferred his cigar to his other hand and wiped off the red substance, looking up at the ceiling in surprise. It was a moment replicated in countless ways across the city. MarsBlock walls, floors, ceilings, staircases, counters — all parts of construction, in all types of buildings — began, very slowly, to melt. It didn't seem caused by a simple change in temperature. The resulting red liquid wasn't corrosive or harmful. But it didn't evaporate, seep into the ground, dry up into flakes, or otherwise disappear. The liquid seems attracted to itself. Often, two nearby red pools will thin and spread out until they connect. Eventually, the substance briefly re-hardens into slabs, and liquefies again. To date, the best scientists have not identified what triggers these cyclical changes in form. Most agree that with each cycle, the substance's molecular structure becomes slightly more complex.

Tourism suffered somewhat. The globby red liquid became known as MarsBlood. Hammer's castle-home and large sections of Las Vegas dripped down. The sticky substance formed large, thick pools around the city, from the Strip to the suburbs, and the National Guard closed streets and performed evacuations. Hammer's financial empire teetered on the brink of disaster.

MarsBlood looked unclean and many were disgusted by it or even afraid. It smelled metallic and had the texture of melting candle wax. Some animals and daring humans tried drinking it, and it wasn't too harmful in small amounts unless the stagnant, thick liquid was infected with Earth-based harmful bacteria. In some respects, it may be healthy. Plants growing near it seem to flourish. Animals are attracted to it, and dogs, in particular, will sit contently near a pool of MarsBlood for hours and protect it. Experts continue to analyze for any sign that the MarsBlood itself may be some kind of intelligent life. Obviously, there is a lot we don't understand. The smartest people in the world are working day and night to unlock the secrets of MarsBlood.

Mr. Hammer faced significant public pressure to address the crisis. He rose to the occasion. His first idea involved delivering huge amounts of sand and cotton to soak up the MarsBlood at the Hammer Interstellar Hotel & Casino and Hammer Interstellar Stadium construction sites. It didn't work. At its worst stage, an astronaut commented that from space, "The lovely blue marble Earth looks like it has a popped, bleeding zit in the area of Vegas."

The Solution. You are standing inside the sublime resolution to the crisis. A soaring, some say cathedral-like, ruby-red museum built with collected MarsBlood. This is a collaborative public and private space designed to implement a policy of respectful containment. Government inspectors assess its safety on a daily basis.

Originally Mr. Hammer's idea, this is how it works: trained experts pour MarsBlood inside specially designed glass cubes. Each cube, a uniform thirty centimeters on each side, has exterior layers of laminated glass strong enough to repel bullets and withstand earthquakes and tornadoes. The inner layer is an ultra-thin, flexible glass that allows sufficient empty space for the MarsBlood's periodic transition to solid form. Each resulting glass container is a brilliant crimson MarsCube. MarsCubes, along with concrete and steel supports, form the walls, floors, ceilings and stairs of this stunning and structurally sound twenty-story museum.

The Future. What's in store for MarsBlood, and ourselves? From the desk of Mr. Hammer himself:

Make no mistake, I believe the rumors about the MarsBlood hands. I've seen one myself. One day, not long ago, I was sitting in my top-floor museum office, where I keep a prototype MarsCube. Before my eyes, the red liquid formed a hand. Its seven fingertips briefly pressed against the glass and dissolved back into formless liquid. Some say that such a hand wants to be free. Remember this — no matter how exquisite, a hand can always close into a fist or wrap around a neck. Perhaps the MarsBlood's mesmerizing, red-apple sheen may itself be an aggressive trait, much like the brightly colored lure of a predatory plant.

We don't know everything about MarsBlood, but we do know ourselves. As human beings, it is our nature to be assertive, inquisitive, and industrious; therefore, development — not just discovery — is our destiny. Now we face something greater than destiny. This is about survival. Some argue that if MarsBlood births into an intelligent, humanoid life in the state of Nevada, the being(s) would have constitutional rights of citizenship. Some want MarsCubes transported to the desert (or even all the way back to Mars!) and emptied in order to allow the MarsBlood to unite and evolve freely.

I disagree! I believe, like many others, that we should put our safety first. Let scientists have more time to analyze the substance. It seems that MarsBlood has no 'MarsBrain', or at least won't for quite some time. If it has no brain, it can have no consciousness or emotion. A four-by-four wood beam was once part of a living tree; do we attribute feelings to it? The MarsCubes are a perfect, sensible solution to allow all of us to view alien life. At the present time, layers of bulletproof glass contain the MarsBlood in a safe, respectful manner. And my solution supports the interest of transparency. All of us, for the price of a plane ticket (Hammer Interstellar Hotel offers excellent hotel/flight packages) get to participate in this journey of discovery. What will happen next? If not for the MarsCube, how long would it have taken to learn that the MarsBlood has concentric whorl fingerprints? Would our own government have told us, or not?

I am happy to announce development of an elegant super-cube that would provide more space for the MarsBlood to evolve into whatever it wishes. If there is enough popular demand, I could unveil the new super-cube as early as next year! Rest assured, I will fight all efforts to close down this museum. Our collective exploration and understanding of our neighbor, the beautiful red planet, has only just begun.

SIGNATURE EXHIBIT – RULES AND GUIDELINES

The Mars Frescoes are located in the Atrium of Adventure, directly ahead. What we ask:

- Be respectful. We don't understand life in all its forms. Keep in mind that MarsBlood may be a living being.
- We discourage touching the glass and use of flash photography in case such actions disturb the MarsBlood in some way we don't understand.
- Do not attempt to break or vandalize the glass, as the MarsCubes function as an integral part of the museum's building structure.
- Notify a museum employee promptly if you see any sign of a MarsCube leak. Keep entrance and exit doors closed in order to help us keep dogs and rodents off the premises.
- Armed private security patrols the museum at all times. Special Forces units assigned by the United States Army are on 24/7/365 standby to respond to any emergency. Pulling an alarm as a prank is subject to prosecution.
- The U.S. Mars Research & Defense Facility is located adjacent to the museum. It is absolutely off-limits. To reach Las Vegas Boulevard from the Atrium of Adventure, simply exit through the MarsCube Skyway. Do not attempt to enter any museum room marked 'Authorized Personnel Only'.

Thank you for your cooperation. Please show your museum ticket at the Hammer Interstellar Hotel & Casino to receive two free MarsBlood martinis (vodka, gin, triple sec, fresh raspberries, and grenadine), with compliments from Mr. Hammer. Enjoy your visit!

BECOME A CREW MEMBER:

As a supporter of the museum, you will help to preserve MarsBlood in a secure and responsible manner. All humans, this generation and the next, deserve the privilege of seeing this strange, unearthly substance. Here at the museum, alien mystery is almost close enough to touch! Please stop at the Crew Member Kiosk for information on membership levels and benefits.

"The Museum of Space Exploration" was originally published as "The Las Vegas Museum of Space Exploration" in *Metaphorosis* in May 2019.

THE MUSEUM OF IDENTITY

Abhijato Sensarma

The tall man in the trenchcoat slipped the Credit ID out of his pocket. It was a rectangular card, bearing just a series of numbers on its black body. But as soon as he placed it on the scanner next to a turnstile, a hologram popped out of it — a likeness of his face.

"Welcome, Dr. Junaid Hamza. Have you come here for a visit by yourself, or with family?" an automated voice asked.

The man let out a sigh. He was asked that question every time he came to visit the museum. "By myself," he said out loud. The display indicated it was buffering for a moment or two, then let out a *clink* as the symbol turned into a circle, with a tick appearing in its middle.

"A ticket fee of fifteen credits has been collected from your account." Dr. Hamza did not mind. He was compensated for the amount spent on these visits at the end of each month. A moment later, the feminine voice added as a pensive afterthought, "Enjoy your visit today."

He would encounter the voice inside as well and gauge its progress, the primary motive for his visit on most days. But for now, the voice subsided as the turnstile moved its bars to let him in. His own voice had matched the wavelengths of the biometric data collected during the issuance of Credit IDs. This was yet another procedure introduced at the museum — inaugurated just this fall — that now worked seamlessly.

Dr. Hamza realised he'd smiled on hearing the voice again, as he stepped over to the other side of the divide. The people waiting behind him glanced towards his heavy frame, then at the holographic portrait projected right above them, then back at the man himself.

The Museum of Identity, the large banner accompanying it said. *Trace the Legacy of Dr. Junaid Hamza and His Invention of CREDIT IDENTITY CARDS.*

🏛

Dr. Hamza visited the museum every day. There was no fixed time during which he did so. On most days, he got off work early and logged in his final hour by surveying the museum. On some others, he began the day by visiting the museum. Today's visit was after work.

Museum visitors noticed him as he walked down the large corridor, covered with a red carpet alongside cream-coloured walls. It opened up to the Dome of Memories that lay ahead, and adhered to the design language of all the Complete Republic's Iconic Personnel Museums.

Even more people identified Dr. Hamza as he neared the Dome, but none approached him. He was a man apart from them, the most famous Innovator in the Complete Republic.

Dr. Hamza didn't deny himself the pleasure of knowing he was the origin of the hushed whispers that went around the room now.

There were newspaper clippings and muted video footage featuring him to be found on these walls, as a preview of what was to be found within the Dome itself. There also was a bar stationed to the right of the corner near the entrance. Here, people sipped wine before making their way to the entrance. Some of them pointed at the pictures — waiting out the attraction of whatever lay inside the Dome — or leaned towards the framed clippings and television monitors interspersed all along the corridor to better read the small print. He was glad they showed the reverence an Iconic Personnel Museum like his deserved.

He walked up to the bar installed right beside the entrance, its counter in the shape of a horseshoe. Other people were already there, so Dr. Hamza sifted his eyes through the collection of wines on display behind it and stationed himself at the very end of the line to be served. He thought about how close inclusion of a bar within the museum was to being disrespectful. But it wasn't, because only the most elite labels of wine were available. Their cost was much higher than what would be expected at a standalone bar — and multiple times the price of the entrance ticket. But most of the visitors who lived in the capital of the Complete Republic did not often take a second glance at their credit balances. Purchasing a glass of wine here was no exception.

It took less than a minute for the efficient bartender to serve these customers, before swiftly moving towards Dr. Hamza at the corner of the bar with a pleasant smile on his face. "Good afternoon, sir. How may I help you?" he said, his lips barely moving, to preserve the structure of his smile.

The bartender was clean-shaven — it was a requirement for being an employee of the state — and his face was square. The bartender pushed the circular glasses he wore up his nose, still smiling without meaning it. Dr. Hamza identified the smile as the quintessential public servant's greeting he had seen everywhere. He exercised it himself whenever the need arose, though he usually reserved it for those higher-ranked than him in the hierarchy, as was procedure.

"A glass of your best wine today, please," Dr. Hamza said eventually.

The bartender nodded, then turned around to fetch an almost full bottle right behind him. "We don't serve this one too often, sir, despite the affluence of most people who come here," the bartender said, bringing it over to the counter along with an empty glass. He proceeded to place it on the counter, then poured the wine into it with a careful deliberation — as if he were extracting a fixed amount out of the bottle, one droplet on either side of which would land him in trouble in the monthly audit conducted by his superiors. After he was done, he gave another smile, though this one was more of professional satisfaction than an attempt at courtesy. "But I'm sure, sir," he said, "that the price wouldn't be a problem for you. And you seem to be in a pleasant enough mood today to not mind it."

Dr. Hamza decided to be generous with his smile. He was indeed indulging in a fancier drink than usual. And as a matter of principle, he never added his bar tab to the refund invoice he sent over to Human Resources at the end of every month.

He plucked out his Credit ID and placed it on top of the portable scanner the bartender had placed on the counter. A moment later, the payment had been made. The bartender wished Dr. Hamza a pleasant trip down memory lane, and as Dr. Hamza entered the Dome, he suddenly felt the slightest bit of giddiness infuse his steps.

First, of course, he had to collect the earpiece that was distributed at the entrance of the Dome through a slot machine — yet another procedure that needed a scan of his Credit ID.

🏛

The Dome itself expanded upwards in a shape true to its name. The floor it loomed over was a perfect circle. Divided by an invisible line running from the entrance and the exit were the two segments of the museum. On the right was the path that led through the journey of Dr. Hamza's life and all his Innovations. On the left of the room was a tour specifically dedicated to the evolution of Credit IDs, as well as his central role in it.

He turned to his right, then plugged the silver-and-blue earpiece onto the upper half of his earlobe. The speaker's size was personalised according to the ear cavity size registered on the biometric data of the Credit ID. It now rested at the most comfortable angle against Dr. Hamza's ear, almost weightless unless he thought about it.

Good morning and welcome to the life and legacy of Dr. Junaid Hamza: the man whose one-stop innovation changed the trajectory of the Complete Republic's economy, raised its stature, and, ultimately, has improved our lives in ways difficult to describe.

The voice was the same woman's voice as at the entry gate — strangely subdued in its pronunciations. But now that its source lay at the tip of his ear, Dr. Hamza gave an involuntary shudder. He still hadn't gotten used to experiencing the connection re-form itself between him and the voice in his ear. The woman spoke with a tone that seemed to lie on the cusp of being either human or artificial, yet somehow felt like neither. Feedback from the visitors suggested this had a 'disorienting' effect — most only learned post-facto that the voice was modelled after Dr. Hamza's late wife. The effort to make the voice more human — and specifically more like Mrs. Hamza's — remained an ongoing one. The Innovator had insisted on using the limited samples of his wife's recorded speech as its source. This meant the AI often had to make leaps in producing some tones it didn't have samples of.

Dr. Hamza stepped across the room, and as he did so, the sensor in the earpiece detected which projection he stood in front of, and relayed information about it. The images were holographic displays, rendered three-dimensional with the use of artificial intelligence, even in the instances where the photographs had originally been flat or of poor quality, as most had been back in the days of Hamza's youth.

The light the holographs emitted filled the entire room with a blue glow. This lent the Dome a celestial ambience. And it added to the serenity of the experience for Dr. Hamza, who by now had been seduced by the voice in his ear. He could never help it; neither did he want to. He felt a strange comfort every time he was bathed in the memories he associated with the voice.

In the past, the earpiece would sometimes fall out of sync with the invisible sensors installed in the wall behind each holograph. Each earpiece emitted a unique wave, and the processor picked it up to dictate the contents of the speech based on the user's location. But now the voice was seamless in its transitions and almost conversational in its tone. Dr. Hamza could almost see the days when he and his wife used to sit in the gardens, have the tea she made for the both of them, and talk about their days as the sun set over the wide lawn she had always maintained was too expensive to keep up. He remembered saying they earned enough to pay the gardeners they'd hired. He remembered saying a lot of things — and her always listening, sipping on her tea and smiling whenever he came to the end of a funny anecdote. He hadn't drunk wine back then.

Remembering this was like a violent tug at the collars of his trench coat. He shook his head to dissipate the remains of the image that had seemed clear to him just a moment ago, then stepped abruptly between pictures of him in third grade and senior high. He wanted to see how much — if at all — this motion would put off the monologue in his ear.

As a child, Dr. Hamza was known among his peers for being formidable at science fairs — where, for his sophomore effort, he built an alternative housing model to save the earth.

He took another step forward, moving from the picture where he was in his uniform to one where he was in an oversized t-shirt and a clumsy tie, with a certificate in one hand even as the other snuggled around the palm of his then-local MP. The voice paused for just a moment as the earpiece was caught in a limbo between two different sensors. Dr. Hamza had not yet made up his mind about whether this was off-putting or added to the AI's naturalism. He feared he had gone through this routine too many times for him to know the difference anymore. What would his wife — timid when meeting new people, yet equally wonderful once she'd started to trust them — think of her voice being used as a guide for countless people in a public space?

The project helped him be recognised within scientific circles at quite a young age. The world did not have much use for his alternative housing model. By this point of the century, most politicians believed sustainable houses would do nothing to prevent the deterioration of the environment. But the abstract model of his innovative thinking itself was appreciated — and Dr. Hamza had not yet escaped his teenage years when he came up with the earliest prototype for an invention the country would be much better served by. In the years since then, the Credit ID has saved billions of credits in money for the Complete Republic, and erased a significant amount of the nation's carbon footprint earlier accrued through paperwork and decentralised systems of identity storage.

Now Dr. Hamza stepped back, sure he was cutting through the woman's monologue at the most awkward phase.

Dr. Hamza would claim to be inspired by the events of his childhood, when he lost his father to a complicated web of debt the old man had entangled himself in while conducting his real estate business. His father was arrested by authorities at the onset of a large national recession. After the seizure of the rest of his property portfolio, there was just one dilapidated house left over. This was where Dr. Hamza spent the rest of his formative years, in the company of his mother.

An improvement in phrasing. His team was often found hard at work on weekends, when the museum was closed to the public. And they hadn't disappointed with this latest batch of updates to the AI's modelling either. They had been working on Dr. Hamza's directives for the better part of the month.

The Innovator himself stared at the picture accompanying this monologue. It was of the family picture they had taken as a ritual. He'd had a few formidable years of growth as soon as he entered adolescence. Coinciding with it had been the disappearance of his broad-shouldered, moustachioed dad. All he'd had left had been his mother, already somehow smaller than him, both her arms wrapped around his shoulders at an awkward angle as she stood next to him.

As the family pictures became more of a farce with each passing year of his childhood, Dr. Hamza slid ever farther from his mother's grasp. Now, he took a couple more steps forward to entirely to cut off the monologue of the woman in his ear.

This home was an ancestral one passed down through generations, and under the ownership of Dr. Hamza's father at the time. The authorities were sympathetic enough to not auction this property off to make up for the debt. Instead, they successfully sought out alternative sour—

Dr. Hamza closed his eyes for a moment, unsure how he felt about cutting off his wife's voice. It wasn't truly hers, he reminded himself once again. But forcing the voice to leave a thought incomplete — no matter how entrenched the words were in his memories — made him reconnect with a pang of guilt he had never been able to brush off.

He slid past photographs of his college years, during which he had been granted a scholarship that saw him emerge with a PhD, and more importantly, the inaugural version of the Credit ID. It would soon be distributed to every upstanding member of the country, thus revolutionising society forever before trickling down to the other classes, as long as they were legitimately recognised with the help of a slew of birth certificates and other documents expected to be in their possession. Anyone who didn't have these was cut off simultaneously from having both an identity and any money to spend — a surgical strike if there ever had been one.

This had also helped the regime at the helm of the government to centralise the information of the people onto its databases. Indeed, Dr. Hamza's childhood story caused him to remain at the forefront to tell the story of his innovation, rather than the Minister of Scientific Innovation who had employed him in the first place. In every interview, he mentioned his inspiration: how inadequate bureaucratic scrutiny over financial details had let his father escape consequences for too long, and how it had fired his drive to hold people and their finances responsible, and to keep the economy of the nation in good health.

The then Minister he'd shared his vision with was now long dead, though the man was in quite a few photographs from this era, and featured even more prominently on the other side of the Dome. *The Minister was a kind man*, Dr. Hamza thought.

But most of the behind-the-scenes agreements between him and the government wouldn't be revealed in any visitor's ear. Dr. Hamza had to consciously remind himself this was because the Museum's sponsors found it more prudent to keep some of the truth unsaid. The woman in his ear said, after a moment, *Please do move ahead and revel in the further glory of Dr. Hamza's life.*

Dr. Hamza made a mental note that this phrasing still sounded a bit too authoritative. He would need to get in touch with the scripting team for an update, and tinker with the AI's algorithm himself. The last update hadn't been enough. The latest set of data available to his department suggested eighty-three percent of the Complete Republic's demographic still disliked the notion of being commanded by a woman's voice.

People kept noticing him inside the Dome. He did his best to move past a growing crowd as the evening approached. They greeted his identification with a hushed enthusiasm conveyed with raised eyebrows and a raised hand to protect the contents of their whispers. They also made sure to turn away before they met the Innovator's eyes as he passed by them.

The recognition of the man in their midst had picked up pace like a wildfire people did not know what to do about, spreading through the room rapidly now. It was a rather strange phenomenon, in Dr. Hamza's mind — it disturbed the quiet reverence expected within the museum, even as the sentiment displaced itself from holographic reproductions to his physical presence. But he only cared for the ambience tangentially now. He'd already been transported to the non-linear world of his recollections instead.

He suddenly did not wish to be seen anymore. Every time he was in the museum, he was giving the project its approval in the eyes of the people who spotted him now. But the government tinkered with every new revised draft about his life. They chiselled away at any factoid that did not advance the story they sought to tell. And he was their heftily paid protagonist.

He took a sip from his glass of wine, then walked and walked till he reached the other end of the curve. He had no interest in the other side of the museum. It was a more in-depth journey through Credit IDs and how he'd worked on it, with different prototypes on display, and archival footage from television shows back when television sets were still manufactured and sold across the breadth of the nation.

The entire museum was too scripted for him to reminisce about with any positive sentiment. He was halfway through his glass of wine, which usually helped him make these trips with relative stolidity. Today, however, he lacked patience for this incomplete narrative of his life. He did continuously try to make the scripts more realistic.

But it had been a battle of passive-aggression between Dr. Hamza's wishes and the government's. A few writers had been caught in the crossfire and paid with their jobs, but this was just the nature of bureaucracy. At least they were freelancers rather than contracted employees — the government's explicit policy barred any artists from being on their permanent payroll, or enjoying any of the benefits and perks that came along with it.

Dr. Hamza instead walked over to a picture right at the end of his biographical section in the Dome. The Complete Republic's incumbent regime had never cared too much for this segment of the museum. There was a reason this picture had been placed at the very end of the museum's journey through his life — it was perhaps the only instance of him positively beaming in any of these pictures, not conforming to the more neutral positivity he'd been trained to emit. But he'd insisted on using this wedding photograph.

He stood next to his wife in it, wearing a black suit with a white handkerchief tucked into its breast pocket. But he did not linger over himself for too long, only remarking how happy he seemed to be in this photograph. Had the picture been edited? He knew it couldn't have been, but it felt strange to him that he'd been this happy once. In any case, his gaze had already moved over to the woman who overshadowed him.

She wore a red-and-ecru dress, as beautiful by itself as one would expect at a wedding. But there was a peculiar feeling people had never been able to pin down with words whenever they were in her physical presence, which Dr. Hamza had been privy to perhaps more than anyone else over the years. Her smiles had always been genuine. Even in sorrow, the sentiment behind them had always borne some truth of its own. It brought a parody of a smile to his own lips. When he realised this, looking at his reflection on one of the screens off which light reflected, he shook his own head to wipe it away.

Her eyes had been another striking feature. They gave off an otherworldly sheen, even through the filter of the photographs she appeared in. This had been experienced even by the most experienced government officials who had met her at their home for the first time. No matter whether they'd seen photographs of her before or not, they were always thrown off from the cultivated indifference they'd perfected in their job profiles over the years.

Their experience meant this disbalance was only momentary, but both Dr. Hamza and his wife had seen them being flustered when she gazed in their direction. She'd laughed about it with him in private, blushing in embarrassment even as she found the humour of these episodes. Dr. Hamza had always claimed there was something supernatural about her presence. Mrs. Hamza had almost always replied that he'd not forgotten how to be a good flirt after their marriage.

Though she usually preserved her silence during these meetings, she was even more hypnotic when she did speak. She'd graduated from a leading university in the capital — but one couldn't trace an academic vocabulary or any posh accent in her speech. And she had been much wiser than him in most matters. For the most part, she'd kept her ideas to herself. She did channel them into her research, but it had never been influential within the country beyond her immediate academic circles. And she had been happy with life in a way that had always eluded Dr. Hamza, a quality reflected in her voice. It possessed a tranquility her husband had basked in whenever she stroked his hair and told him about her day during their evenings together.

Dr. Hamza met his wife — a remarkable woman in her own right — while they pursued their bachelor's degrees. They married soon after graduation, with her one year senior to him. While the Doctor would then go on to refine Credit Identity Cards till the system was ready to be implemented across the breadth of the nation, she wrote a thesis on the Sociological Background of Economic Satire in Western Literature. Despite their divergent academic interests — he a respected economist, she a sociologist crucial to advancing the anthropological analysis of language in comparative literature — the two grew together in their own inimitable way. Until, of course, their marriage met with tragedy when his wife decided to leave the country. And the flight taking her to America crashed.

The holograph on display transitioned to show a picture of the wreckage of the plane she'd been aboard. The script the voice in his ear followed to the letter made no mention of the fact that she had decided to leave him, as well as the Complete Republic, just a few days before her death. It had been a direct result of the Parliament's passing legislation that outlawed the discussion of satire in any context, except when analysing it within the classroom — or in a political speech — to deride it for the low literature it was. 'It is engaged in only by dissidents with no positive contributions of their own to help with the growth of the Complete Republic', the Anti-national Satire Censorship Bill had gone on to say.

The official report mentioned the cause of her death to be that the plane she was travelling on had run into a sudden hurricane while attempting to land at the airport. It was a natural phenomenon that had become hazardously common across the globe by then, but especially in the continent she was heading towards. Dr. Hamza, on the other hand, had thought her to be dead as soon as she chose her identity as an academician with ideas of her own over that of a woman with a man she could love for the rest of her life.

You'd never have to make that decision for yourself, would you? If you insist on not letting me make it either, perhaps the both of us are truly better off separated the moment I step out of this door tomorrow. Just know I'll love you all the same.

The imagined voice shook him off his feet. It was one of the last things she'd ever said to him, with no smile accompanying her sorrow when she'd left. And the lines popped into his head now as if he'd just heard them, though he knew it was only a hallucination. He took a sip from the glass of wine he'd been carrying, wiped his brows with the kerchief in his trench coat's pocket, and listened to the voice in his ear resume speaking. Yes, Dr. Hamza heard it now — even if incrementally, the voice had improved in resembling his wife's. That counted for progress.

The entire endeavour might have been less time-consuming if they'd just resorted to a living, professional voice actor. But no, despite often pondering whether his wife would have approved of the entire venture, he remained steadfast about the correctness of his decision.

Dr. Hamza used this inspiration to fuel his journey into artificial-intelligence-driven speech research. Within five years, he developed fully functional, responsive speech software based on his late wife's famously magnetic voice, as a tribute to her. It is being beta-tested for improvement within select Iconic Personal Museums, including this one. A full-fledged launch across all AI services offered by the Complete Republic is expected to take place by the end of the year...

Dr. Hamza peered down at his toes, then at the bubbles rising to the top of his glass of wine, before sipping on it and continuing onward. The voice had moved on from his marriage already, and he did not particularly care for whichever achievements of his had been listed out as having been achieved after her death — a sign for the public that he was coping well with her passing. He wasn't.

He had thought including her in the project would be a way of keeping her alive. But the words that reverberated in his ears, sourced from an imitation of her voice, reminded him she would've never talked about him — or anyone else — in this manner. *Should he have done this?* It was too late to back away and start from scratch now. For one thing, he had done this as a way of getting back at the regime, which he blamed for having driven his wife and their marriage to the brink. But he knew that wasn't the truth. Not the complete truth, anyway, just as the words that kept streaming into his conscience weren't.

How often had she spoken about herself during their shared evenings? She did let him know about how her day had been, but only after he'd gone through the narration of his. And by then, his mind had often drifted away to the beauty of the sunsets, with her voice entrancing him as a background score rather than the ideas and fears and hopes of the woman he loved the most.

Somewhere along the way, he had come to the erroneous conclusion that she didn't really have anything new to say. But right now, he would have done anything he could to get her back. Her everyday truth had been more precious to him than the pale imitation he heard of her voice now, recycling the same words off a script he grew to despise more with every passing minute, again and again.

He knew all the same that he wouldn't give the latter up for anything in the world either. But no matter how hard he thought about it, or how much he drank after going back home in the evenings now, he did not know how to live with it.

Suddenly, he did not feel like completing the rest of the tour to test for any bugs or glitches in the software. He wasn't in the mood to listen to the voice anymore. As it was, he already had enough mental notes from today's visit to send his team's way. He made an abrupt move towards the exit, draining his glass of wine and placing it on a designated tray protruding from the wall, from where it would soon be collected.

A tour of Dr. Hamza's journey towards the invention and release of Credit IDs remains, if you are interested.

He did not respond. The voice in the ear took it for the rejection it was.

Thank you for visiting us today. Please fill out the feedback survey when you deposit this earpiece before exiting the museum. This will go a long way in helping me improve my AI conditioning for any future visits.

For a few moments, Dr. Hamza wanted to say something in return. But he paused, coughing to clear away the remnants of any embarrassment he felt collecting itself near the bottom of his throat. A response would have been futile, because the voice neither recorded nor understood any speech directed towards it by the user. Not just yet.

Dr. Hamza hadn't focused on the verbal interaction capabilities of the AI during development, citing budget restrictions at the early stages of the project. But he had not admitted his deeper reluctance to anyone in his team. Once upon a time, her enigmatic voice had mostly been reserved for his ears only. Countless people listened to it now — but his wife did not *speak back* to them. Not in the way she'd spoken back to him when she was alive, with such understated affection and tenderness in her every syllable.

At that moment, he made a final mental note on this trip: he'd like to keep the tone of the AI just as it was. A bit of authority, he reasoned after all, was necessary in even the loveliest of voices. He heard it even now, as it spoke for a final time at the verge edge of the exit: *I hope you visit us again.*

THE MUSEUM OF INSPIRATION

Pauline Yates

I stir memories of my father into my tea with a spoonful of raw sugar and sip the bittersweet sadness that lingers. Two weeks have passed since I laid him to rest next to Mum, but I haven't had the heart to go through his things. The retirement village staff packed the last of his belongings into a box, but it sits undisturbed in my study. I'm not ready to revisit anything that reminds me of him.

Sighing, I place my cup on the table. I'm putting off what needs to be done, but the task refreshes memories of what happened when Mum died. I thought Dad and I would laugh and cry and reminisce about family times as we navigated life without her. Instead, he withdrew and grew increasingly sullen, very different to the happy-go-lucky father I remember. I blamed grief. Then I blamed him for not dealing with it. During a time when our father-daughter relationship should have strengthened, his moodiness pushed us apart.

He may have realized his mistake. In the weeks leading up to his death, his eyes often shimmered with regret. I take no joy in knowing that he may have felt guilty about the strain he caused. Mostly, I just feel sad that whenever we spent time together, his mind always seemed to be elsewhere.

"But I won't be like you, Dad," I whisper. "I'll deal with my grief and move on, what you should've done."

Resigning to the awful task of putting Dad's belongings to rest with him, I go to the study and open the box. Inside is a folder secured by a thick rubber band, his

Bible, an address book, the last novel he read (science fiction, his favorite), his watch, a plain glass vase he used for flowers, and a bundle of old letters.

Pulling out the folder, I remove the rubber band and slide out a ream of paper. My lips part in astonishment. Typed on the first page is 'Beneath a Starless Sky', the title I thought of for a story he told when I was a child. We used to sit in the garden at night and he'd point at stars and tell me the names of fictional planets and where they were in the sky, but one night there was a thin layer of fog and we couldn't see anything.

I flip through the pages, but as I read what he typed, Dad's voice fills my mind and I'm transported into his fictional world. Again, I'm the intrepid Starfleet commander sent to rescue a group of space explorers who crash-landed on a mysterious planet inside a black hole. My heart swells with exhilaration, but I drag myself out of Dad's world and close the pages.

I shouldn't read this now. Being happy so soon after Dad's death doesn't feel right. But the story is all here, with chapters and page numbers — a complete novel. I had no idea he'd typed this up. He should have tried to get it published. It was a fantastic story, and I can't wait to read this fuller version when I'm ready.

Wiping a wistful tear that escaped my eye, I return the manuscript to the folder, then sift through the bundle of letters. The envelopes are yellowing and postmarked years ago. Turning over a letter, my heart jolts. The sender is a publishing company. Opening the envelope, I unfold the letter and read.

"Thank you for sending us 'Beneath a Starless Sky'. Regretfully, we will pass..."

Dad *did* try to get his novel published. How devastating to receive a rejection. Returning the letter to the envelope, I open the next letter. It's another rejection from a different publisher. The next letter is the same. And the next.

"Oh, Dad," I say. "Why didn't you say anything?"

I would have helped if I'd known. Maybe he gave up the idea of publishing a novel when computers replaced typewriters. He didn't own a computer and was always grumbling about emails and how nobody writes letters these days, which frustrated me to no end. Or maybe retyping his story into a Word doc was too daunting for someone his age. I assume manuscripts are sent by email now. But even if I had offered to help, I doubt he would have accepted. He was a proud man and asked no one for help, preferring to handle things himself.

"And look where that landed you, Dad," I say, sighing. "You're gone, and so is the chance to get your book published." A dream slipped away, as many dreams do.

Who am I to talk? Don't I have a dream that I let slip away? It used to sing in my heart, but I haven't hummed the tune in years. It's still there, but it's muted and buried beneath layers of lost hope born from the pressure of life's responsibilities. Even if I found the desire to resurrect it, I'm too old to start a new venture. I'm not even sure I'm capable.

"Or maybe I'm too like you, Dad, stubborn and unwilling to embrace change." Huffing at that uncomfortable thought, I bundle up the letters and continue to sort through the box. The phone rings, an unwelcome interruption, but I answer it.

"Hello?"

"Am I speaking with Susan Flannery?"

I don't recognize the woman's voice. "Yes, I'm Susan."

"Good morning. My name is Beryl Marsh, from the Museum of Inspiration. Please accept my condolences for your father's passing."

"Thank you. Um, how can I help you?" I don't recall dad mentioning a Beryl, and I certainly don't know the museum. I hope she's not calling for charity and thinks I'm easy prey for a donation so soon after the funeral.

"Susan, forgive my intrusion into what must be a difficult time for you. However, I've come into possession of something belonging to your late father. I'd love to display it in my museum, but require your permission as his living next-of-kin. Is it possible for us to meet so we can discuss the details?"

What's she talking about? Dad owned nothing worth displaying in a museum. I don't think. He didn't tell me about the novel. What other secrets did he keep from me?

Or has this woman stolen something from his retirement unit?

"What is it, and how did you get it?" I ask, dreading the thought of Dad's belongings in a stranger's hands.

"I'd rather discuss this with you in person," Beryl says. "It's quite personal and will be easier to understand when you see it."

This has to be a scam. I have all of Dad's belongings, the items in this box the last of them. I should hang up and ignore this woman, but if she's stolen something, I want it back.

"I'd be happy to meet with you," I say, keeping my tone pleasant so I don't scare her off. I want to know who and where she is in case I need to report her to the police.

"Lovely," Beryl says. "Would 2 pm today work for you? This is the address."

Snatching a pen and paper off my desk, I scribble it down: 115 Lexington Avenue. I know that street. It's on the edge of the town. I don't recall a museum, though. It's mostly heritage-listed brick houses on tiny allotments. This is definitely a scam.

"I'll see you at two. I look forward to meeting you."

"Lovely," Beryl says again. The line goes dead.

I tap the pen on the paper. How safe am I, going to a strange address to meet a person I don't know? Needing more information, I open the computer and search for the museum online. A website pops up: The Museum of Inspiration.

The website shows a photo of a red brick house behind a decorative wrought-iron fence, with stained-glass windows and French front doors. Crammed onto the smallest lot in the street, it's dwarfed by its larger neighboring estates. A sign on the gate reads 'The Museum of Inspiration, Open Tuesdays and Thursdays, 10am-2pm. Tour bookings essential'. There's no phone number on the sign or on the website, though the website has a booking form. I check my phone. Beryl called from a private number.

I close the computer, wondering what to do. Today is Wednesday. Maybe I should wait until tomorrow and turn up during the opening times when other people are likely to be around? That would be safest, but I can't ignore the tug at my heart. If Beryl has something belonging to Dad, I want it back now.

I check the time on my watch. It's after one, so I quickly change into fresh clothes, then drive across town. Lexington Avenue is narrow, so I park in an adjoining street and walk to the address. Stopping at the gate, I study the house. It looks exactly like the photo on the website, but it's the saddest house in the street. Lost in shadows cast from the neighboring houses, the museum, if that's what it is, is anything but inspiring; the brickwork crumbles, the gate creaks open, the cement path leading to the front door is a patchwork of cracks. The door opens and a spindly, gray-haired woman I assume is Beryl smiles through wrinkles so deep it's hard to tell if her mouth curves.

She's a tiny woman, but her eyes are sharp and there's a toughness about her that puts me on edge. A warning jumps to mind — scammers are the least likely person you'd expect. If that's true, this woman fits the bill.

"It's lovely to meet you, Susan," Beryl says. "Please, come inside."

I step through the door into a dingy sunroom. A narrow hallway runs through the centre of the house. On either side of the hall, doors to other rooms are closed. The walls are a deep shade of maroon that adds to the claustrophobic atmosphere. There's no furniture, no artwork, nothing to suggest a museum.

"I thought this was a museum?" I say, wondering if coming here was a mistake.

"It is," Beryl says, closing the door and shutting out the little light that crept in with me. "I'm glad you came today. It's quite busy on tour days."

"Tuesdays and Thursdays, right?" I hope she hears my skepticism.

"Ten till two, but it's never nearly enough time," Beryl says. "Come. I'll show you around. It will help to explain my request."

She flits along the hallway, a busy bee despite her fragility. I follow, more curious than cautious. I can't see where she'd set up a museum display, unless the house is long, with rooms at the back that I couldn't see from the street. A door on the right is marked OFFICE, but Beryl walks past it to another door at the end of the hallway. Stopping, she flicks a switch on the wall, opens the door, and waves me through.

Stepping past her, I enter a living room. Heavy black curtains cover the windows, blocking all light from the outside. Other than the curtains, the room is bare. No paintings, no sculptures, no displays of historical artifacts. My stomach does a nervous flip-flop. What have I walked into?

"Walk around, take your time," Beryl says.

"There's nothing to see." Anger courses through me. Dad would turn in his grave knowing I'm here. I was always warning him about scams.

"The exhibits are motion-activated," Beryl says. "I suggest starting at the wall on my left and working your way around."

The only way I want to go is out the front door. But I'll play along. I'm not leaving until I find my father's belongings.

Stepping to the left, I walk along the wall. A light flickers overhead, then an image appears in front of me, a hologram of a woman wearing a university cap and holding a diploma. Stopping, I stare at the woman, wondering who she was and what her historical significance is. This woman could be anyone who graduated from a university.

"That's Mary Stevenson," Beryl says. "She raised three children with her husband, Charles. After her children left home, Mary worked in a dry-cleaning shop until she died aged seventy-six."

"Did she do something historically notable?"

"No, nothing."

"Why are you showing her, then?"

"You'll see. Go on." She waves me along the wall.

Confused, I follow the wall around. Mary's image snaps off, and I trigger the next hologram. This one shows a man standing at the top of a mountain, arms raised in jubilation. I have to admit, the hologram is impressive. The image is so clear I can see the ice clinging to the man's eyelashes.

"Who's this?" I ask.

"Peter Mannering," Beryl says. "His dream was to climb Mount Everest. Sadly, his dream died with him in a car accident, age forty-seven."

"I don't understand. You have a picture of him standing on top of a mountain."

Beryl says nothing.

Frowning, I continue along the wall. Another hologram appears, activated by my movement. This one shows a woman sitting in a vehicle, staring across an open plain at the reddest sunset I've ever seen. I still don't understand the significance. Continuing along the wall, the next hologram shows a woman standing in a garden holding a basket of rosemary sprigs.

Reaching out, I touch the hologram. My hand takes on the colors in the image. It's just light, nothing solid. "What are these?"

Beryl comes over and stands next to me. "They're unrealized dreams. The woman in the vehicle dreamed of seeing an African sunset, but left it too late to travel abroad. This woman in the garden, her dream was to live in the country and make a living from growing herbs, but she never left the city. The first woman, Mary, dreamed of obtaining a university degree, but found excuses to delay her study plans. And though it was in Peter Mannering's heart to scale the largest mountain, the closet he got to the summit was reading about others who had made the trek, instead of doing it himself."

"Yet you have pictures of these people achieving their dreams?"

"What you see was in their heart, nothing more."

An icy chill creeps over my skin. "What is this place? How do you know what's inside someone's heart?"

"It's what I do," Beryl says. "For inspirational purposes."

"By displaying dead dreams? How is that inspirational?" I wave my hand at the woman in the garden. "I think you made her up and you're selling fake stories to people foolish enough to believe them. This isn't a museum. You're a con-artist."

"Perhaps your father's personal effect will help you understand what it is we display here?"

"Yes. Where is it?" My face flushes with furious heat. "Whatever you have, I'm taking it and leaving. I'll take no more part in this nonsense."

"As you wish. This way, please."

Showing no emotion at my angry outburst, Beryl walks back to the door. I hurry after her, triggering the holograms as I pass — the woman and her sunset; Peter and his mountain; Mary and her diploma. Even if these dreams are true, all they inspire is sadness.

Beryl goes to the office and pushes open the door. I follow her inside, bristling with fury at her insensitive play-on-dreams con-job. Unlike the empty hall and museum room, the office is cluttered. Filing cabinets take the wall space on both sides of the room. A narrow timber desk lines the back wall. It's covered in stacks of manila folders held together with rubber bands. Above the desk is a bookshelf holding a collection of square metal canisters.

Beryl reaches for a canister and pulls it down. Turning, she hands it to me.

"What's this?" The canister is warm and stirs an odd sense of longing.

"Your father's dream," Beryl says.

Does this crazy woman seriously expect me to believe my father's dream is inside? I know all his dreams. Don't I?

"Perhaps you'd like to view it in private?" Beryl says. "Unrealized dreams belonging to someone close can be confronting. I'll be outside if you need me." Stepping past, she goes outside and closes the door.

Alone with the canister, I don't know what to do. The rational part of my brain is telling me that this is all part of the scam. That Beryl has concocted some crock show and then she'll fleece me out of money to display it. But another part of my brain whispers doubt into my mind. That perhaps I didn't know Dad's dreams, because dreams are private and never shared with anyone. Don't I have a dream I didn't share with him?

Listening to the whisper, I open the lid.

Light blooms from inside the canister. A hologram pops up in front of me. It shows my father sitting at a table signing books, his eyes bright and a wide grin on his face. Seeing the book's cover, tears spring to my eyes. 'Beneath A

Starless Sky' — the title of his unpublished manuscript printed on a picture of a man and a child stargazing — what Dad and I used to do.

I scramble for an explanation. Beryl could have read the manuscript at the retirement village and guessed that he wanted to be a published author. But there's no way she could have conjured the front cover. The child could be me, because she wears her hair in a ponytail like I did at that age. I don't know how this is possible, but this hologram shows the dream in Dad's heart and it's as real as I am.

Reflecting back, I wonder how long he dreamed to be a published author. Did the idea bloom during those early storytelling days, or did it unfurl later in life? I don't recall Mum mentioning it, though I do remember her saying that Dad was off in his world whenever he didn't respond to a question. I remember, too, how the story used to keep me awake long after I should have fallen asleep, but Dad never got angry. His eyes would shine brighter than the stars as he tucked me beneath the blankets and shushed me to sleep as though he didn't want to leave his world, either.

Having read some of his manuscript and experienced how uplifted the story made me feel, despite my melancholy, I wonder if Dad revisited his story as a way to escape his grief after Mum died. Isn't that what stories do, transport you to another world and give you a break from the pressures of real life? Maybe the publishing idea grew from a desire to share his story with everyone so other people could escape their misery, too.

If all that is true, I was wrong to think Dad withdrew because he couldn't overcome his grief when Mum died. I don't doubt he missed her. He kept her photo by his bedside from the moment she passed. But seeing this hologram explains a lot. Many times when I rang to check on him, Dad would make excuses about being too busy to talk, if he answered the phone at all. He wasn't shutting me out, or withdrawing because of grief. He must have been putting all his efforts into finishing his novel. He also would have known time was running out to fulfill something he longed to do, especially after Mum's passing. But after multiple rejection letters, no wonder he grew sullen. It must have broken his heart to think his efforts had gone to waste.

"I'm so sorry, Dad. I didn't realize how much publishing that story meant to you." If only he hadn't given up, though trying again after having his confidence crushed would have been difficult. But the Dad I know wasn't one to give up easily. His stubbornness extended in more ways than refusing help. What if he wanted to continue his search for a publisher, but age got the better of him? The regret he wore on his deathbed might have been because he left it too late to resume and he was forced to resign to the reality that his dream would die with him.

An uncomfortable prickle creeps up the back of my neck. How would I feel reaching my deathbed, knowing I'd left it too late to chase my dream? Now that I understand the significance of these holograms, I've no doubt achieving my dream would make me happier beyond measure. I must want to. Why else would my song still be in my heart?

"There are many reasons we don't fulfill our dreams," Beryl says from behind me. "But I hope that by displaying unrealized dreams, it will inspire people to strive for theirs."

"How did you get this?" I ask, my voice thick with emotion.

"It's what I do," Beryl says.

She gives no further explanation, but there's no need to understand the how when I know the why. The exhibits in this museum are to remind us that if we don't want our dreams to die, we should breathe life into them before we can't.

I gaze at Dad's triumphant expression, then close the lid and hug the canister to my heart. "If you don't mind, I'd like to keep this. Dad's dream is precious to me and it's..."

"Inspiring?" Beryl offers.

I sigh. "It's given me a lot to think about."

Like striving for my dream before it's too late. It's still possible. I know my song by heart. But it won't be heard without me. I should stop finding reasons not to pursue it, because there are no reasons. The only thing preventing my dream from becoming a reality is the excuses I make.

Clutching the canister, I hurry from the office. Strangely, the sunroom doesn't appear dingy, as when I first arrived. It's warm and welcoming, and sunlight gleams through the stained-glass windows, casting rainbows across the floor. I jump over them, the lightness in my heart spreading to my feet. Pausing at the door, I glance over my shoulder. Beryl stands at the office door, hands clasped in front of her waist.

"It's an apt name for your museum," I say.

Her smile irons out her wrinkles, if they were there at all. "I'm glad you think so, dear."

Opening the door, I step outside, humming the song in my heart.

The Museum of Living Color

Ryan Cole

Red lust, as usual, comes in the morning. Red in the way that you whisper my name, in the tender caress of your fingers on my neck, where my dry skin soaks up your technicolor world. Where you are my brush, and I am your canvas: pliant, eager, ready to be drawn.

I smile as your scorched-earth skin comes to life. I swallow the vermilion heat on your tongue.

And I take. I steal as much of you as I can.

But it's never enough. Not for me, or your family, or the portrait of us that they want you to create. The one that will hang in their gallery forever.

And you and I both know that your red never lasts.

🏛

Revised placard text for: *The Portrait of Maurice and Henrietta Mildrin* (1925; Great Falls, VA; property of the Mildrin Family Gallery).

Maurice and Henrietta are pictured along with their six children on the azalea garden lawn of the Mildrin family estate. As is shown by the way that they gaze into each other's eyes, red played a prominent role in the artists' lives. Note the crimson undertones, the unabashed desire. Red lust is used to hide all of their flaws.

Note also, however, the smear on Henrietta's chin — the dark-golden anger, the same gold that glimmers in Maurice's right pupil. The artists claimed that these were due to the aging of the portrait, and that they never would have used such an impure color — especially gold — to paint themselves. Mrs. Henrietta Mildrin, the original curator of this Gallery, took pride in showing which colors made an appropriate marriage. And until her recent death, that marriage — and its portrait — was what every Mildrin relative strove to achieve.

🏛

Gold creeps in like the sun between the clouds. Your lust becomes a shadow of the fire that it was when you sculpted my skin with red-smeared hands. When you hadn't yet dipped into your palette of emotions, the reminders of who you are and who you have to be — who *we* have to be — to have a place in your family.

"I don't think we should go," you say through your tie. You wrangle the ends into a paisley knot around your throat. "You're still not ready."

"*I'm* not ready?" I say, unsurprised, because I am no stranger to your swiftly changing colors — the inconvenient shades that you aren't allowed to show. "It's been seven years. I've learned what I need to know."

"Maybe it's not enough."

I pull on my loafers, absorbing the words. Your gold never comes without a fine, serrated edge, forged in the heat of your growing frustration. At me. Your parents. Your bottled-up emotions. "I'm as ready as I'll ever be," I say with years of practice.

You sigh and rest the back of your hand on my cheek, staining me with all of your dark, dirty gold. One of the scant few colors you can share. "Alfie," you whisper. "Don't make me do this."

I try to pull away, but the color won't let me. It continues to flow. "You can't just cancel," I say, my cheek burning. "We've had this scheduled for months." As if there weren't anything strange about scheduling an appointment to see your great-aunt, whom you've known since you were a child, who has probably already seen what you're trying to hide. Don't blame *me* for showing you who you really are.

But since when did the canvas give advice to the brush?

"We're going," I say. "She even purchased our portrait frame."

You pucker your lips into an irritated pout, and you let your color slide all the way down my back, under my blazer, where nobody can see.

My canvas skin shivers. I drink in the anger that you feel, but don't want to. A piece of yourself that you would rather not own. And like a good husband, I let it all in.

I let it seep into the wrinkles in my stomach, the folds in my thighs that your scarlet-self adores. I stow it in my armpits, under my toenails. Tiny pieces slip under the flaps of my eyelids, so that when I go to sleep, my vision is a black field with bright golden stars.

But that doesn't matter. You don't need to hide from me.

The one we have to fool is your Great-Aunt Suzannah, and I'm starting to worry that you may be right.

Are the two of us prepared to join the Mildrin Family Gallery?

🏛

Revised placard text for: *The Portrait of Malachi and Joanne Mildrin* (1939; Richmond, VA; property of the Mildrin Family Gallery).

Malachi Mildrin, the youngest of Maurice and Henrietta's six children, is pictured with his betrothed, the smiling Joanne Mildrin, who is seven months pregnant. When the artists finished painting their official self-portrait — an act often saved for several years into a marriage — they had only been engaged for two and a half months.

Note the pale-yellow angst, the silhouette of displeasure that surrounds both their shoulders. It is worth noting that their union was one of necessity, a product of Mrs. Henrietta Mildrin, who disapproved of the artists' premarital activities. Which begs the question: was Joanne's smile genuine?

🏛

Dots of faded yellow trickle from you in a haze as we step out of the car and onto the driveway. Your unruly blonde curls, slicked into submission, cast you as a man that I don't normally see: tamed, dampened, willing to suffer the necktie that binds you.

We walk past the fountain, up the granite steps that fan out in waves, and we stand on the threshold of a door that dwarfs us. It morphs into turrets and stained-glass windows and balconies that overlook a garden of azaleas.

Your fingers scrape mine, but they aren't really there. They vanish, brushless, into what we haven't achieved, into how you haven't shaped us into what we should be. You simmer in your worries. And I simmer with you.

You knock on the door, and you cringe when it opens.

"My little Maverick," says Suzannah, who is almost three times your age, pinching her over-plump lips into a smile. She inspects you like I do when you aren't paying attention, searching for a shade that you haven't shown before, as if she knows that what we've crafted isn't worthy of display. Then she squeezes my shoulder with a splotchy, brittle hand, betraying a strength that her thin frame hides.

"And Alfie, my dear, it's been far too long. I haven't seen you since the wedding. I'm *so* glad you're here. Commissioning a portrait is a Mildrin family tradition, and you're the first couple that I get to sink my teeth into." She grins, veneers flashing, and she guides us inside.

You hesitate, afraid to walk into the building that will commemorate our marriage for generations to come, and like a fading ray of sunlight, you cling to the wall. Hover by the portraits that are hanging in the entryway. There is one, in particular, that captures your interest.

"Ah," says Suzannah, shuffling over. "There's your Aunt Melanie, back when she was pretty. And you, cute as a button." She points at a much younger version of yourself, clothed only in colors that the Gallery condones. "But come on over here. Take a look at this one."

She guides us to the other side of the sprawling foyer, where an oversized portrait hangs over the staircase. "See that one there, right over the banister? That's your Great-Uncle Milton and his wife, Genevieve."

This gets your attention. "Is that one new?"

"Oh, you know Henrietta, always hiding things away. I found it down in the basement in an unmarked crate, and once I knew you were coming, I chose to dust it off."

"It looks different than the others. Doesn't it?" you say. More erratic, you mean. Showing all the wrong colors. But you leave that unsaid.

"Each of us is unique," says Suzannah, smiling coyly. She leaves it at that, doesn't wait for you to answer. The two of us shuffle from the chandeliered foyer, leaving you alone with your long-dead relatives, and with a wrinkled hand on my waist, your great-aunt guides me into a cavernous sitting room, where a tray of miniature sandwiches and teacups is arranged.

Along with a large, empty square of oiled wood.

"Is this ours?" I say.

Suzannah nods with me. The empty frame rests grandly on an easel, and not just *any* frame. The frame to officiate our place in the Mildrin family.

"It's beautiful," I say, because truly, it is. A masterwork of cedar planks, intricately carved.

My eyes start to glisten, but I *cannot* cry. Not near Suzannah.

When I cry, I lose control. My canvas unfurls. The colors that you give me escape in all directions. They emerge from my dozens of carefully crafted hideaways: my wrinkles, my eyelids, the crease between my shoulderblades.

And maybe it's the stress, or the guilt from our lies, but the teardrops that flow start to crack my façade.

"Alfie, what's wrong, dear?" says Suzannah, her voice smooth. "Come over here, sit with me."

I follow the trail of her hand to the sofa, because it's already too late. Our secret is revealed.

"Miss Suzannah," I say, "I apologize, *really*, I don't know what's come over me."

"Well, *I* do," she says, wiping my cheek. "And you can call me Suz. I'm not like my mother."

"You do?" I croak.

She nods, her fingers dyed a burnt, rusty gold as she soaks up my color. "Maverick needs to accept that nobody is perfect. Not you, not me, not him, *not even them.*" She says that last with a sweep of her arms, to encompass all the portraits on the walls around us.

I wonder what secrets that sentence could hold. But she doesn't elaborate. She taps me on the knee and motions to the foyer. "Why don't you try to get Mav to come in here? The Gallery has some new rules that I've created, and I think he'll want to hear them." Another coy smile, knowing more than she lets on.

I leave her on the sofa. And I find you standing right where we left you before.

Your arms are crossed, eyes on the portrait of your Great-Uncle Milton — the one that, until now, no one knew existed — on the gold flowing out of his oil-sketched features. The gold so similar to what you repress, to what you've been taught isn't clean, isn't right. And around that gold, a hint of hopeful green, and a midnight-blue sadness that looks nearly black.

🏛

Revised placard text for: *The Portrait of Hugo and Melanie Mildrin* (1966; Great Falls, VA; property of the Mildrin Family Gallery).

Hugo and Melanie are pictured in the conservatory of the Mildrin family estate. They are joined by Maverick, their newly adopted nephew, aged three years old on the date of commission, only six months after the tragic passing of his parents, the late Beatrice Mildrin and her husband, Murphy.

Hugo and Melanie are blatant in their optimism. Note the dandelion stems that dangle from their fingers, the effervescent turquoise that bubbles from their lips, the wilderness of too-happy weeds at their feet. The promise of rebirth — a commendable theme — is strong in this rendition. Green hope drowns out their sordid, blue past.

Of particular importance: these artists were prone to feeling a wide range of emotions, the command of which, some would say, was less than ironclad, and which, for better or worse, they passed down to their children.

🏛

As you emerge from your reverie, you touch my arm and say, "Alfie, I'm sorry."

I'm sorry, too. I'm sorry that your parents didn't teach you restraint, to summon one color when you don't need them all.

But then again, those colors are what drew us together.

"It's alright, Mav," I say. "Our portrait will be the most spectacular one of them all."

You smile at my smile. You allow yourself to relax. The golden anger fizzles to a cool, plain white, as fresh as new soil. Complacent and tired from the storm of emotion. And out of that soil springs a leaf, and a stem. A hopeful bud of green wriggles out from your eyebrow, another from the curlicue swirl in your ear.

I allow them to blossom. You smell of crisp spearmint and rosemary thistle. You sparkle like a newly chiseled emerald jewel. And the green flows freely, into my canvas, brimming with all of the innocent positivity that your childhood-self on the wall exudes. This is one color that I gladly soak up.

"This portrait of Milton," you say, your voice shaking. "It's what I wanted *us* to be. But he's so... sloppy. His colors bleed everywhere."

You turn your eyes inward, not thinking of Milton.

"Mav," I say quickly, reaching through your storm, the green so wild that it doesn't let me through. "Suzannah said it's okay, that we don't need to hide it anymore."

But you're already lost. The green is too fragile. Your emerald retracts, compounding on itself, and with all of the pressure that comes with too much hope, it shatters.

"I'm going to take a walk," you say, pulling away. You let go of my hand and descend the staircase.

When you slam the door behind you, it squashes the garden that we almost let grow.

🏛

Revised placard text for: *The Portrait of Abigail Mildrin* (1993; Herndon, VA; property of the Mildrin Family Gallery).

Abigail, the daughter of Hugo and Melanie Mildrin, and the cousin to her adopted brother, Maverick Mildrin, is pictured alone. She is the only Mildrin artist to abstain from marriage, as part of a vow taken on her twenty-fifth birthday, and which the prior curator, Mrs. Henrietta Mildrin, took great issue with.

Given that the artist took her vow with conviction, it seems odd that blue sadness would dominate the portrait. Notice the sapphire ripples in her frown-lines, the dark-navy tears that cover her cheeks. Could it be, perhaps, that Henrietta made certain rehabilitations? Those that show Abigail as Henrietta saw her: sad, lonely, unworthy of happiness? The Gallery shall never know, for Abigail has since estranged herself from the Mildrin family.

🏛

I make my way back into the sitting room, alone, and I collapse on the sofa.

"Feeling a little bit *Abigail*?" says Suz, repeating the joke that once spread through your family. As if blue grief — that none of you show — were something to laugh about. "Believe me, I've been there. We all have at some point."

She picks up a sandwich and shoves it into my hand. She watches me eat as she sips her tea.

I nibble on the miniature ham-and-cheese triangle. "How did you hide it?"

"I didn't," she says. "Why do you think Henrietta hated me so much? She would die all over again if she knew I were in charge now."

I inspect her skin; there are no scars of blue, no pockets of sadness. Wrinkled cream flows from her fingers to her neck — and not the cream of worry, but the cream of contentment, a product of years' worth of blending and refining, of honing her palette to a balanced spectrum. One in which each of her colors is welcome, but none so violent they burn out the rest.

"I wish he could be like you."

"But he *can*," says Suz. "Alfie, my dear, ours is a family of visceral emotions. Maverick needs to learn how to let himself out — not just the red, and not just the green.

Once he can accept that the other colors have a place, he can learn to control them."

I sigh and set my half-eaten sandwich on the table. "You make it sound so easy."

Suz just laughs. "It can be," she says. "All you need to do is show him."

"Show him?" I say. "I'm no artist."

Suz leans all the way over to my cushion, and she dramatically cocks one of her over-penciled eyebrows. "What do you plan to do with all of his colors? Hide them forever?" She slowly shakes her head. "My dear, you can *use* them. It may not be pretty, and it may take some time, but Mav needs to see that his emotions are valid. That all of them, together, make you both something special."

"But Mav's supposed to guide me. The brush on the canvas."

"Traditionally, yes." Suz winks at me and smiles. "Every other Mildrin artist has painted their own portrait. But in this case, I think we can make an exception."

I chew on my lip, unsure what to do.

Suz seems to notice. "Here, take this," she says and reaches for my cheek, pinching it with all of the compassion I can hold. "It's something I wish Henrietta had given me. It'll help you see the best in what you already have — if you're brave enough to reveal it."

I feel the smear of color that oozes from her fingers, pink mixed with red mixed with cotton-candy-fuchsia, that clings to the surface of my skin like oil. She gives me a color that I've never felt before — one that you've never had the power to share — and my canvas isn't sure what to do, how to act.

The violet is alive, pulsing with potential.

"Now, get out of here," she says, patting me gently. "And don't forget the frame."

🏛

We don't see each other much over the next few days. You are as normal, drowning in yourself. I am in the basement, drowning as well — but this time, not in you. I wade through the sketches that I've practiced over the years; I study the rules that you've taught me that we need. Then, I crumple those up and throw them in the trash can.

And I start something new.

On the first day, I stare at the frame on the wall, the carved-cedar treasure that we brought home from Suzannah's.

On the second day, I trace the wooden planks with my fingers, memorizing the lines that will one day define us.

On the third day, I lay my hands bare in the center. I press on the canvas.

And I let you all out.

Every searing touch of red, every ember of gold, every muted, not-good-enough drop of tainted yellow. The emerald smiles that give me false hope and the deep-blue despair that always comes after. I swirl these colors that you've given me to hold, and I give them back to you, with some of my own. Some that I've created, and some that I've discovered. And under them all, a streak of violet burns — the violet of love, a messy, tangled thing.

Later that evening, you come downstairs, and you find me in the basement. "Alfie," you say. "Wha — what are you doing?"

Rather than answer, I hold out my hand. I wait for you to wrap your fingers in my own. And with the hint of a smile, I lead you to our portrait frame. Both of us shaking, slick with sweat. Both of us scared to see what we'll create.

With my palm in the flurry of colors on the wall, I allow you to guide me. Your brush to my canvas, as it always should have been. There are deep, wide strokes. There are colors that bleed. There are tears and emotions we've never acknowledged. And for the first time in seven long years, I don't care.

And I hope, in time, neither will you.

When we are done, I lean back, and I stare at our portrait. The me that I see is raw and pure and covered in all of the scars that I've earned, from the red-fire lust and the golden-anger blade and the indigo sadness that blooms when we fight.

"That's us," you say, as you let your shoulders sag. Not in a good way, but not like before, when your colors were stifled. Now, they run free. Now, your whole family will see us as we are.

"That's us," I say, holding your hand.

I smile and know that I wouldn't change a thing.

Original placard text for: *The Portrait of Maverick and Alfie Mildrin* (2003; Fredericksburg, VA; property of the Mildrin Family Gallery).

Maverick and Alfie are pictured in their home on the eve of their seventh wedding anniversary. These are two bold, daring artists. The maelstrom of colors is a sign of their honesty, an acceptance of their flaws. They are vulnerable, something much needed in these halls. Their portrait is unique, in the hundred-year history of the Mildrin Family Gallery, in being the only one to incorporate true violet. And by embracing their own chaos, they make it a masterpiece.

THE MUSEUM OF FOG

Alexander Danner

The sign posted to the door read, 'Drive Slowly: Hazardous Conditions', which was true as far as it went. Had Benny driven her car into the museum, hazards could not have failed to present themselves, most obviously her own car barreling across the lobby to smash through the lucite donation box at the center of the room before destroying the glass door to the exhibit itself, and potentially the attending security guard who stood beside it. Obviously, Benny wasn't driving her car. She had come up the stairs and into the museum on foot, as anyone would. So the sign was just dumb.

"That sign is really dumb," she said out loud to the security guard, whose name was Carlos. It said so on his embroidered name tag.

"Yeah," said Carlos. "I know. You think I don't know how dumb that sign is? I stand right here next to it every day. All day. I know how dumb the sign is."

"Well. Good," said Benny. "I'm glad you've been paying attention." She dropped a tenner into the lucite box.

The door to the exhibit hall was closed. This was necessary to keep the exhibit itself contained. Benny wasn't sure what she'd expected to find inside the museum, but she certainly hadn't expected anything so literal. An art collection, perhaps. Or a historical display. She'd assumed that 'Fog' was the name of the founder, one Arturo Q. Fog, or Melinda Rockefeller Van Fog, or even just John Fog. But no, The Fog Museum was a purely descriptive name. A few wisps of the roiling mist snaked out through the crack beneath the glass door. The lobby floor was slightly hazy.

"Thank you for your donation," said Carlos. "Generosity like yours makes all the difference for institutions like ours."

"I'll be right back," said Benny, then she retreated to the restroom.

Peeing is an essential first step to exploring any museum. Benny knew the disappointment of reaching the most captivating exhibit, only to have the experience undercut by an agony of the bladder. It had happened to her while walking the length of the Apollo rocket at Kennedy Spaceport, forcing her to break the viewing into two legs. She'd had the mystique of Elvis Presley's gallstones ruined by her bodily needs in White River Junction, in a museum so tiny she could still have seen the exhibits from the toilet, if she'd left the door open. In Columbus, Ohio, she'd gotten so completely lost that by the time she'd found the International Drainage Hall of Fame, she'd barely glanced at the black and white photos of old men on display before hurrying off to find a restroom. Now she knew: 'Always tinkle before you tour.' That was Benny's motto.

She also took the opportunity to check her phone. No messages, but she sent out a quick tweet to her friends and followers of her travel adventures.

> **Benicia Deluca** @VagaBondGirl90
> Checking out @fogmuseum. Seems a
> little sketchy. Anyone else been here?
> #traveltips

Her phone pinged, signaling a new message tweeted at her.

> **The Fog Museum** (@fogmuseum) is
> now following you on Twitter!

Great. A few more messages followed, nothing useful — friends telling her to be careful if it seemed weird, followers looking forward to her report on a new attraction. It didn't seem that anyone in her circle knew anything about it. She stuffed her phone back in her bag, finished her business, and returned to the lobby.

"Feeling better?" Carlos asked.

"Always tinkle before you tour," she said. "That's my motto."

"Wow," said Carlos. "That's a terrible motto."

"Anyway," she continued, "your Twitter person sure is eager."

"She's just a kid. I think she's somebody's niece."

"How big is the exhibit?"

"Smaller than it feels. Stick to the walls if you get nervous."

"I'm not the nervous sort."

"So you'll be going in sometime soon?"

"Yeah," she said.

"Shall I open the door?"

"Go for it."

Carlos reached over to grab the handle.

"You're sure you're ready?"

"Come on, dude, just open it."

"Dude? Who says dude anymore?"

"Fine, Carlos, please let me into the damn exhibit."

He opened the door and gave a small bow, ushering her in. The wall of fog against the door fell immediately, poured to the floor and spread out, engulfing Benny's sandals. She wiggled her toes, wondering how far into the hall she would have to go before she lost sight of her purple nail polish. She snapped a pic of Carlos holding the door for her, #snarkybutcute.

"The display's getting away," said Carlos. "I need to close the door."

She stepped inside and Carlos closed the door behind her. She was tempted to wait there while the fog refilled the space that had emptied, but she imagined Carlos laughing at her for looking petrified. At that thought, she pushed directly into the fog, no skirting the walls. She could still see into the lobby when she looked back, five feet in, but the triumphant grin she brandished for Carlos' benefit was wasted; his back stayed to the room, completely disinterested.

Her phone pinged, three times in succession.

The Fog Museum @fogmuseum
@VagaBondGirl90   Welcome,   and enjoy your tour!

The Fog Museum @fogmuseum
@VagaBondGirl90 You are now in Radiation Fog Hall. Don't worry — it's not radioactive!

The Fog Museum @fogmuseum
@VagaBondGirl90 Radiation Fog is formed by ground-level humidity cooling as heat radiates from the Earth at day's end.

She debated silencing her phone. She didn't need some digital tour guide to explain fog to her. The appeal here was experience, not education. But as she moved farther in, her view of the lobby faded quickly. It wouldn't take much to lose all frame of reference. A connection to the outside world might be nice, she decided. She set it to vibrate, stuffed it back into her purse, and continued walking. There was nothing particular to walk toward, so far as she could tell, just a soft grey expanse that she trusted would reveal something sooner or later. At the very least, she would hit the wall on the opposite side before long.

Or not.

After ten minutes, she had encountered nothing. No displays, no walls, no other people. There wasn't even much sound, save for the clopping of her own flip-flops on the floor, which was muted and echoless, despite the seemingly cavernous space. She reached her arms out to her sides; if she was passing anything, she didn't want to miss it. It was oppressive, not even knowing how large a space she was in. It could be the size of a football stadium, or just a hallway. And why was there no echo? Were the walls really that far away?

"Hello?" she called out, but no response came from the space around her. Her purse buzzed against her hip. She sighed and took her phone back out.

The Fog Museum @fogmuseum
@VagaBondGirl90 Hello!

"Yeah, hi!" she called back. "That's not at all creepy, by the way!"

She began to worry that she might be walking in circles, and as soon as she thought it, she realized that of course she was. She'd read all about it, how blindfolded people move in spirals, never in straight lines. She should have thought of it right away, but whatever, it was a problem easily fixed. She pulled up the app store on her phone, downloaded a free compass app, et voila: Navigation! She was currently facing northeast, so she turned to face true north, and struck off again. She had no special reason for choosing north, but it had worked for the magi, so why not?

Two minutes later, she felt something crunch beneath her feet. She bent to examine it, using her phone to light the ground. She was surprised to find she was standing on black asphalt, which was littered with translucent pebbles. Glass, most likely. Safety glass. She stood up and took just two more steps before she found the wrecked car. It was a Civic, just like the car she'd been living out of the past few years, though this one was a couple models older. The entire front end was caved in by some collision, and the windshield was shattered outward. Benny took a step closer. A deflated airbag, spotted with long-dried blood, dangled from the steering column. She took a photo, #YIKES.

Her phone buzzed.

The Fog Museum @fogmuseum
@VagaBondGirl90 Radiation Fog is a particular hazard for night drivers — remember, when visibility drops, SLOW DOWN!

"Sorry I stepped on the glass," said Benny. "I didn't see it."

The Fog Museum @fogmuseum
@VagaBondGirl90 No worries! All exhibits are fully interactive. Please touch, interact, and explore.

Benny reached out and opened the driver's side door, then bent to look inside. There was a dirty travel mug in the cup holder and some old CDs scattered across the back seat. She popped the trunk, then headed around the back. The trunk was mostly empty, except for a couple of toppled grocery bags, their contents splayed across the trunk. The produce had long since collapsed into moldy puddles, but there was a box of peanut butter chocolate chip granola bars, still unexpired, if not exactly fresh. "Is it okay if I take these?"

> **The Fog Museum** @fogmuseum
> @VagaBondGirl90 Take whatever you
> think you'll need on your journey!

She continued north for an hour, an hour and a half, two hours, with little to see, save for an old mayonnaise jar abandoned on the ground, filled will a dark yellow liquid that could only be one thing, #doubleYIKES. Apparently the restrooms in here were really hard to find. Obviously. "Who's got the terrible motto now, Carlos?" This made a great update for her followers — the photo earned her a succession of grossed-out responses and retweets.

After another hour of walking, she sat down on the floor and unwrapped a granola bar. It was ten minutes to five. What would they do if she was still in here at closing time, whenever that was? Would they vacuum out all the fog to reveal the exits? She plugged her phone into a portable charge stick she'd brought with her, thankful that she'd had the foresight to drop that into her bag before leaving her car.

"Okay, I give," she said around a mouthful of food. "Am I actually getting anywhere?"

A reply came immediately:

> **The Fog Museum** @fogmuseum
> @VagaBondGirl90 Of course! You're
> getting farther north! Mostly nobody
> thinks   to   bring   a   compass.
> #alwaysbeprepared

"Is that the right way to go?"

> **The Fog Museum** @fogmuseum
> @VagaBondGirl90 Depends. Are you
> looking for something specific?

"Not really. But I haven't found an exhibit in hours. Can you point to the next one?"

> **The Fog Museum** @fogmuseum
> @VagaBondGirl90 Of course! Head
> NNE. It's kind of a hike, but you've
> been making awesome time.

"Sweet. It'd better be good, though."

> **The Fog Museum** @fogmuseum

@VagaBondGirl90   It   totally   is!
Anyway, gotta go. Dinner at 5:30, and
Dad flips if I'm not there on the dot.
The Fog Museum @fogmuseum
@VagaBondGirl90 See you tomorrow!
"Tomorrow?" Benny repeated, confused. "Tomorrow?!"
Benicia Deluca @VagaBondGirl90
They've locked me in @fogmuseum. I
wouldn't even mind, but I haven't
seen anything since the jar of pee.

She ignored the barrage of pings on her phone,
various messages of concern and outrage. It was good to
give her audience some suspense. She'd probably have a
couple dozen new followers by morning. Instead she
focussed on her snack, wishing she'd brought a bottle of
water, but oh well. She'd find a water fountain or something
deeper in.

It was another forty-five minutes before she began to
see a glimmer of something ahead. There were faint lights,
floating halos in the air — regularly spaced, like lampposts,
which was exactly what they turned out to be. They stood
above a row of gas pumps, alongside a pair of small
buildings, the station office and a small travel center hung
with signage for restrooms and vending machines. A pair of
cars were parked outside the travel center, old ones, an
early model Caravan and that kind of station wagon with
the fake wood panelling on the sides. There was even an
eighteen-wheeler parked over by the diesel pumps. Nothing
moved. This stillness unnerved Benny more than any of the
previous emptiness she'd encountered. Serial killers don't
haunt empty plains. They haunt isolated gas stations. She
pulled her keychain from her purse, her tiny keyring-can of
pepper spray held at the ready.

Benny's first stop was the travel center — she wasn't
about to miss an opportunity for indoor plumbing — but
she entered tentatively, peeking through a window before
testing the door. The building was small, just the two
bathrooms and a lobby with vending machines, a plaque on
a podium at the center of the room, and a wall map of
Connecticut highways, dated 1993, too old to be much help
even if she were in Connecticut. She called into both

bathrooms before entering, and checked for feet under the divider walls. Nothing and nobody. The bathrooms were surprisingly cleanish for a rundown rest stop, and the vending machines were well stocked. From the first, she bought a packet of Nutter Butters, a lemon pie, and some beef jerky. Not the most appetizing meal, but as close to balanced as she could manage. From the second, she bought two bottles of water, stuffed one in her purse, and twisted the top off the second to drink while she read the plaque:

> Night driving through heavy fog is especially hazardous. Smart motorists, including even professional cross-country truck drivers, will take the first opportunity to safely exit the highway and wait out limited visibility conditions. Manmade oases like this late twentieth-century roadside rest stop offer travelers much needed comfort and refreshment.

She snapped a bunch of pics to post later, then moved on to the station office. The door opened into a tiny space with a small desk, chair, and cash register. There was a mini-fridge under the desk— filled to capacity with frozen burritos — and a tiny microwave in the corner. Benny settled herself at the desk to heat and eat a beef and bean supreme. Back outside, the two cars offered nothing of interest, save another mayonnaise jar in the station wagon, empty this time, thankfully. Her next stop was the truck, which she had saved for last precisely because it seemed most promising. Truckers spent days at a time in their rigs, so they treated them like little mobile houses. She might find more food, some useful electronics, even a bed to spend the night in. It was still early for sleeping, but with her only guide gone for the evening, it seemed best to stay put until morning.

The truck was reasonably clean — no one had used it as their home away from home in years. From inside the cab, the fog seemed even more impenetrable for the sharp contrast between seeing and not seeing created by the windshield. The truck's electronics were useless — all nineties-era stuff, including a four-inch black-and-white cathode-ray television that plugged into the lighter for power, but picked up nothing on its silly little antenna. The CB likewise seemed to work, but no one responded to her calls. Another little fridge offered several Jolt soda bottles, which she saved for morning, when she'd be glad for the caffeine.

She spent the next hour on her phone, responding to students in an online class she was teaching, answering questions about money management software and online services. After that she logged into her banking, where she saw that she'd received payment for an article she'd sold on roadside museums and novelty attractions. It was a nice little lump that she didn't actually need right now, so she moved it into savings. Finally, she plugged her stick charger into the dashboard lighter and turned her phone off. She locked the doors, then climbed into the rear compartment, where a thin mattress with a scruffy blanket and pillow waited. She pulled the curtains of the sleeping compartment closed, tucked herself down, and began the process of willing herself to sleep — something she'd become very good at while sleeping in odd places at odd times. As she drifted off, she almost — almost — allowed herself to feel a moment of worry over the strange circumstances she found herself in. But then she was asleep, and all worries abated.

🏛

In the morning, she woke to a rising rumble that shook through the entire truck. She wasn't even sure if it was the noise or the motion that had woken her. Her first thought was of thunder, until the sound was followed by the distinct slap of shoes hitting asphalt — someone had just opened the rear door of the trailer, then jumped out. There had been people back there all night, just feet from where she'd slept.

Benny turned on her phone, although at five in the morning, it was unlikely anyone was on the other end yet. She dashed off a tweet that she was 'off to meet the neighbors', then slipped through the curtains into the driver's seat. There was nothing to see through the windows, and the mirror was little help — there was movement at the back of the truck, but the fog obscured any details.

Armed with her pepper spray, she opened the door and lowered herself to the ground as quietly as she could. She moved along the side of the truck slowly, hoping to get a look at her neighbors before they saw her. She could hear them chewing something crunchy, an oddly reassuring sound, immediately familiar: the sounds of breakfast cereal. There were two people, a man and a woman, seated in folding lawn chairs, eating out of bowls. The man spotted her first.

"Dude!" he called, barely intelligible around his mouthful of cereal, giving her a friendly wave with his spoon.

The woman looked up, and immediately smiled: "Hey. Hey! You want some Froot Loops? We've got plenty!"

These people were no threat, she decided. The couple were old, forties at least, and dressed in period costume, with ripped jeans and flannel over t-shirts — the guy's was a band shirt, with some kind of screaming claymation pig. The back of the trailer was outfitted as a makeshift apartment, with a mattress and a chest of drawers, and posters on the walls. The front was something else entirely, with a full drum kit, a keyboard, and an electric guitar on a stand by the wall. It looked like a stage.

"Can you play?" asked the man, who introduced himself as Mikey. "Jennifer's got drums, and I play keyboards, but we haven't found anyone for lead guitar yet."

Benny shook her head.

"That's too bad. You can still hang with us if you want," said Mikey. "We've got Froot Loops to last forever."

"What about vocals?" asked Jennifer. "We need a front man even more than guitar."

"I'm the front man!" said Mikey.

"You can't sing, Mikey."

"Can too."

"Nuh uh. You sound like you got a goat biting your ass when you sing."

"Yeah, well you just watch me burn the charts, then tell me I can't sing."

"It was good to have a bed for the night," Benny said. "But I think I need to keep moving."

Benny excused herself to use the restroom, while the two 'musicians' bickered over vocals. When she returned to the truck, Jennifer and Mikey told her what they could about the surrounding area, mostly the locations of several more abandoned cars. They also mentioned a directory, northwest of the rest stop, with indicators pointing to other parts of the museum. Due north was the Upslope Fog exhibit. They'd gone that way once, years ago, but found it impassible; it was a mountain with icy crevices that funneled fog down from the peak. To the west was the Advection Fog exhibit. That one they couldn't explain — they'd never dared go near it, for fear of what 'Advection' might be.

"It sounds nuclear," said Mikey in awed tones.

Benny Googled it. "It means there's probably a lake there," she reported, to dumbfounded stares.

"Once you leave, there's no finding your way back," said Jennifer.

"I'll just set a GPS marker," said Benny, and did so. "Why don't you come with me?" she encouraged. "Maybe we can get you out of here, and back into the real world."

"Nah, we're good," said Mikey. "Cereal in the morning, rockin' out at night. Total freedom, you know?"

Benny took a selfie with them, #stuckinthe90s, then struck out for the directory, to see if it offered any more information. She reached it after only half an hour, finding a tall, rectangular structure with a plaque sporting the museum logo on one side. On the next side was a history of the museum, founded in nineteen-whatever by Dr. John Jacob something or other, blah blah blah. Nothing useful. The third side sported arrows pointing to the next exhibits, exactly as Jennifer had described them, Upslope to the north and Advection to the east. Nothing new there, but confirmation was appreciated.

On the fourth side hung the prize — a rack of informational brochures, with the same boring history, naturally, but more importantly: a map. She could see that she had travelled nearly the entire way through the Radiation Fog exhibit, and was near the boundaries of both the Upslope and Advection exhibits. Beyond Upslope was Evaporation, after which the map indicated an exit. Likewise, Advection was followed by Ice Fog, which also offered an exit. But for all her walking, she was still closer to the entrance than she was to either of the other exits. It made more sense to go back than to go forward.

Her phone vibrated.

> **The Fog Museum** @fogmuseum
> @VagaBondGirl90 Good morning, Benicia! Did you enjoy the '90s rest stop preservation exhibit?

"Sure, it worked out. Met a couple of grunge rockers. Have a nice dinner with your folks?"

> **The Fog Museum** @fogmuseum
> @VagaBondGirl90 Yes! Ever do roll-your-own sushi?

"No, but it sounds fun."

> **The Fog Museum** @fogmuseum
> @VagaBondGirl90 You should try it! But you gotta get tobiko. My dad always forgets the tobiko, but it's no fun without it.

"That's the roe, right? The little orange fish sprinkles?"

> **The Fog Museum** @fogmuseum
> @VagaBondGirl90 Yah! They don't taste like much, but they make the rice look happy!

"Once I get out of here, I'll make roll-your-own sushi a priority."

> **The Fog Museum** @fogmuseum
> @VagaBondGirl90 My dad says knowing how to cook for yourself is the first step to independence.

"What's the second?"

> **The Fog Museum** @fogmuseum
> @VagaBondGirl90 Job security.

"Hmm. I guess that depends on what you're looking for independence from."

> **The Fog Museum** @fogmuseum

@VagaBondGirl90 I see you made it to
the directory. Have you picked a
direction?

"I've ruled out the north. Climbing a mountain in sandals seems like a bad idea. Turning back the way I came would be quickest. So that's tempting."

The Fog Museum @fogmuseum
@VagaBondGirl90 Yeah, I guess. That
makes sense.

"But not that tempting. I'm headed east."

The Fog Museum @fogmuseum
@VagaBondGirl90   Ohhhh,   you're
heading for the lake! I love the lake!

"The ice field on the other side sounds rough, but I see there's a gift shop before the polar wasteland. I'm hoping I can get boots and a coat."

The Fog Museum @fogmuseum
@VagaBondGirl90 Absolutely! Our gift
shops offer a wide selection of Fog
Museum logo Ts and outerwear.

"Done deal."

She folded the brochure and stuffed it in her purse, then set out for Advection Lake. Beneath her feet, asphalt gradually gave way to gravel, followed by dirt, then grass, until after two hours, she found her toes squelching into mud. In the fog, she'd very nearly stepped into the lake before she saw it. The water was cold, but rippled slightly, moved by a steady current of air above it. She rolled up the cuffs of her jeans so she could wade a little without getting her clothes wet. She turned south to reach a dock the map showed on the water's edge. She could follow the lake shore, which meant she could stow her compass and relax while she enjoyed the chill of the water on her feet.

The Fog Museum @fogmuseum
@VagaBondGirl90 You're on the shore
of Advection Lake! Advection Fog is
formed by warm air blowing over cold
bodies of water.

When Benny reached the docks, she found exactly what she expected — a touristy rental stand beside a half-dozen moored rowboats. The attendant was asleep in his chair, head lolled back, breathing wetly through the gaping maw in the middle of a scruffy grey beard, a tattered Harlequin romance lying open on his chest.

"Excuse me," she said, but the man didn't budge.

"Hello," she said louder, and knocked hard on the low wooden counter. Still nothing.

"Hey!" she shouted. "I need a boat!"

He finally grunted and lifted his head, looking groggily at Benny.

"How much?" she asked, as she dug in her purse for some cash.

"For a boat? Just a sawbuck. Includes life vests and paddles."

She passed him the bill, and he passed back two oars and two vests.

"I just need the one," she said, pushing the extra vest back at him.

"The other's for your fella," he said.

"Haven't got a 'fella', thanks."

"Your boyfriend, I mean."

"Yeah, I wasn't confused by the vocabulary."

"How're you gonna row the boat?" he asked.

"With these," she said, and waggled her arms at him, before grabbing the oars off the counter and tromping off.

The Fog Museum @fogmuseum
@VagaBondGirl90 *Snrk!*

"Oh you liked that, did you?" She was warming to the museum's Twitter girl, she decided.

The lake was much larger than Benny anticipated. She rowed for hours, ignoring the occasional buzzing in her purse. Eventually, she saw a lighted beacon in the distance, and made for it. The light was atop an iron signpost that stood straight up from the water. She pulled at it, and found that it was sunk immovably into the lakebed, however far down that might be. She unclipped the shoulder strap from her purse, looped it around the sign and through one of the oarlocks, and then clipped the ends together. Her makeshift mooring held solidly enough, so long as the water stayed as calm as it had been thus far.

She stowed the oars in the bottom of the boat before eating more vending machine loot. She removed the life vest, opting to use it as a pillow rather than a life preserver. The boat was unlikely to topple while she was lying down, with her weight relatively low and stable. The air was much colder now, and she regretted the light blouse she'd worn into the museum. But navigating was the biggest issue. She had kept the boat facing due east the entire time, but a southerly wind had pushed the boat perpendicular to her rowing. She had no way of knowing how far she had gone or how far she had left to go. She could be ten feet from the shore right now. Or ten miles. She might not ever get there, she realized. The sign she had moored to warned of the dangers advection fog posed to sailors; how ships would drift aimlessly, crash into unseen rocks, drowning sailors by the hundreds only meters from shore.

Her telephone rang. Not the brief buzz of a Twitter notification, but the prolonged pulse of an incoming call. Of course — it was the fifteenth of the month.

"Hi Dad," she said into the phone.

"Hey, you're still alive! Do I hear water?"

"What? Oh, uh, yeah. I'm in a boat. A rowboat."

"Oh, a rowboat! You know the one about Pete and Re-Pete, right?"

"Yes, I know the one about Pete and..."

"They went out in a boat..."

"I know, and Pete fell out..."

"So who was left?"

"Dad..."

"No, I wasn't even there, Pete told me about it later. But you know who was there?"

Benny sighed, and gave in.

"Re-Pete."

"So Pete and Re-Pete went out in a boat. Pete fell out. Who was left?"

"Ha ha, Dad, yeah, that's a good one."

"Seriously, though, you're wearing a life jacket, right?"

"Of course!" she said, hastily putting it back on to undo the lie.

"It's a little late to be out on the water, isn't it? It'll be dark soon."

"Yeah, I'm about to pack it in. Make camp for the night."

"Oh, that sounds nice. I'm glad you're not sleeping in the car."

"Not tonight."

"You know, you don't have to sleep in your car any night. Your bed's here waiting for you."

"I know that, Dad."

"Do you need some money?

"Nah, I just got paid for a couple of articles — I'll be in beer and pizza for a month."

"I'm already logged into PayPal."

"No, really, I'm good."

"I'm already sending it."

"Alright, a few extra bucks couldn't hurt. Thank you."

"Maybe get you into a hotel for a few nights."

"Listen, Dad, I should go. I kinda need both hands to row."

"Going in circles, are you?"

"This whole time, Dad, yeah. Ha ha."

"Okay, honey, I love you. Have a good night."

"I love you too."

She sat in silence for a while, feeling the boat sway beneath her. All around, there was nothing to see save the light atop the signpost.

> **The Fog Museum** @fogmuseum
> @VagaBondGirl90 DADS. #amiright

"Dads. Totally."

> **The Fog Museum** @fogmuseum
> @VagaBondGirl90 Anyway, I gotta get home. Try not to capsize in your sleep, okay?

"Promise. Hey, give your dad a hug for me, okay?"

> **The Fog Museum** @fogmuseum
> @VagaBondGirl90 Yeah. I can do that.
> See you tomorrow.

Benny looked briefly at her navigation app, confirming that the GPS marker for the rest stop was still there. She could still return to that fixed point and go back the easy way. She was tempted. She was also tempted to delete the marker, to take that option away from herself entirely, leaving no way out but forward. She turned the phone off for the night, making no decision yet. She didn't even tweet her aquatic bedroom — that could wait for morning too. She returned the life vest to the floor of the boat and lay down to sleep.

🏛

In the morning, she neither deleted the marker, nor turned around. As disconcerting as the museum was, the lake was the first true obstacle she had faced. Was she really going to be put off her path so easily? She was not. She downed some ibuprofen from the bottle in her purse, then unmoored and set the oars back in their oarlocks. With arms aching miserably from the previous night's efforts, and still a good twenty minutes out from feeling the relief of her painkillers, she resumed rowing. After an hour, she realized that the sign had likely marked the halfway point. There was no way she could have done the full length of the lake in one go, so it was good she had stopped. But the realization renewed her determination — she only had to do again what she had already done once. Easy.

Well, not 'easy'. But 'achievable' at least. It took several hours, and another dose of painkillers, but she got there, feeling the boat slide onto the sand before she had seen any hint that land was before her. With her jeans still rolled up, she stepped out of the boat into the water — an icy shock immediately cramped her feet — and dragged the boat the rest of the way up through the mud. She left her life vest in the boat with the oars.

The cold was much worse on shore. She didn't think she was quite into ice fog territory, but there was snow on the ground, and thin crusts of ice extending out onto the lake surface. It wasn't so cold that it would kill her — at least not quickly — but frostbitten toes were a very real possibility. She started back north along the shore at the quickest pace she could maintain, arms wrapped tightly around her body, trying to ignore the snow that invaded her sandals with every step. The pain of the cold passed quickly enough — by the time half an hour had passed, she no longer felt anything in her feet at all.

"Well," she said, unsteadily, through chattering teeth, "I have officially made a mistake." Her phone immediately buzzed.

The Fog Museum @fogmuseum
@VagaBondGirl90 Don't give up now! You're just minutes from commemorative keepsake ornaments and a convenient snack bar!

"I'd love a hot coffee."

The Fog Museum @fogmuseum
@VagaBondGirl90 We have @Starbucks!

"Of course you do."

Starbucks Coffee @Starbucks
@VagaBondGirl90 Starbucks is proud to sponsor @fogmuseum and other fine educational and cultural institutions!

Starbucks Coffee @Starbucks
@VagaBondGirl90 Use this e-coupon for a free small hot coffee, only at @fogmuseum! http://ow.ly/KZxIY

Benny kept pushing. She could see something above her — had been seeing it for a while, gradually coming clearer. A blip of light high up in the sky. It was a lighthouse. If not for the wind blowing her southward, she'd have rowed right to it. So, she had a beacon to follow, but of course it wasn't as close as it seemed. It was another twenty minutes before she felt the ground beneath the snow change from frozen mud to pavement, which led eventually to the building's entrance. Which was locked, of course. The lighthouse itself was off limits, a historical piece to be seen, but not entered. The gift shop sat beside it, well-lit and welcoming. Benny walked the extra fifteen feet to the revolving glass door.

The wonderful rush of warmth quickly became unpleasant as the burning sensation of skin thawing settled into her feet and fingers. Her first stop was the restroom, where she ran her digits under cool water to help them acclimate to normal temperatures. From there, she went straight to the Starbuck's kiosk for a venti skim toffee-nut latte. At the snack bar, she bought a cheeseburger and fries from a bored teen in a Fog Museum polo shirt. It was the first hot meal Benny had eaten since the microwave burrito two nights earlier. She was halfway through her meal when her phone pinged.

> **The Fog Museum** @fogmuseum
> @VagaBondGirl90 Can I ask you a question?

"Sure."

> **The Fog Museum** @fogmuseum
> @VagaBondGirl90 Are you homeless?

"I'm... nomadic."

> **The Fog Museum** @fogmuseum
> @VagaBondGirl90   What's   the difference?

"Choice."

> **The Fog Museum** @fogmuseum
> @VagaBondGirl90 Your dad sounded worried about you on the phone last night.

"Yeah, that's how dads sound."

> **The Fog Museum** @fogmuseum
> @VagaBondGirl90 How do you deal with that?

Benny sighed. She had an answer, of course, but not one she especially liked. "Sometimes you just have to let them worry."

After her meal, Benny pulled out her map. The first, most important point to note was that the map was not to scale. The lake had taken much longer to cross than its dimensions on paper suggested it should have. The ice fog exhibit might be similarly underrepresented. It wasn't enough to buy a sweatshirt — she needed equipment for a good, long hike in the cold. At the gift shop she procured a heavy coat, gloves, socks and boots, leggings, a hat, and even a pair of snowshoes. She hated to drop so much of her money on gear she was only going to need once, but this wasn't the time for frugality. And anyway, her dad had plonked an extra $300 into her bank account overnight. She took her purchases to the ladies' room and put everything on, two pairs of thick socks, a fur-lined hood over a wool hat, goggles, and a scarf wrapped several layers around her face. When she was fully transformed, she snapped a photo of herself in the mirror.

Benicia Deluca @VagaBondGirl90
I'm ready to slay a f***ing dragon! #GearedUp!

She felt powerful and protected, and also actually, honestly terrified. Like that first day when she'd packed her things into her trunk, and driven off into America.

The Fog Museum @fogmuseum
@VagaBondGirl90   Dragons   aren't real, silly! Watch out for polar bears, though. #notkidding

Right. She waved goodbye to the barista and the shop clerk and the burger girl. None of them waved back. She returned to the damp cold of the lake shore, checked her compass and started off for the Antarctic base camp. The cold came on quickly. The temperatures near the water had been merely freezing; as she moved farther west, she found a whole new world of cold. She was glad for the snowshoes. She couldn't tell how deep the snow went, but sinking would have slowed her down regardless. Not that she could run, exactly, with the broad paddles strapped to her feet, but at least she wasn't struggling to pluck her feet from the snow with every step.

The Fog Museum @fogmuseum
@VagaBondGirl90 You are now in Ice Fog Expanse — our least-visited region! Ice fog is made of frozen vapor. You are literally breathing ice!

"That's not as exciting as you think."

Benny kept moving, pausing as rarely as possible. She knew slowing down was bad. Stopping would be lethal. She felt the cold despite her many layers of protection. Her legs, where she wore the thinnest layers, felt chilled clear through. She occasionally slapped at her thighs to encourage circulation. It didn't help, but it was satisfying to know that she could still feel the pain and the tingling warmth that spidered out from it. She walked for hours. She couldn't drink anything — her water had frozen solid, an obvious problem that she couldn't believe she hadn't anticipated. She had slipped a strip of beef jerky down into her bra to thaw — the shock of it against her skin had been almost enough to send her into seizures right then, but it was the only way she could soften it enough to eat. The past few days had done absolutely nothing to diminish her lifelong dislike for beef jerky, but she needed the calories, and the calories helped.

She should have stayed the night in the gift shop, then started fresh in the morning. Maybe claimed her free small coffee. She was about to say as much to her Twitter followers, but her attention was stolen by the sound of quacking. Or not quacking exactly, but kind of like that. Some weirdly throaty bird noise that bore no resemblance to song. She soon found herself in the midst of their swarming mass, and grinned as they meandered around her legs, bumping against her, disinterested in her passing. She thought to try petting them, but didn't dare take off her glove. Instead, she snapped a photo, straight down, capturing her own knees in their midst.

> **Benicia Deluca** @VagaBondGirl90
> Probably going to die. But look: #Penguins!
> **Benicia Deluca** @VagaBondGirl90
> If you don't hear from me again, feel free to put that last tweet on my tombstone.

Her post was followed by a string of responses questioning her senses. She knew she deserved it. Why had she been in such a hurry? She couldn't even have offered an excuse that made sense. If she said she was just eager to be out of this place, feeling trapped or lost or frightened, anyone could have understood that. But none of that was true. Oh, there were moments of it, sure, but she'd just rowed herself across an entire lake, and was caught up in the spirit of being awesome. She'd done that! And now she wanted to slay a fucking dragon! Or a polar bear. Or whatever. And she'd run off into the cold to do that too. More hours passed. She was frozen and exhausted and almost certainly going to die. Of being frozen. In a museum. For real. She felt herself drifting toward sleep, even as she kept moving. Her tweet about penguins might actually end up on her tombstone, she realized. That was kind of a consolation; she'd always hoped that her dying comment would be something bravely flippant.

Her mulling over her epitaph had been running through her mind for several minutes before she realized she wasn't walking anymore. Wasn't standing up. She was lying flat on her face in the snow, and couldn't recall how long ago she'd fallen there. She couldn't feel her face, or anything else, save an insistent thrum against her thigh, coming at regular intervals, over and over. It was that vibration that had broken her reverie, woken her from her lethal sleep. Automatically, she reached into her coat pocket and pulled out the phone, and there was a string of tweets:

>**The Fog Museum** @fogmuseum
>@VagaBondGirl90 Hey, get up!
>**The Fog Museum** @fogmuseum
>@VagaBondGirl90 Wake up!
>**The Fog Museum** @fogmuseum
>@VagaBondGirl90 Benicia, wake up!
>**The Fog Museum** @fogmuseum
>@VagaBondGirl90 Please wake up!!!

And so on for twenty, thirty tweets. The intern hadn't stopped buzzing her until she'd gotten through.

"I'm up," said Benny.

And she pulled herself up.

And she started walking.

Again.

She made it to the base camp. Numb and hobbling. But she made it.

The camp was little more than a trailer surrounded by additional gear and storage. There was a light in the window. She hoped whoever lived there was welcoming. And alive. Unable to lift her arms, she knocked on the door with her shoulder, banging clumsily. This prompted an immediate startled clatter from inside. That was fair, she supposed — they probably didn't receive visitors very often. When the door finally opened, it revealed an old woman with scraggly gray hair tied into a clump behind her head. She was wrapped in a thick, brown, cigarette-pocked robe that looked almost as old as the woman, worn over a tank top and pink boxer shorts.

Benny didn't say anything. She couldn't move her jaw.

"If you're coming in," the woman barked, "come in fast and shut the damn door behind you."

Benny tried to do as she was told, but couldn't manage the steps. The woman eventually took pity, and hefted Benny up the steps by her armpits, like she was picking up a toddler.

Inside, she helped Benny strip off her layers to give the trailer's warmth direct access to her skin. Her body tingled with the sensation of a thousand bee stings as it reacclimated to room temperature.

"Thank you," said Benny, once she had warmed enough to speak again. "It's such a relief to get out of the cold."

"Better get used to that," said the woman. "We've got a lot of it."

The woman took a seat in an undersized desk chair by the computer, ignoring Benny entirely for a good half hour, while Benny revived and casually looked around the room. The trailer itself was a well-organized disaster — piles of unwashed dishes and discarded containers confined to the kitchen area, mounds of clothes circling the single bed. Books and papers demarcated the woman's workspace, a desk sporting an old PC and dot-matrix printer, among other technical paraphernalia, various scanners and what looked like an old-fashioned GPS monitor. The whole space reeked of cigarettes, and indeed, the woman was lighting one now.

The Fog Museum @fogmuseum
@VagaBondGirl90 Are you okay?
Benicia Deluca @VagaBondGirl90
@Fogmuseum I am now. I owe you one.
The Fog Museum @fogmuseum
@VagaBondGirl90 You really scared me.
Benicia Deluca @VagaBondGirl90
@Fogmuseum I really scared myself.
The Fog Museum @fogmuseum
@VagaBondGirl90 It's my fault. I didn't warn you how bad it would be.

I was too excited. I didn't think
anything could stop you.
Benicia Deluca @VagaBondGirl90
@Fogmuseum Hey, no. I took my own
risks. And I made it. It was close, but
here I am.

"There's water in the fridge," said the woman, after
some time had passed. "And a bag of pork rinds on the
counter, if you're hungry."

Benny looked longingly at the bowl of fresh fruit that
sat beside the pork rinds, but helped herself only to what
had been offered. No sense testing the bounds of the
woman's hospitality.

"Well, let me tell you a little about what we do here,
while you're still getting warmed up."

Benny nodded agreeably and crunched a pork rind.

"I'm Dr. Denise Fülnkholme, director of simul-
Antarctic research. As I'm sure you know, we've been
studying native simul-Antarctic fauna in their natural
habitat of the simul-Antarctic tundra since the museum
was founded in 1972. I've been here since the beginning,
originally as chief research assistant under the founding
director, Dr. Bill Wurlitzer-Evans, god rest his miserable
soul, taking over as director myself after the unfortunate
simul-orca incident in 1989." She paused to take a drag on
her cigarette. "We've improved safety protocols
tremendously since then. Let me just throw that out there,
dispel some of the concerns you very reasonably must have
about such things. No more simul-orca incidents for us."

Benny swallowed her pork rind.

"Uh... it's nice to meet you Dr. Fülnkholme," said
Benny. "I'm Benny."

"So why don't you start by telling me about your
education."

"Uh... sure," said Benny. "I dual-majored in Business
and Communications."

"No scientific background?"

"I watch a lot of Discovery Channel. Speaking of, I was
told there are polar bears."

"That's right."

"But you just said this is the Antarctic. There are no polar bears in the Antarctic. The word literally means 'no bears'."

"Not the Antarctic. The simul-Antarctic. The 'simul-' is key."

"Okay, sure."

"Tell me more about your communications experience."

"I've published some personal finance pieces, but mostly I'm interested in travel writing."

"Well, I have to tell you, I'm conflicted. I'm reluctant to hire someone without a scientific background, but the truth is, there just aren't many applicants, and it sounds like you could take the grant writing and external communications off my hands. I think a three-month probationary employment might be worth a go."

"So that's three months of hanging out in an Antarctic base camp, playing with penguins?"

"We don't play with the penguins," said the scientist, before letting a small smile escape. "We conduct interactive studies."

"Room and board included?"

"You'd live here. Supplies are provided."

"Can I get direct deposit?"

Dr. Fülnkholme looked confused, but Benny's phone chimed almost immediately.

The Fog Museum @fogmuseum
@VagaBondGirl90 I can set that up!
The Fog Museum @fogmuseum
@VagaBondGirl90 You should do it!

"Three months?" Benny repeated.

"Probationary."

She thought about it for a moment. Short term contract, and a chance to develop her skills in grant writing and wilderness survival?

"Done deal," said Benny, and shook Dr. Fülnkholme's hand.

"I do wish I'd gotten to see a polar bear," she lamented, after the three months had come to an end.

The Fog Museum @fogmuseum
@VagaBondGirl90 Don't go! You still could!

"I'm very happy with your work," said Dr. Fülnkholme. "I've decided to offer you the full thirty-year contract. You just need to sign."

"Thirty years! That is an awfully long commitment."

"You don't get to be the best in your field by spreading yourself thin."

"Don't get me wrong, Dr. Fülnkholme, I've had a blast working here. But it's time for me to head west. There's an exit out that way."

"You won't make it on your own."

"Maybe I won't. I've got a map, though, and I'd really like to try."

The Fog Museum @fogmuseum
@VagaBondGirl90 The penguins will miss you, Benny.

"The penguins will get by."

Benny set out with her map, gear, and snowshoes, as well as a fleece-lined pair of pants. She was better prepared for this outing than her previous, but the cold was no less brutal, the fog no less blinding. She followed her compass due west. Three hours' travel brought her to the first exhibit she'd seen since leaving the research station — an abandoned sleeping bag, unrolled on the ground, with no other signs of life. It looked very old, decades old. She snapped a photo, #RIP.

Her phone buzzed.

The Fog Museum @fogmuseum
@VagaBondGirl90 You could still go back. It's not too late to take the contract.

"I've already got what I needed out of this. It's time for the next thing."

The Fog Museum @fogmuseum
@VagaBondGirl90 You found another job already?

"I've had other jobs all along."

The Fog Museum @fogmuseum
@VagaBondGirl90 My dad says you
have to be realistic. He says you don't
need to be in love with your job.

"I'm not in love with my job. I don't teach classes in personal finance for jollies. I'm not even that crazy about travel writing. But it keeps me traveling, you know? It's the option I can live with."

It was another half hour before Benny began to hear the sound of breathing behind her. A sort of snuffling, heavy and low, as of something large. A crunching trudge accompanied it, the sounds of feet in snow, feet much larger than Benny's.

"I'm almost there," she said eventually. It wasn't a question.

The Fog Museum @fogmuseum
@VagaBondGirl90 The exit is just
ahead, if that's really what you want.

And indeed, there appeared to be a hovering pink bit in the haze ahead — it would soon reconcile itself into a glowing 'exit' sign. Just a few feet farther.

"My mind's made up."

She could hear the steps growing louder, the breath growing louder. Something was coming close behind her. She wasn't going to run. Running would be a mistake. Instead, she pulled her keys from her purse.

The Fog Museum @fogmuseum
@VagaBondGirl90 You owe me one.
Remember?

"Sure," said Benny. "You can still talk to me, you know. You know how to reach me." The thing behind her was grunting now as it snuffled in the snow. Was it tracking her, lifting her scent from the ice she had disturbed? It was too close. She turned to look, and saw nothing. No, almost nothing; there was a single blemish on the otherwise perfect blankness of the fog, a dark spot hovering in the air, moving up and down, searching. She snapped a photo, but even that one feature disappeared in the flash, leaving only a soft white image of nothing, #polarbearinasnowstorm. The animal grunted again in response to the flash, and she held out her pepper spray, ready to take the only desperate action available to her.

> **The Fog Museum** @fogmuseum
> @VagaBondGirl90 I'm not supposed to. I'm just supposed to be the museum. I get in trouble when I break character.

She heard more grunts, but farther off — another bear in another place. A more protracted guttural roar followed. The dark spot of the closer bear's nose jumped to attention at the sound — it vacillated between the prey it had been stalking and the call of its own kind. Benny hoped it was mating season. She had wanted to see a polar bear, but just the nose was plenty, she decided now. She was gripping the pepper spray too tightly — a fine mist escaped the can, blending invisibly into the fog.

"So don't break character," said Benny. "Just follow me from your own account."

The more distant bear called again, and this time the one before her made no attempt to resist. The nose darted away, followed by the quieting sounds of the bear's bulk barreling across the snow. She let out her breath and released her grip on the pepper spray. On her next breath, her throat stung slightly, as the residue of pepper spray wafted back in her direction. Her eyes as well. She turned away from it, back to her path. There was the light, just a short distance ahead. It was right in front of her.

> **Benicia Deluca** @VagaBondGirl90
> Now exiting @fogmuseum — highly recommended! (But bring your serious walking shoes.)
> **The Fog Museum** @fogmuseum
> @VagaBondGirl90 Thank you! And don't forget to rate us on Yelp!

Benny pulled the door open and stepped out of the fog.

The lobby was exactly as she remembered it, though she was coming to it from a different angle through an unmarked and opaque door. She also saw Carlos, still standing at attention.

"Hey, Tinkles!" he shouted to her from his post. "You're letting the exhibit out! Shut the door!"

After stomping the snow from her boots she made straight for the restroom, across the lobby, pausing only to flip Carlos the bird and a smile. Then she exited the museum and circled around the building to the parking lot, where her car still waited. She hoped the battery would start after three months of disuse, but if not, that was solvable. Nothing to worry about. She popped the trunk, began stripping off layers — coat, scarf, sweater, boots — until she felt the summer heat bleeding up into her bare feet from the asphalt.

Her phone buzzed. She had a new follower on Twitter. She smiled, and followed back. Then she silenced the phone and put it away.

"The Museum of Fog" was originally published as "The Fog Museum" in *Rivet: The Journal of Writing that Risks* in May 2019.

The Museum Nihilo

Eve Morton

The museum was located in a former Motel 6 alongside the notorious 401 highway, between two former fur-trapping stations in the wild Canadian north. Sherry read and reread the description in the guidebook, but she was still stumped. These directions had meant something, long before Sherry was born. Now they had faded into the background and formed an archaic portrait of a time before Time in her consciousness. Sort of like how people used to use 'horsepower' to describe cars. Not only had there been no horses whatsoever involved with those cars, they'd still used fossil fuels.

"So strange," Sherry murmured. "Almost as strange as fur-trapping."

She clicked off her green and energy-efficient car. She verified the address in the guidebook once again. The yellowed pages were the same shade as her corn-silk hair, and almost as brittle, thanks to how much UV light exposure they were receiving on this small jaunt. Sherry sighed as she looked around. No one else was here. But odd as it was, this was the correct address. The Museum Nihilo awaited. "What the fuck is Jerry *thinking*?"

Over the past six weeks, Sherry's boss at the newspaper had sent her on a series of adventures to 'go and grab the next greatest clickbait'. She'd done road trips like this for him in the past, gathering video and blurbs on adopted dogs (flesh and robotic alike), and she'd covered so many centenarians' birthdays she was sick of marveling at the array of candles and then asking another Emma or

Aiden about their special 100th birthday wish. Then again, she was never one for celebrations or sentimentality.

But this task, going around to old roadside museums and oddities, and scanning them for a 3D display the newspaper planned to have online, was a cut above the previous puff pieces. It had made her extend her travel beyond the safe and crowded city, talk to people she didn't know in places she'd only read about, and it meant she needed to engage in face-to-face extended conversations — with the possibility of shaking hands — with those people. Which, as much as being in the field was cool and real work as a journalist, all that contact with people made Sherry feel icky, bizarre, and straight-up gross.

"At least it's a living," her mother and sister, and, well, everyone told her. "You should feel lucky."

"I don't feel anything but annoyed," she'd often respond.

Before slipping out of her car for this latest mission, Sherry retrieved her gloves and a sleek, black mask. She tied her curly hair back with a tie, and, for the sake of her own safety, sent Jerry a quick audio message to let him know she'd arrived.

"Great," he responded right away, and then called her for an extended news brief. "Glad you arrived safely. But remind me again. Is this the giant twine?"

"No. Saw that yesterday. Didn't message you because, well, I could stay in my car. But this place is weird. It's a museum. Something about —"

"Death? Violence? Medical experiments?" He listed many more options in a rapid-fire, and much too excited, manner. "The Americas used to do a lot of strange things to their citizens. So you may see remaining wax figures or mannequins in odd poses. Don't worry, no one is trapped inside. We made sure of that during the wax shortage, when we melted most of them down. Broadcast it, too, for a lot of viewers. Many really liked to watch certain celebrities melt."

"Live or wax version?" Sherry joked. She was unnerved when Jerry didn't reply right away. She looked at the guidebook once again, flipped a page over, and then read the contents of this particular museum aloud to him. " 'The Museum Nihilo. This roadside attraction in the middle of the Canadian wilderness boasts any number of fascinating displays, all leading to and remaining supplied with nothing. Come inside and see for yourself: we really do have nothing to our name!' " She furrowed her brows again. "What the fuck is that supposed to mean?"

"I think it's a pun," Jerry said. She heard his typing as a series of faint clicks on the other side. When he came up with the translation of the Latin name, his suspicion was confirmed. "Yeah. It's a pun. The name means Museum of Nothing. So there really is nothing to their name."

"Nothing?" Sherry eyed the wooden sign on the front of the door. A single circle. *Or was that a zero?* "I don't get it."

"Well, go inside. See what you can find. Then write me an amazing article on it."

"But what if it's really..." She didn't finish.

Jerry chuckled as he completed for her. "Nothing? Well, you'll still write something. And that nothing becomes something. Like always."

"Ugh." Sherry touched her forehead. "I hate this job."

"No, you love it. Why? Because you're that kid who, when given the prompt for a philosophy exam asking why, you would write 'why not?' Right?"

"Well, yeah. But that's obviously a trick. Like those whoopee cushions and hand buzzers I saw in the Idaho Joke Museum. And so —" Sherry bit her lip. Through a darkened front window of the museum, a figure moved. Curtains fluttered, white as hospital bed sheets. "Oh. This is like the Joke Museum, too, isn't it?"

"Probably. Don't know. Never been. That's why I have you."

"How lovely."

"Yeah. But it does remind me of something I did in school." When Sherry was silent, hoping to end their conversation and lackluster sparring, Jerry disappointed her and went on. "There was one time I didn't study for an English exam. I know, shock and horror. I shouldn't be an editor. Or maybe this was the thing that made me one.

"Anyway, when I got to the last question and realized I could not write a 1,000 word essay on the main character of the novel we were studying, I pivoted. And so I basically wrote an essay on how I should have studied, but didn't. It was exactly 1,000 words. Had a thesis statement, good spelling, arguments, grammar, and so on. All that nice stuff. And it worked! I got an A. Teacher used it as an example, too, for years to come. 'See, kiddos,' Mrs. Abernathy would say, as she held up my marvelous words to the class. 'You really can write, even if you have nothing on your mind.' "

"Ew." Sherry made another face. "Your teacher held it up? As an example?"

"Yeah. A lotta humiliation as teaching back then."

"Ugh." Sherry still couldn't believe people used to learn like this — and shit like that — in government-sanctioned schools. Complete with desks and chalkboards and all that other unpleasantness of mean kids. She shuddered. Then she smiled wide as Jerry's incidental lesson sank in. "Hey. Why can't I do the same thing for my article? I can just say I never went inside, just imagined the Museum of Nothing and bam. Done. No handshakes and certainly no touching. And ironic, too, which our younger audience—"

"No."

"No?"

"No," Jerry repeated. A beat of silence passed on the other end. Sherry filled it with something more meaningful, with all her hopes of clocking out early and streaming media on her device until the wee hours. Nope, she had a scan to complete. An article to write. A museum to be inspired by. The more Jerry stayed silent, and the more he breathed without language, the more Sherry filled in the blanks with all she desired.

Then her gaze crossed over to the museum in front of her. The door outside clicked shut. She was about to say something — anything — when a hard knock came from her passenger door.

She cursed. A lot. She nearly dropped her device, but caught it in her hand and pressed it against her chest. Jerry's disembodied voice shouted from the other end, muffled by her palm. "What was that? Are you okay? Your articles will go viral when you're dead, but I don't think you want to be known for listicles and —"

"Hello." The woman outside spoke softly, but still somehow managed to drown out Jerry and project through the safety glass of the vehicle. Her hair was long and bone white. Her face contained what seemed like ten thousand separate wrinkles, deeply etched into her dark skin like dry riverbeds. She wore a white dress that ended at her bony elbows and her knobby knees. When she smiled, she revealed a small gap between her front teeth. "Are you here for a visit?"

"Um. Yes." Sherry disconnected her device entirely. Jerry would call back, she knew, so she blocked his call for an hour on her device's controls. The mask and gloves made her feel protected enough without the connection to her boss and her mission. She stepped out of the car and spoke to the woman over the hood. "Am I the only customer? Are there others inside?"

"No customers, only visitors."

"Oh. Well. Are there any other visitors inside?"

"Nothing's inside." The woman smiled. "Not a single thing."

"Okay. But you're open?"

"Of course. What else would I do?"

"I... don't know." Sherry's smile was tight. This was weird. Beyond-her-pay-grade weird. The woman walked a slow circle around the car towards Sherry's side. When she extended her hand for a shake, she exposed skin that was a complex map of blue veins and even more wrinkles. Sherry didn't want to shake, but for the sake of appearances, she did. The woman's hand was cold. Weird again. Surely it couldn't get worse.

"I'm Millicent, by the way. Please call me Millie."

"Sherry. It's not short for anything. Just Sherry."

"Nice to meet you, Just Sherry."

Millie let go of Sherry's still-gloved hand, and then gestured to the front door. Sherry did not bother to correct her name or play along with the joke. Once they stepped inside, and Sherry's eyes adjusted to the dark, the extent of the museum came into focus. The floors were hardwood, immaculately clean, but worn down under the high-traffic areas like the front door. Along one wall was a long desk that contained a computer with a bouncing circle on it, like an older version of what Sherry had heard people at her office call screen savers. Papers were haphazardly scattered on the desk. Beyond it were a series of coat and hat hooks, including a coat tree that extended its arms upwards towards the popcorn ceiling. All the hooks were empty. Outlines of bare feet and all-black shoeprints led from this area to several large, aquarium-size tanks, then further into the small museum and its displays. Water filled the first aquarium, but there were no fish or other life inside. Not even a castle or a neon scuba diver. Sand and grasses filled the second tank, though there was plastic mixed with the detritus. The third contained the charred remains of a large grass fire, plus a mini tiki torch that could be lighted.

"Our elemental display," Millie whispered. She was suddenly right behind Sherry. When Sherry jumped and touched her chest, Millie added, "My apologies. Sometimes I forget that people do not want to hear the commentary."

"The elements," Sherry asked, and pointed to the three tanks. "Shouldn't there be four? Five, depending on who you are?"

"The air cannot be contained." Millie inhaled deeply, making her nostrils flex open and close. "It is inside of us. We are the biggest tanks of air I've ever seen."

"That sure is one way to put it," Sherry said. When Millie did not laugh, Sherry added, "Aren't we more water than air?"

"True. Would you like to be in a display?"

"Oh, no. That's not what I meant."

"What did you mean, then?"

Sherry smiled, forced and painful. Millie's gaze unnerved her. What the hell was this place? Then she remembered — *nothing!* — and she became coy once again. "I meant nothing. Don't worry."

"Ah, okay." Millie went around a corner, and soon added, "We did have a fourth display for air. A vacuum for all the junk people leave behind. But we needed it for the front hallway. It's now in the back closet. Much better shelf life there."

"I see."

As they wove among more unsolved riddles and strange symbols, Sherry fiddled with her phone and the scanning device in her pocket. She hadn't yet caught the front entrance for the replicated simulation online, but she could get it when she left. A recording app was running in the background as well, so Sherry could have a record of this impromptu interview to write her article later on.

Sherry feigned interest in most of the items, though it was difficult. These were strange and bizarre — which *could have* been good enough for a story in and of itself — but Millie's ongoing, uncanny commentary drained the life from them. Sherry had to struggle to pay attention and keep her eyes open. She yawned. She frowned. *How can talking about nothing be so damn boring?* Sherry chuckled dimly as she thought of Jerry's story from high school. She wondered how to start her own essay on the museum. *I am completely unprepared for all of the Americas and so I shall write to you a nothing story of the museum of nothing. I will write to you of our hot air-filled lungs. Of empty coat hooks for invisible mice and small children. For the night elf that clearly keeps this woman alive on ambrosia and other substances that do not exist.* As Sherry continued to follow the patterned footprints behind Millie, she recorded her own observations by speaking aloud. Millie often answered Sherry in return, elaborating on what was written on some slabs, or confirming a suspicion that Sherry had voiced.

When they reached the glass case that held a piece of paper with a simple zero written on it, Sherry was surprised that the number zero had been an Arabian concept. "Would have thought they'd be more famous for 1001 as a number, given all those tales."

"They were brilliant mathematicians," Millie said seriously. "They deserve a spot in all museums, even in this one of nothing. Such an important concept, you know."

"Oh?" Sherry snickered. "Or should I say Zero?"

"Yes. We cannot have something without the concept of nothing. Like we cannot have freedom without the concept of slavery."

"Whoa, that's a rough comparison."

"True, though."

"Well, okay. But who said anything about slavery?"

"It is always at the back of anyone's mind. One concept must have an opposing idea, a matched force. And since the scales always must balance, a slave must exist if we are to understand freedom. Zero is the highest concept there can be. Without its creation, we would not have the division of wealth, the concept of intelligence, and even the concept of beauty. Without something as simple as a zero. As nothing. Nihilo. Nothing creates something, always."

"Nihilo," Sherry repeated. "Is that what the sign out front means? Because it's Latin for 'nothing'?"

"And Latin's a dead language. No one speaks it," Millie added. "So yes. It is a nothing language and so nothing inside of it takes on new meaning. Like two negatives always making a positive."

"They do? I was never good at math."

"Then come, let's examine the rest of the mathematical concepts and displays." Millie continued to guide Sherry through equations on various flashcards and kept under glass. Sherry shuddered at a blue painted '0 x 0 = 0', then a test by a grade-seven student who had correctly answered a long series of equations with zero. This was a test? What was it supposed to prove, other than that one student was smarter than the other?

"Man, life was strange back then," she said into her recorder. She had a glimmer of an idea of how to frame a museum like this — endless trivia, making it a banal place to keep a child docile while travelling, like teachers used to do for kids in school — but she lost the thought as Millie answered her.

"Not any stranger than now. Different names for the same things, all around. Life always strives for the same ending, I think."

"Annihilation?" Sherry asked.

"Not exactly. Though that, too, is also on display." Millie gestured to one of the later cases by a back door, filled with wilted flowers that had once been a funeral display. A character named The Grim Reaper was in a black robe. His face was skeletal, a body of starvation, and one of his arms was raised in a wave. Next to these displays was a mushroom cloud. Sherry blinked. She knew that image well enough. Too well. *Annihilation, indeed.*

"I think," Millie spoke again, "that life is dictated by two main events: creation and survival."

"Okay," Sherry said slowly. She didn't bother hiding her derision, even while recording. "Those aren't opposites, but —"

"No, but they are the antithesis of nothing. And so they are all that remains. That is the point of life, and a place like this. We *must* have two concepts for them to balance one another. Black *and* white. Men *and* women. Something *and* nothing. In fact... Yes, this is perfect. We need a new type of museum-goer in order for our business to boom again. Come." Millie grasped Sherry's hand. Her skin was still cold. Or did that mean that Sherry was hot? Millie tugged her towards the Death display, then beyond that wall and into a storage area that was filled with former displays of chalkboards, a tall bottle of Wite-Out, an array of deflated black balloons, and many leashes for invisible dogs. Millie led Sherry along a single line of the footprints through the remaining museum space until they burst out a back door and into an empty lot next to a barren field.

"Hey." Sherry stepped into a puddle. Her shoe was caked with mud and some kind of sticky resin.

The garbage bin for the museum, like the museum itself, contained nothing of any worth. But the same sticky resin was inside, as were pieces of trash that had stuck to its surface. Each layer was like a geological dig; Sherry could see old candy-bar wrappers from companies that no longer existed; horns and scales and skins of extinct animals; along with pieces of covers for DVDs, VHSs, magazines; and finally other items that simply didn't exist in stores or products any longer, such as batteries and gas cans.

"Dead stock, overstock, just stock." Millie ran her hand along the dumpster without a qualm. Sherry winced, but Millie only smiled as she brought out a series of flecked pieces of trash. "This is what life was like when we had so many things. We had everything. We kept everything. Even our garbage was located on the same planet, tucked inside our houses, right next to us. We loved trash so much, we filled an ocean with it. We made plastics that remained around forever and ever. Oh, we had *everything*." Millie's eyes grew larger, her adoration clear. "And everything had us. It was lovely. It was —"

"A climate crisis," Sherry said. "We had an addiction to crap. To capitalism. To stupid rules like not wearing white after Labor Day. We had deaths and extinctions and sickness and —"

"We had creation. And in that creation, we survived."

"But —"

Millie waved her hand at Sherry's qualms. She pointed to the field in the distance. Sherry followed. Millie pointed to the shifting, overcast clouds above them. Then back to the pavement, rocks, puddles. She pointed to everything. Sherry looked at everything.

Then Sherry realized she was pointing at nothing, this time around.

Deliberately.

"It is always a paradox," Millie said, her arms now placid at her side, "that the truest things in life make no sense. We cannot have something without nothing. And when we think we have everything, we really do have nothing. We almost lost our entire world to having everything. We put something before nothing, and it almost cost us everything. We could not survive or create. Don't you see?"

"That's great," Sherry said. She gave another forced smile. She didn't mean Millie's beady eyes. "Just great."

"Great," Millie repeated. "We must now put nothing before something, to win back everything. To create and survive again."

"You bet."

Millie leaned closer, her eyes conspiratorial dots. "Do you understand?"

"Yep."

"You don't."

"Nope. I do. Very much." Sherry nodded. She faked a smile.

While Millie ranted and raved, Sherry wished she could forget everything that had brought her here. Hadn't that scientist created that drug that allowed you to pick and choose childhood memories? They should use it on global memory — once called history — and destroy all museums that bent timelines to the curators' will and gave out fables instead of facts. She longed to discard all objects people clung to that had no worth whatsoever, and eradicate all sentimentality. Wouldn't everyone be better off?

But then a few of Millie's stray words became stuck in her mind, like an earworm or an echo. So did Jerry's. So did all the previous words she'd ever written that had now been flung into cyberspace. She wanted to stamp them out. Cross them out. Ignore, forget, move on. But she turned around, and since this was still technically part of the museum, she marveled. She looked. The clouds shifted. The light changed. Or maybe that was a trick of her own mind and memory, because, suddenly, the iridescent plastics, the resin that kept them in place, and the fading covers of old magazines were stunning. They were real. They had been held in hands. Now this was all that was left. But it had still existed.

All at once, the theme for her article came to her, like a vision from another time. Creation. Creation despite destruction. Despite utter failure, people still made things. People still did things. They put them on display and then watched as they all fell down, decayed, and were destroyed by any number of forces.

Then they did it all again.

A part of that seemed futile. Destructive. Boring.

But another part of that process seemed like breathing. Like walking. Stunning when you focused on it, but otherwise nothing much at all.

"Do you mind," Sherry asked slowly, and fearing that her own desire would fade if she didn't spit it out fast enough, "if I get into the dumpster? I just think that I'll, um, be able to capture this story —"

"Of course! That is what it is there for: appreciation!"

Millie's dark eyes watched as Sherry gripped the edges and slipped inside. Her shoes stuck to the bottom and made a squelching noise as she shifted away from particularly bad patches. She was only a little stuck by the resin as she shifted to the other side and around all corners. Her phone in her pocket recorded the thwacks and ticks of her movement; the scanner also recorded the 3D rendering that she would put on the newspaper's website. *Behold, the Museum Nihilo! A garbage can filled with nothing. This is the future of technology, of discovery — wading through the layers of what has come before.*

Part of her had expected her thoughts, her prewriting in her mind, to be sarcastic like Jerry's story of his essay. But the more she moved, the more her fingers touched the sticky edges of all that had come before, the more she was enchanted. Genuine. *Behold, the Museum Nihilo! A garbage can filled with everything you once left behind! Come inside and look around, and maybe take a few trinkets back to your home! Take everything, take nothing! It's all the same in the end.*

"Would you like help out?" Millie asked once Sherry had walked around all four corners of the garbage bin.

Her mind was still buzzing, still glowing with all she wanted to write — but Sherry accepted the help. On the sidewalk again, her balance felt precarious. Her shoes made several more sticky sounds.

Then they were silent.

"All right," Millie said. "If you understand our mission and our message, then maybe there will be some hope for the future."

"You know what they say: children are the future," Sherry said, but held off on adding that she, personally, wanted none from her loins. "Our readers online tend to be of the younger demographic. They should like this place. I think, at least."

"One can hope," Millie said. "Though as long as all new customers are like you, we will be more than satisfied."

"Like me?"

Millie didn't respond beyond a simple nod. She led Sherry back inside, waxing philosophic once again about her display cases.

"Would you like to see the vacuum?" Millie held her hand on a doorknob to a closet.

Sherry struggled to remember what Millie was talking about. The element display seemed far away now, though it was only two feet ahead. "No, thanks. I should go. Have to write a story on this place."

She expected Millie to ask more about the report, but the woman was silent.

Sherry felt that silence like a wall. Like the first time Jerry brought her into the office, showed Sherry her reader stats online, and demanded more. Always more, more, more. More eyeballs, more attention, more cash and credit with vendors online. She remembered when she'd pitched the museum story — *hey, wouldn't it be neat to drive more people online if we had virtual displays?* — and the resounding silence that followed. Nothing, everything, beat in that moment, before he told her the idea sucked, only to present her with it the next week during a meeting. Fine. That was all fine. It was a living, and she should feel lucky.

Sherry looked behind herself yet again. The dumpster was behind that wall. The dumpster would always be there. Or garbage would be, at the very least. Garbage was the only thing that survived long enough to mean something and matter. *Like creation and survival.* She recalled Millie's words about the only things people needed. Sherry got it now. She'd survived for a long time, but for what purpose? To create. Even if it was to create listicles. To create clickbait for yet another sideshow freak attraction. It had meant something once, so why not again? She wanted to do it. Oh, did she want to, more than ever before.

"I get it," Sherry whispered. "Oh, I get it now. The Museum of Nothing. You're really —"

"Do you want a picture?" Millie asked.

Sherry looked at her device. Everything was still recording. *Right. Yes. A photo.* She still had a job to do. For now.

Sherry held her device up with the camera feature on. Millie's image appeared with a strange aura around her. "Hmm. Can you move a bit to the left?"

Millie did so. She was now under the sign for the museum. No one would read it, Sherry figured, since it was in Latin — but then again, maybe she could even bring back Latin from obscurity.

As she took a series of shots on burst, Sherry imagined hashtags in Latin accompanying her piece. So many visitors — so many eyeballs! — on her article. They'd browse through her museum online, marveling in the same way she had. A chill ran through her spine. She saw the same dark footprints leading the way through this digital museum, algorithms and code guiding them before their own unique impulses, text-to-speech software illuminating each display. A part of her was saddened by this — didn't that wandering, like to the dumpster, produce interesting experiences? — but she focused on her job.

"That was great. Let me take a look and this should be all I need," Sherry said. She flipped to her device without looking up. Millie's image was before her, her teeth in a jagged smile, imperfectly spaced. Cute, if not a little deranged. Perfect for the online crowd who grew up seeking out quirks like this. Sherry flipped her device down, about to give her praise to Millie and say her goodbyes — possibly through a gift shop — but Millie was gone.

"Millie?" Sherry gasped. "What? Where?"

She snapped her head in all directions, taking in the scene. There was no museum any longer. She was outside, her car parked a few feet away, untouched. There was no front door, no strange hallway with a dozen black footprints to follow, weird displays, or an older woman with gap teeth named Millie.

There was... nothing.

"Oh. Very funny." Sherry folded her arms over her chest. She waited. Millie was going to come back. This was another one of her nothing/something shticks she'd been doing all day, a meme that would surely be curated online. Although this disappearing act was far more advanced than her cryptic lines, Sherry was positive this woman could conjure an entire museum and then make it disappear. Maybe the whole thing had been a hologram, and this was a glitch. Yes, Sherry was sure. Very sure.

She waited.

Five minutes passed. Ten minutes. Jerry called in, but she delayed his message. She opened her device to the photo she had taken of Millie; it was still there, her dark skin and bright white mane a haunting contrast. The title of the museum glowed behind her. As did something behind Sherry's device. She lowered her screen to behold the garbage bin, a few paces ahead of her. She waited to see if anything else would reappear, but the dumpster was it.

Sherry walked over slowly, fearful it might disappear once more. When she approached the familiar edges, her heart rate climbed with familiarity and adoration. *Behold! Behold! Behold...* She ran her hands along the edge, grasped something the same color and texture as her corn-silk hair, and smiled. She held that hair, knowing it to be her own, and let out a deep breath. *This is my creation. I will not be forgotten.*

This way, I will survive.

In her car, ungloved and unmasked, Sherry reviewed the photos of the Museum Nihilo, along with her recording and 3D scan. All of it was still there, functional, and no different than she'd experienced it. She would turn this in to the tech guys for the newspaper online, and they'd digitize it next to the Gigantic Ball of Twine. The museum would be one of many, all digital, driving attention and traffic online. It would make Jerry, their advertisers, and everyone else happy. It would not be the full truth, but enough to entice. Maybe even enough to satisfy even the more callous viewer strolling the internet.

Sherry knew it was the right decision. Hand in the story as she experienced it. Leave out the disappearance and inevitable ending. The dumpster — and her place inside its history— would remain hers a little longer. It would be her museum, like it had once been Millie's museum. *But what next?* Sherry wondered, her journalistic mind always reaching for the next deadline and the next. *Maybe, like a bad chain letter or computer virus, there will be another me.* The thought delighted her. Almost like children, almost like having a future, there would always be another person here.

Eventually, anyway. How likely were real people to visit? Everything would be online. This place would remain a dumpster in the middle of nowhere, located by a former Motel 6 alongside the notorious 401 highway, between two former fur-trapping stations in the wild Canadian north. Meaningless. Nothing. Sherry smiled. She got comfortable. She would, she decided, like it here.

She was still in her car when Jerry phoned her back. She answered slowly, and sighed so heavily between her greetings that Jerry finally asked her point-blank, "Hey, what's gotten into your ass? Did you go to the Dildo Museum, too?"

"No."

"Then what's up? You know, I should be mad at you and giving you the cold shoulder. You're the one that hung up on me."

"I know. I'm sorry."

"Ick. I hate apologies. Means we're getting too close."

"Right. Suck it, then."

"So, what's up?" Jerry pressed when silence followed for a beat too long. "Sherry, please. What's going on?"

Sherry looked at her phone. She looked at the dumpster. A lot of time must have passed, as Jerry was repeatedly calling out her name. It sounded so far away, even with her phone to her ear. "Sherry. Sherry? Sherry. What's wrong?"

"Nothing, Jerry," she said, and meant it. "I'll send in the scans. I'll write the story by tomorrow morning. Don't worry, Jerry. Everything's all right now."

"Oh, good then."

"Yes. But then I quit." Sherry waited, her device to her ear, for sounds and signs of objection.

Not surprisingly, she heard nothing.

THE MUSEUM OF GLASS

Marisca Pichette

At the bottom left corner of the cornfield, there is a museum of glass. Of course, it is not always a cornfield. Every other season, we grow potatoes there, and before that it was tousled and free, a rolling expanse of aster and daisies and black-eyed Susans, their bodies warping with the wind and springing back again, bright and glittering in the sun. Before that, we expect it was just another section of wood — maple and birch and oak and spruce, grape vines tangling in their branches, reaching for the sun. The space where the museum is now would have been covered in leaves, their bodies swish-swishing when the wind stirred them into action, curling in pirouettes before snow came to cover them up for half the year.

And you should see it in the snow. When the corn has been harvested and all the leaves swept off to the north, the snow descends on the hard brown soil and blankets everything in silence. Only a handful of sticks peek through, punctuating the landscape with the slashes of their bodies. They lean this way and that, frozen in place, immobilized by the snow. Their stumbling forms create a stage on which the museum rests, its doors flung wide in every direction, no matter the season, or the weather.

Maybe our museum is not unique. Maybe there is one at the bottom left corner of every corn or potato field, reflecting the sprouts as they grow, and the seeds as they fall. Maybe there are brick museums, and wood museums, and museums made entirely of doors. We do not know.

We only know that every year, hundreds of people come to visit the Museum of Glass. They come from other farms, and from the woods, and the hills. They come from families or from lives of solitude. They come with nothing. They come wanting nothing. They come.

When they come, they ask where it is. They skirt along the edges of the field, peering through the cornstalks, and they roll up to our door. We are the keepers of the museum.

We did not build it. We did not find it, either. It was there when we were born, and it will continue to exist, so long as the field is there, marking its place on the world.

When people come, we guide them. We take them through the open doors, and we show them all the wonders of the Museum of Glass.

🏛

Everything is transparent in the Museum of Glass. Your footsteps echo on the floors, but when you look down, all you see is grass, moist and green in the hothouse atmosphere beneath the museum's foundations. Your shoes leave flecks of dirt in the space between your feet and the ground. You wonder if the air will clear them away.

Inside the Museum of Glass, there is always a fresh breeze. Your guide tells you this is because the doors and windows are always left open. The museum is always open to visitors. You shuffle forward with your group. There is no fee, which is good — as you have no money. All you have are your pockets, which hold only your hands. Everyone around you is the same. There is no need for money when everything you work for has substance, and dirt.

Your guide leads you through the front hall of the museum and you marvel at the displays. Your guide is dressed similar to you. They wear a wrinkled flannel, rolled up to the elbows. Their arms are dirty from working the land. Their skin is dark like yours. Their hair is covered to protect it from the sun.

And the sun reaches you even here, in the museum. When you look up, you see clouds and blue sky. Slight distortions where panels meet are the only indication that the museum has a roof; its glass is pristine, invisible. You wonder at the craftsmanship that created such a thing. It far surpasses any ability you ever thought to hold.

Your group shuffles forward into the first room. Next to you, an old woman runs her fingers along the wall to keep her bearings and balance. Her skin leaves light trails of dirt behind, like breadcrumbs.

"Here is the Hall of History," your guide proclaims, backing out of the way as your group files in. You look around, seeing the cornfield and trees outside. Then, as your focus adjusts, you light on the objects.

Cases dot the space, with glass pedestals and glass covers. Some have twisting glass stands to support their cargo, and every piece is labelled with a small white card. The cards stand out clearest — a flock of suspended white squares filling the room like leaves paralyzed in scattered descent. You notice a case very near to you, and step close to read the card.

It describes a work of exquisitely blown glass etched with clouds and stars. You read the name: Divinity. Your eyes slide up to consider the form. If you squint, you can just make out the edges of the sphere, bending in and over themselves. The air between is warped, and slight fuzziness indicates an atmosphere within. You blink, and lose focus. You move on.

The old woman behind you takes your place, fumbling with her glasses.

You wander through the room, using the placement of the little cards to guide you and keep you from blundering inadvertently into one of the delicate cases. As you tiptoe around a dais, your gaze slips to an especially small piece near the wall. You walk over and stoop to see the object.

It is freestanding, within a tall box case. As you try to decipher the shape within, another visitor comes around the other side, and you find yourself looking at them through the glass.

Their face is distorted by layers of transparency and creased in concentration you feel reflected in your own features. While you watch, they study the object within the case, their eyes roving up and down its contours. Then they look up, and meet your gaze.

You are locked in this act of looking, observing each other through the panes. Confusion and discomfort are on their face, and you know they were unable to unlock the secret behind the object. Instead, you contemplate each other, searching for answers in a stranger's face. Before either of you finds anything, they straighten, and move off to the next piece. You watch them through the glass, forgetting to alter your stance to see them without the object in between.

When they have left, you pull your focus back to the piece before you. You can see the trees standing uncertainly outside of the museum, their leaves lush and green. You try to rein in your sight, focusing on the dimensions of the art, but they seem to constantly be changing. First, you think the piece is as tall as its case, glass tickling glass in a gesture that you can hear in your mind. Next, it is almost invisible, huddled at the bottom of the box, barely peeking over the lip of the white card.

While your group mills about the room, you remain exactly where you are. There is something that draws you to this particular piece, to its waves of light, the way it seems to alter the air between you, and the trees beyond. You try to determine its shape, fancying you can make out jagged lines that fracture the world on the other side, but each time you shift your eyes, they are gone, and the piece is invisible once more.

Exhausted by looking, you resort to reading the card. It states the medium in clear black script: Glass. And the artist: Kelly. You turn to the title, and even that is enigmatic, speaking of some elusive, intangible word — whose only image is in its letters: Integrity, 2010. It's not clear whether this is the model or the year in which it was made.

You continue to stare at it, to try to uncover its secrets, even after the guide has moved on to the next room, and your group has followed. Because the walls are clear, they have never once moved out of your sight. Through the glass, you watch them, dark figures pirouetting around tiny white cards.

🏛

When they are ready, they leave, and go back to the lands that birthed them. We watch them go — standing at the bottom left corner of the cornfield. Often, they leave things with us.

Headscarf — blue, with yellow trim.
Gloves — wool, hand-knitted, green.
Apples — four, speckled and uneven.
Rice — red, one pound.
Mirror — silver and black, small.
Pitcher — ceramic, grey with blue flowers.
Glass — in pieces.

We take these gifts and give what we can in return. We give them corn, and potatoes, and herbs from our garden. We give them cloth made with our hands. We give them words of encouragement, and validation. We give them memories to bring back to their homes.

And when they are gone and it is night, we bring their gifts back to our house. We sit down and write notes.

We write about their faces, their hands, their words. We write about the lands they came from and the lands they went to. We write about their stature, their requests, their exclamations. We write about their eyes. We write about everything we can remember, and then we put labels on everything they have given us. In the morning, we separate the items into what we can use, and what must be kept.

The useful things sustain us until the next group comes. We nourish ourselves on gifts of food and read the notes with each bite we take. What cannot be used, we wrap up, and we take it to the bottom of the field.

Next to the Museum of Glass there is a place that has no name. In this place, we put everything we want to remember.

When the season changes, and the corn shifts to potatoes, we go back to that place.

Sitting on the ground between the swaying stalks of two asters, we find a neat stack of white cards. Written on each in a tidy, black hand, is something that cannot be described, along with a name.

Hope, Marilyn
Compassion, Omar
Levity, Harriet
Humanity, Anonymous

We bring them to the museum, and we discover always a new room, and pedestals on which to set the cards. Each word, and each name, finds a place in the Museum of Glass.

"The Museum of Glass" was originally published in *Unsung Stories* in March 2020.

THE MUSEUM OF SHIFTING HISTORIES

Nathan Milner

Washington. Delaware. Leutze.
   Repeat it.
   Washington. Delaware. Leutze.
   With a sound like casting a fishing line, the curator stretched the cord that connected her key card to her belt and pressed the card flat against a panel next to the door. A red light on the panel flashed green. A magnet lock disengaged with a snap and she pulled open the door, stepping into the museum.
   Each of these actions and reactions had been repeated thousands of times. One followed the other with the inexorable force of gravity. The curator didn't mind. She liked the routine; it allowed her to focus on other things.
   Washington. Delaware. Leutze.
   She was listening to the sound of her own footsteps feebly beating on the marble floor when she was interrupted.
   "Good morning, Ms. Costa." The new security guard sat at a desk behind a tall counter, newspaper in his left hand, a dented thermal mug in his right.
   The guard was new in a relative sense. Althea had hired him nearly two months previous, but that hadn't provided her enough time to pick up on his patterns yet — when he arrived, when he left, how much he liked to talk — and for that reason he remained an irritant, a distraction.
   The curator paused for a moment in front of the front desk. She very nearly said, "Good morning, Leutze," but

stopped herself. "Good morning, Tim," she said and resumed walking.

As the curator passed Tim and the welcome desk, she moved into the first gallery and there she performed her first inspection.

Washington. Delaware. Leutze. There it hung, against an eggshell wall.

The words, her recitations, were only a part — the most basic part — of a process. The curator now reviewed the painting in detail: the steadfast man poised at the bow of the ship. The frozen waters. The Grand Union Flag shriveled in the cold.

She checked every piece of it against the gallery in her mind and everything appeared to be in place.

The curator skated into the next gallery with graceful, practiced steps, while her mind moved to the next object of its focus.

Lighthouse. Two Lights. Hopper.

She tried not to have favorites. It had been her first life's ambition to reach this position and, as the curator, she cherished the museum and everything in it. But this was her favorite.

She could almost see herself standing there in the tower, peering out at that horizon. Her hand gripping the cold rail. Her lips casting incantations into the wind.

Lighthouse. Two Lights. Hopper.

For here she stood perched upon a stronghold of art, history, and culture, watching for waves. More accurately, the curator was tasked with watching for ripples and ensuring that they never became waves.

With Hopper's lighthouse inspected and approved, the curator moved on to the European gallery. Striding toward the van Eyck where she would begin her review of this gallery, she glanced at the Vermeer and spotted an inconsistency. A young woman with a water jug. The pitcher sat atop a table draped in a pale-yellow rug.

The curator pulled a square of paper from the breast pocket of her shirt where she kept a stack of the same. She uncapped a fine-tipped blue pen and began to write. She detailed in precise language the changes she observed. What the painting had looked like every day up to this one and what it looked like now. In the bottom corner, right-aligned, she added today's date.

Finished reporting her findings, the curator ducked under the velvet rope and, after folding her note exactly five times, carefully tucked it into the back corner of the painting's frame. By the time she had finished straightening the painting and took a step back to check her work, the correction had been made. The rug beneath the girl's pitcher was once again red.

As the day progressed, the curator completed her tour of the museum, examining each exhibit and artifact, comparing it to the day before and the day before that. She passed like a displaced spirit through corridors and halls and exchanged short, polite greetings with her employees, first, and then, as the day progressed, with guests.

Her employees considered her cold, aloof, but they also considered this one of the easiest jobs they had ever had. The curator didn't micromanage, made few demands of them. She was easy with raises and generous with vacations. From their vantage, she seemed to have an enlightened approach to money, to work, to time — to all of the things that weighed so heavily on them.

She didn't overly concern herself with ticket sales or the planning of new exhibitions. As much attention as she declined to pay to the larger operations of the museum, she devoted to the objects and artwork within, inspecting each piece through a narrow pair of glasses resting at the base camp of her long, hawkish nose.

The cleaning staff believed she was checking their work and felt a pressure that the donations coordinator never would, but at the end of her meticulous review, the curator never complained of dusty frames or smudged display cases, so they told themselves that their efforts had been successful.

She never took lunch, interfering as it would with her patrol of the museum. In the late afternoon, once every exhibit had been checked, the curator would retire to her office to sign documents and make decisions about the running of the museum.

Then the last guests would leave, the museum's lights would dim, the employees would file out the back door to the parking lot and to their cars.

Day by day, she lived in this way until, at the age of sixty-four, three years before her death, a man arrived at the museum and presented her an opportunity. He ignored the art, even the Hopper, and made straight for the curator.

"Are you Ms. Althea Costa?"

"Yes."

"I'd like to discuss with you an interesting opportunity."

"I know, Matthew. This isn't the first time, anymore."

He always looked surprised. But he always recovered quickly. "How many?"

"This one makes seventeen." The number visibly rattled him and he fell back to his notes.

"So you know that tachyons..."

"Are no longer hypothetical. I don't know all of the details. The message, as you know, must be short, but I've pieced together the rest reading Einstein — seems like he had it all figured out. And I've had plenty of time to work through it. Please continue, though." She'd grown fond of Matthew after all of these lives and she wanted to be encouraging.

"Well, I'll just hit the bullet points, then... Tachyons are particles that always move faster than light. Um, using tachyons, signals can be sent faster than light and therefore travel, uh, into the past..."

"Slow down. There's no hurry."

"Sorry. Okay. Into the past in a relative sense. Relative to an observer traveling conventionally through time. Forward. You, if you said yes, would be that observer. You would be the fixed point to whom the sending of the first signal would appear to happen after the receiving of the second signal and vice versa; you'll receive before it's sent or in the past, your message. You'll create a loop, between when you place the call and when you receive it." He made a circle with the thumb and forefinger of his left hand. "They tell me, in time, I'll have a loop of my own." He made another circle with his right hand then linked one circle inside the other. "Together, we make a chain, you and I, two loops."

Althea smiled. She appreciated that he was trying to simplify it for her. In fact, there were many more than two loops. For what is a chain with only two loops? Not long after the technology was invented, there would be dozens of loops strung together, reaching both forward and back. And men like Matthew bound them together.

He fumbled with something clipped to his belt. He managed to pull free a white plastic rectangle the size of a paperback novel and held it out to her. "It can't send anything with mass, only information. But information is enough to cause changes. Changes to the timestream, incongruities, can be subtle. It calls for an expert." He seemed to be finding his footing now. "Your position would be to watch the museum and report any incongruities you notice. And I, in turn, will watch you. I'm an observer of observers. I'll receive your reports and carry your observations into the future where the necessary steps will be taken to repair any damage done to the timestream."

"Excellent," she said, taking his hand and patting it gently. "I understand completely. I can record a short message and at the time of my death it will be sent back into my past."

"Has to be after death. Fractures the psyche otherwise. Have to close the loop."

"I'll receive a telephone call when I was forty-two that will, in my own voice, explain my mission and everything I've learned in this life. If I say yes, correct?"

"Yes."

"Well, Matthew, I've already said yes. So if you'll pass me your recorder, let's get started."

🏛

Washington. Delaware. Leutze.
Good morning, Tim.

The curator's footsteps clicked down the museum's side entranceway. The guard at the front desk hadn't lifted his head from his newspaper yet, but she called out, "Good morning, Tim," and kept moving. A faint "Good morning,

Ms. Costa," chased after her through the front hall as she glided into the first gallery.

Washington. Delaware. Leutze.

She began her check: The steadfast man. The frozen waters. The American flag.

The American flag...

The stars and stripes. Designed in 1777, a year after Washington crossed the Delaware in 1776.

The curator jotted a quick note explaining the issue and secreted it behind the painting's frame. She stepped back a few paces to check her work and noticed that the incongruity remained. The stars and stripes still hung from the side of the overstuffed boat.

A dim uneasiness gripped her, but she tried to brush it away. *Such are the vagaries of time,* she told herself. Most corrections occurred instantaneously, but she had seen a few take as long as five minutes.

Nothing to worry about. Move along... Lighthouse. Two Lights. Hopper.

The words and the images they conjured drowned out all other thought. She stood before the lighthouse and felt a sense of quiet wash over her to see its waves and coast just as she remembered them.

Guests began to shuffle into the hall around her as the museum opened for the day. The curator floated among the visitors as weightless and opaque as a plume of mist.

The Egyptian gallery beckoned, but the curator couldn't help thinking, *Washington, Delaware, Leutze.* Until she confirmed the correction, she couldn't move on.

Her thoughts occupied, the curator nearly collided with a guest in the doorway between galleries. The curator found herself looking into the face of an unwell man. His skin was too loose and bunched around his eyes and neck. Stubble erupted from flesh the color of wet clay.

"Excuse me," she said and crept around the man, who did not move, but stood wheezing in the doorway.

Returning to the first gallery, she discovered a crowd of visitors now milling in front of the Leutze. She could no longer see the frozen waters above their heads but she could see the flag and it remained unchanged.

She sliced through the throng of guests then turned to face them. "Greetings, welcome. I'm the museum's curator, Althea Costa. I'd like to tell you a little about this piece." She ducked under the rope and stood next to the painting. "It was painted in 1850 by Emanuel Leutze..." Information spilled mindlessly from her mouth while she stepped gradually closer to the painting. When she had arrived next to it, she continued speaking and gesturing with her left hand while her right snaked behind the painting's frame searching for her note. It was gone.

The curator felt her heart begin to pound.

"Well, that's the Leutze. If you have any questions, our assistants can be of... assistance. Please enjoy the rest of the museum. Thank you." She yanked the rope high to walk underneath, nearly toppling the brass stands to which it was affixed. She strode into the front hall.

"Samantha!" The curator called frantically to the young woman leaning over the front desk laughing at something Tim had said.

"Yes, Ms. Costa." Samantha stood abruptly and hurried through the front hall shocked by the first hint of urgency she had ever heard in her employer's voice.

"Samantha, that painting, the Leutze, has it been cleaned recently?"

"Yes, Ms. Costa. Custodial cleans every night." She looked carefully at the painting. "Is something wrong?"

"This morning. Has it been cleaned this morning or jostled in any way?"

"No," Samantha said. "We try to stay out of the way once the guests arrive."

The curator bustled off, trying hard to slow her breathing. Gliding past the European gallery, she saw the sick man once more. He lingered before a display case that held a violin the color of honey. After their first awkward encounter, she had hoped not to run into the man again, but when she saw the violin, even at a distance, she nearly sprinted to stand beside him.

Moving swiftly, but firmly in control, the curator joined the sick man by the display case and stared at what she saw inside: Gut strings instead of wire. No chin rest. A short fingerboard. A Baroque configuration.

The Gould violin, one of the finest examples of Antonio Stradivari's work, had been given a Baroque configuration overnight.

"It's something, isn't it?" the sick man asked, and then his hands flew to his mouth to stifle a long string of rattling coughs.

"Yes... yes, it is," she said and turned quickly away. She pulled a square of paper from her pocket and, using her hand as a solid surface, scribbled a rambling, unsteady note.

Returning to the violin, she found that the sick man had moved on. She knelt and inconspicuously fed the note under the plinth upon which the violin stood.

She closed her eyes hard and held them closed for a count of ten before slowly, tentatively opening them. Nothing had changed.

Two incongruities in one day and a vanished note. What could it mean?

The room began to spin around her. The curator reeled through the gallery, trying to remember the words, looking for something, anything, that matched her memory — some solid thing. The paintings all seemed to mock her. *Grape Trees at Collioure* instead of olives. *I Saw the Figure 6 in Gold,* not the figure 5.

Her eyes fixed on the art, the curator careened between guests, and slammed into a garbage can. The sound reverberated through the gallery and everyone in Art of the Ancient Near East turned to look at her.

"Pardon me," she said steadying the wobbling trash can. She looked down into the can and there, atop soft pretzel wrappers and empty bottles of soda, lay a note detailing the many historical inaccuracies of the Gould violin.

She felt stranded, lost. She had no other choice. She pulled a square of paper from her shirt pocket and in fine small handwriting wrote, 'Matthew, I'm scared. Something is wrong. Please come immediately.' At the bottom of the note, right-aligned, she printed today's date, then stuffed it behind the first painting she passed, a depiction of a Persian prince.

The curator sat on a bench in the front hall and waited. He would come. She was sure of it. He would get the message and get it back to himself, loop by loop if necessary. He would come and he would know what to do. But not until the guests had left. When they could speak in private.

The day wore on until the guests began to file past her out of the museum. The museum's lights dimmed.

Tim the security guard approached her hesitantly. "We're heading out, Ms. Costa. You working late?"

She looked up as if waking from a dream. "Working late... yes. Goodnight, Tim."

He backed away from her and fell in with a group of employees heading toward the back exit. She listened to their footsteps fade and then lapse into silence.

The curator hopped up from the bench and dashed to the museum's front glass doors. She watched as the last headlights left the parking lot and a figure emerged from the darkness. Matthew marched up the museum's front stairs.

The curator unlocked the front door and held it open for him. "Oh, Matthew. Thank goodness. Something strange is happening."

"I got your message. What's the matter?" He sounded a touch annoyed. "We really shouldn't meet like this unless it's an emergency."

As he hurried toward the doorway, Matthew faltered for a moment, breaking his stride. He gasped, then stumbled and fell into the curator. The two of them dropped to the floor in a heap. When she had managed to shift Matthew's weight off her, the curator looked up and saw the sick man standing in the doorway, holding a knife that dripped red like an overladen paintbrush.

"Now the chain is broken," he said. He knelt and rummaged through Matthew's clothes until he found a white plastic rectangle.

The sick man stepped into the museum.

The curator scooted away from him, backing through the front hall, leaving a trail of Matthew's blood like a ragged brushstroke.

"No more watcher. No more reports. They won't know what's happened until it's too late," the sick man said pursuing the curator through the front hall. "I can do whatever I want. Even... this." He gave a pedestal a soft shove. The pedestal tipped, dropping the sculpted head of Ptolemy II to the floor where it shattered to pieces.

The curator continued crawling backward through the first gallery where a time-tarnished Leutze hung.

"They promised me my own loop," he said, "which sounded pretty good to me. And, let's be honest, what choice did I have? My time is running out." He tried for a smile, but a coughing fit overtook him, contorting his face and dropping him to one knee.

The curator stood and fled down the back hallway. At the end of this hallway was a wooden door, its glass window stenciled with her name and title. She remembered the first time she had seen it that way — *her* name, followed by *her* title — and the pride she had felt. These had been the best years of her life.

The sick man followed ploddingly, holding his knife out in front of him like a divining rod.

She dove inside her office and had just managed to swing the door shut behind her when it exploded inward. The sick man, leading with his shoulder, had thrown his weight against the door, and now tumbled in as it gave way.

The curator circled behind her desk, setting an obstacle between herself and the sick man. He began to circle too, his lips and chin glistening with spit. They turned slowly around the desk in synchronous orbit.

The curator heard the sick man's breath, ragged and primal. She heard herself whimpering against her will. Then a peal of bells split the distance between them as the telephone on her desk began to ring.

The curator and the sick man both froze in place. Their eyes shot to the phone. It rang again.

"Who do you think it is?" the curator asked. She saw uncertainty for the first time in the sick man's face and maybe... fear. "It's already over. It's already happened. I mean, if it's you on the phone, then I guess you won. But if it's me..." The man's eyes swung violently between the curator and the telephone.

"Do you want to find out?" she asked. "Let's see how this ended."

The curator reached for the phone but the sick man, stock-still since the phone began to ring, suddenly surged to life. He leapt down on the phone before the curator could touch it, spilling the receiver off its cradle and dropping his knife in the process.

He gathered the receiver up and held it to his ear. His voice choked with dread, the sick man said: "Hello?"

He listened, his face twisting. His eyes went wide. "No... how?" His hand dropped away from his ear and the receiver clattered across the desk.

"Once you picked up the phone, it had already happened. Uncertainty collapsed."

"Well, I guess, that's it then," he said with a note of resignation. "Nothing left to do." The sick man bent and picked the knife up off the floor where he'd dropped it. He extended it with both hands toward the curator, as if offering it to her. When the curator didn't move, he turned the blade inward and slammed the knife into his chest. Air seeped through his lips like a punctured tire and he slumped to the floor.

The curator picked the receiver up off her desk and listened to the remainder of the message. She knelt and rummaged through the sick man's clothes until she found a white plastic rectangle. She tuned it in the way she had watched Matthew do seventeen times before, then left her office and returned to the museum. Now all that was left was to press the soft, thumb-shaped button at the bottom of the device, record her message, and send it back to twenty-four minutes ago.

At sunrise, she thought. *At sunrise, I'll place the call and start a new loop.*

At the end of all of her previous lives, Matthew had pressed the button and placed the call. This time, she'd have to do it herself. She'd have to do it all herself. With Matthew gone, there was too much uncertainty. If she put it off, lived a little longer, anything could happen — heart failure, car accident, they could try again. She would close the loop. Tonight.

She would borrow the sick man's knife. Then, she would hold something heavy just above the button. *Once I pass, gravity will do the rest*, she thought. *The statue of Isis and her son Horus should work perfectly.*

The chain was broken, but her loop remained, though it had tightened quite a bit. She would never again touch the future. She would have only the time between when she received the call in her office and when she placed it a few hours from now, forever. Until then, she would enjoy the museum.

She floated through the galleries. She drifted toward her favorite, the Hopper, but it had changed. A figure, just a silhouette, standing at the lighthouse rail where none had been before — trapped there, helpless to light the lamp, to raise a warning.

The silent figure stood at the lighthouse rail and watched waves crash endlessly below.

THE MUSEUM OF HYDROLOGICAL PHENOMENA

Lori J. Torone

Jack biked the riverbank path to the museum, the evening city lights shining in the water like sunken stars. The Museum of Hydrological Phenomena was affiliated with the university and situated in the park at the city's end. There, the river narrowed into a wide stream and then a creek, wending its way through manicured lawns, box hedges, and willow trees that had been strategically placed by the municipal parks department. He passed the playground he had frequented as a child. Eventually the traffic sounds faded, and he could hear the birds and the river murmuring. Jack shifted the bag of groceries he was delivering, breathing deeply in the relative quiet and exhaling stress and hopefully whatever smog was stuck in his lungs.

He looked forward to this grocery delivery route, twice a week, through the park. He hated the city, even though he had grown up here; hated the buildings crowded together, the noise pollution, the aggressive artificial lights that outshone the stars. The city was a thousand-piece puzzle, and his individual piece was from a different box. He felt misplaced.

The park, at least, was something to loosen the stagnation in his chest and quiet the turmoil in his mind, even though it too had been cultivated by the city, long ago clearing a forest in order to plant flower beds and metal swings. The creek was the only original landscape feature, and he found its murmuring brought him temporary peace like nothing else did.

Jack veered away from the water and turned up the path for the museum, coasting to a stop and leaning the bike against the stone wall. He hefted the grocery bags from the wire basket. The Museum of Hydrological Phenomena had originally been a church, before the university acquired the building, although there was a vague account that it had been built over an earlier, pre-colonial structure. Most of the old-timer professors called it by its original name, Our Lady of the Waters.

Sarah opened the private back door when he knocked. "Hi, Jack! Lentil soup tonight." The professor looked like an old hippie, with her flowing dress, rows of crystal bracelets, and long white braid. She was very down-to-earth with Jack, but the seniors were intimidated by her bluntness and demanding expectations of their theses. She only taught the thesis class and gave the occasional special lecture; she was on campus in the mornings and curated the museum in the afternoons. Even the other professors seemed to be in awe of her, and her lectures were talked about for weeks. They blended archaeological findings with her two doctoral fields, hydrology and anthropology.

"Peaches are in season now, so I added a few to your order, if that's okay," he said, handing her the brown paper bags. She had been thrilled when the stores stopped using plastic bags, almost like it was a personal victory, and remarked how she hoped those plastic six-pack rings were next.

"More than okay. Very much appreciated! I love baking peach cobbler." She entered the small kitchen of the old rectory to take his plate out of the oven, and he followed.

He remembered the first time he had delivered to her, before he had heard the stories about her and the mysterious special collection. He had been a freshman and needed a job for books and food. No one else at the store wanted to take the hour-long bike ride down to the museum. When she opened the door, she had scrutinized him, and he met her murky hazel gaze unflinching until she finally nodded and said, "Well, then. What would you prefer as a tip, money, or a home-cooked meal? I have leftovers."

He had been taken aback, but something — maybe loneliness, maybe the fact he was no longer welcome at his family dinner table — made him accept her dinner of broiled salmon and mashed potatoes.

They had their ritual. As she put away the groceries, he sat at her table and ate whatever food she had made. They would talk, mostly about his second-year anthropology courses. She had ceased asking him personal questions a while ago, he assumed because she could see they made him uncomfortable. His parents were no longer speaking to him, and he wasn't sure if the hurt was lessening as time went on or he was just getting used to it. He wasn't into the bar scene; he avoided any city life, really, unlike most of his dorm-mates, so he had no exciting social life to tell of. He spent a lot of free time in the library, researching anything he was interested in, just to spend as little time in the dorm and as much time as possible in what quiet and solitude he could find.

Once he had finished eating, they would move into the main collection room, which closed to the public at dusk, so it was cool and quiet, with its dim lighting and stained-glass windows. Sarah sat at her desk with the newspaper, and Jack examined the exhibits.

There were cases of local artifacts: broken pottery, coins, bones both human and animal, arrowheads, daggers, cutlery, jewelry, statuettes. An educational section for school groups contained 3D displays of the river's tides and sediment levels, with charts of fish and birds, some long gone from the river. Pamphlets of basic hydrology and river folklore, arts and crafts projects, and coloring pages lay scattered nearby on a large table.

A few doors, what students said were the old chapel and two confessional booths, were always locked. Rumors on campus were that they were secret collection and archival rooms, accessible only to a chosen few thesis students, who were handpicked by Professor Sarah, and who subsequently disappeared after entering them, never to be seen on campus again. Jack thought it was more likely they were storage or utility rooms, as he had seen Sarah pull a broom from one before.

When he had gotten up the courage to mention these rumors to Sarah, she had laughed, saying, "You've got to be kidding me. An archive of missing-thesis-student skeletons?

I'm not a monster, no matter what the seniors think!" She had unlocked the coin display for him to peruse, adding, "At least mysteries are healthy for human nature."

Jack pulled on white cotton gloves to handle the pottery pieces he was currently exploring. He had already jotted down in his small notebook: *#35: broken water pitcher, dredged up near southwest bank decades ago; spout intact, handles missing (?); clay; serpent etching — blue paint? plant material?* — look up. He handled each broken shard, trying to fit them together. They matched with each other, but not the pitcher. He sighed and picked up the pen.

He had never felt such a kinship with pottery shards before.

#36-43 broken pottery pieces, similar clay and coloring, found in vicinity of #35 but not fitting it. A second matching pitcher? Cups?

Sarah rattled the pages of her newspaper and made a noise of mild disgust. "Pollution levels are up, both air and water, not surprising," she said, and a few minutes later added, "And they are dredging again and widening the banks up by the market district to allow more cargo boats to pass. Ridiculous!"

"Maybe they'll find new artifacts."

Sarah snorted. "Not there, they won't. And that's not the point, even if archaeology weren't the furthest thing from the city government's mind." She peered at him over her reading glasses. "Here's a question: What does everything in this museum have in common?"

"Uh... they are all part of the city's history? Human experience?" He had a sudden insight as to what the senior thesis students felt. Her eyes were suddenly intense, like at their first meeting. "These are all items that people made and used, like this pitcher."

"Not quite," she said, "although most people come to that first conclusion, despite the museum's name, because people tend to think of nature and history through the lens of human experience. That pottery you are studying was found in the river, not far from here, actually. Every item on display was either dredged up from the river or discovered in the mud of its banks. The river is the current underneath every exhibit here, and its movement is time passing. The river as muse."

She watched him for a minute, as if expecting him to reply, then sighed and pulled her sweater closer around her and went back to her newspaper. A draft hit Jack's neck, made him shiver. He looked around at the exhibits. Suddenly the room felt damper as well, almost as if he could feel the remembered presence of water, carried by each relic that had once been submerged in one time period only to be hauled up dripping into another one.

It must be less quiet, less musical at the bottom of the riverbed now than it had been hundreds of years ago, when the only honking was made by geese. He wrote these thoughts in his notebook.

"What are you looking for, Jack?" Sarah asked, startling him into straightening up from his notebook so abruptly that his back cracked. "I can tell you aren't researching for a paper. So, what is it? I can point you in a certain direction if you need. After all, that's my job."

Jack paused. What was he looking for? She was right. He didn't have a paper due, nor was he doing fieldwork yet. His dorm mates teased him that he fell down research rabbit holes, but it was the perfect excuse not to go out, really. He hated the crowds, the fluorescent lights, the diesel smell and noise of the city; the clubs and bars seemed a microcosm of the city itself — overwhelming, grasping, fake.

What was he looking for? What didn't he have? His classes interested him enough. He certainly had his own electric kettle, hot plate, and even a small microwave, but Sarah's meals were better than fast food, and the only real home-cooked food he could get.

He didn't know how to answer her. And he didn't want to say he didn't know. And he couldn't say he just liked it here, in the cool, quiet museum, that the exhibits grounded him and made him forget about his own broken pieces.

What he said was, "I think I'll know it when I see it."

Her eyebrows raised, and she seemed oddly satisfied with that answer. "I think it's time for a pot of tea. The museum seems extra drafty tonight," she said, rising from her desk. "I'll be back in a bit."

It did seem draftier to Jack than usual. He stood up and walked around, trying to find the source. He passed the locked doors. One had a definite breeze exuding from its frame, the other just a presence of cold seeping out, like from an icebox.

He paused. The draft became a cold breath upon his face, whispering his name. *"Jack..."*

A prickle of anticipation ran down his spine, that feeling of a discovery just within reach. His fingers grazed the doorknob. What if his answers lay behind these doors? He should just ask Sarah for access.

But he was certain she would say no. Not every thesis student was allowed into the collection. And he had a sinking feeling that their friendship wouldn't matter in this case.

The keys were in her desk drawer. He bit his lip. It would be a breaking of trust. Sarah was one of the few people he felt comfortable with. He dropped his hand, turned away. *"Jack,"* he heard again, consonants crisp and urgent.

She wouldn't know if it was just a quick peek to assess the contents, he told himself. And then he could figure out if or how to approach her about letting him study the collection. It was a reasonable, academic decision. He darted over to Sarah's desk, opening the wooden drawer where he knew the keys were. It stuck, and he yanked too hard in his haste, sending it crashing to the floor with a resonating thud, spilling its contents. Jack heard fast footsteps and jumped up, side-stepping around the desk.

"Jack?" she called. "Is everything okay? Did something fall?" She stood at the threshold of the rectory door.

"My notebook, and I fell over in the chair trying to get it. Nothing broke," he called back, walking towards her to intercept her if need be.

"Are you sure?" she said, and stepped forward, her brow furrowing. "That sounded —" The teapot started to whistle. "Okay. Let me just steep this."

"Can you pop some biscuits in the stove, too? Maybe I can take some back with me, for breakfast, if you don't mind?"

She contemplated him for a moment, then nodded and turned away.

He stuffed everything back in the drawer, except for the keyring, and shoved the drawer back in the desk. He ran to the closest door, the one that felt like a freezer, and tried the keys until he found one that fits. The door opened, and an icy gush of air whistled over him. Just a peek...

It was pitch black. He couldn't see anything. He felt along the wall for a light switch and couldn't find one, so he slid himself all the way into the room until he found it and flicked it on.

He had been holding his breath without realizing it. No skeletons, Jack observed with a small inward laugh at himself. Only very old paintings in carved wooden frames hanging on the walls, some sepia photographs, and a few glass cabinets.

The paintings seemed to mesmerize him, and the cold numbed him. Forgetting himself, forgetting Sarah who was going to come out of the kitchen at any moment, he walked the room's perimeter slowly. The paintings, he realized, were a historical record: river landscapes showing the progression of the city growth in the background, the changes in bank width, water depth and flow, and boat types. One in particular, noticeably different from the others, made him stop to scrutinize it. It was a simple forest creek landscape. Brushstrokes of oil paint gave texture to the canvas, bringing the whorls of its current to life. A fish leapt, breaking the surface. Jack blinked, and it was gone. He rubbed his eyes; the painting was so vivid it was sparking his imagination, had him wishing he was there, so he could experience the landscape in its purest form.

The river as muse, Jack thought. *Or in this case, the creek. Where the river begins?*

He was getting colder as he stood still, so he went to the cabinets, which contained a yellowed quarto of poetry, the personal diary of the archaeologist for whom the university department was named, a nineteenth-century anthology of river folklore illustrated with woodcut engravings, and a shelf of bound thesis papers. Behind them were the old photographs, mostly of the university being built in the 1800s and the founding faculty, who stood in a group, staring stoically at the camera in their academic attire.

One of them looked exactly like Professor Sarah.

The cold became suddenly painful; his teeth chattered. Jack blinked, but it still looked like her, and his brain seemed to become as numb as his hands and feet. *It's not possible.* But somewhere in the back of his mind, he remembered her saying, 'I'm not a monster.'

"Find anything?"

He startled, almost falling over. Sarah stood behind him, at the door. "So now you've seen the special collection that everyone loves to speculate about," she continued, gesturing around the room, her tone sharp. "The room is temperature- and light-regulated for preservation. That's why it's not open to the public. To keep damage at a minimum." Abashed, Jack kept his head down as he put the keys in her outstretched hand and followed her out of the room to her desk, where she put a steaming mug of tea into his hands. "Well, I can't say I blame you. If you had asked me to see it, I would probably have said no, not until your thesis, and maybe not even then. Not every thesis student can handle what's inside that room." She gave him a pointed look. "So, did you at least find anything for your trouble? Have any questions answered?"

He paused before shaking his head, gulping the tea. He couldn't look at her out of guilt and apprehension, but he felt her eyes on him, felt an energy emanating from her that he had never before. It was unnerving.

But she's not a monster. I believe her, he thought. *So who — or what — is she?*

Sarah's tone was demanding, ripping him out of his thoughts. "Then I'll pose a question that I'd like you to answer instead, to make up a bit for pilfering my keys. What does human nature do to Nature itself?"

"Is... is that a rhetorical question?" he asked in return, stammering, so flustered by her that when he put the empty mug down on his work table, his elbow hit the pitcher he had been studying. It tipped, dangerously close to the edge of the table. Gasping, he caught it before it fell, and something clinked inside.

It was a coin, with a smooth silver patina, cool and silky between his fingers, etched with a salmon on one side and three undulating lines on the other, like snakes. "This is new," he said.

Sarah laughed. "Nothing here is new."

Jack had a moment of disorientation, in which the room's shadows seemed to flow over the floor much like the lines on the coin. "No, I mean, this wasn't here. In the pitcher. And I've been through the coin display. I've never seen this coin." He paged quickly through his notes, then stood and walked over to that display. There was an empty spot next to a card that read:

#111 silver coin, unknown date and origin.
Find where the coin belongs and find yourself.

"Where does it belong?" Jack whispered, as he racked his brain. He did not recall this coin at all.

"Finally," Sarah said. "You are starting to ask worthy questions, to look beneath the surface. Take the coin with you. No, leave the gloves, you don't need them."

She walked across the room and unlocked a second door. With a pull of a string and a click, a bare light bulb illuminated stone steps descending into the earth. "That one," she pointed across Jack's shoulder at the third door, "is the real utility closet."

Sarah went first, and Jack hesitated before crossing the threshold and putting his foot on the first step. *I believe her.*

"Going back to my non-rhetorical question," Sarah said, as they took the rough-hewn steps carefully, submerging into cool, dank air saturated with the musty scent of stone and earth. "Participate in my impromptu lesson and perhaps you can redeem yourself. Let's begin. What created civilization?"

Jack opened his mouth to give her the textbook answer of the key components of a civilization, then closed it so hard his teeth clacked. He thought about her wording of the question, and the museum's exhibits, and he had that wonderful sensation of academic revelation, the symbolic light bulb over his head which he loved so much. It chased away any remaining shame and apprehension he felt. "The rivers," he said triumphantly. "Civilization was born in river valleys. Mesopotamia's Tigris and Euphrates, the Nile, the Indus, the Yellow River. And then the great European cities grew on rivers: Rome on the Tiber, London on the Thames, Paris on the Seine."

They had reached the bottom of the steps and emerged into a cellar. Jack heard water trickling. Sarah fiddled with a lantern set atop a crate, its light spluttering. "Well done. The river goddesses fed their people with water, fish, fowl, and fertile soil. Upon their currents they gave them a means to travel, and thus grow and spread their civilizations through trade." The dark room gave her voice a hollow, echoing quality. "The river goddesses, all daughters of Mother Earth, gave humans the gifts of resources and resourcefulness."

The lantern beamed, diminishing the darkness into shadows. "Ah, there we go. The bulb was loose." The cellar walls and floors were uneven, like a natural cavern; Jack saw a few more crates, as well as old wooden pews stacked unevenly on top of each other.

"This way," Sarah said, leading him into a narrow passageway. "Unfortunately, that wonderful human trait of resourcefulness too often has a negative effect. Especially on our water resources." She paused and glanced back at him, eyebrows raised. The sound of water had grown louder.

"Exploitation," he said. "Dams and dredging to control water flow. Pollution, factory waste runoff. The ramifications on wildlife."

Nodding, she said, "As civilizations grew, they no longer saw their water sources as divine, or even as sacred, no longer viewed what the goddess gave them as gifts, but as rightfully theirs. And that's why, when explorers like Henry Hudson followed the rivers, they believed everything they saw was theirs for the taking. Even now, rights to water sources are a constant legal battle." Sarah stopped abruptly and turned, almost blinding Jack with the lantern. "People refuse to listen to the water's voice anymore. Why?"

This time he did not hesitate to answer. "Maybe because they make too much of their own noise to really listen to anything else." The bitterness in his own voice startled him.

Sarah's face lit up and she smiled broadly. "That's an excellent way of putting it, Jack. That's definitely one answer. Here we are." The passageway opened into a grotto. She swept her arm with the lantern outwards, beckoning him to enter first.

A spring burbled up from the rocky back wall, forming a pool. Sarah placed the lantern on the floor near the entrance and drew a matchbox from her sweater pocket, lighting votives that were nestled among the rocks. The candle flames reflected in the water and sent white light dancing around the grotto, illuminating several statues that were interspersed among the rocks.

A carved porcelain woman, dressed in white robes with a blue sash around her waist, held her arms outstretched to Jack. Other statues seemed older: a severely chipped marble woman bearing a water jug on her shoulder; a bronze statue, stained green with time, of a woman in front of a cauldron; a squat clay statuette with a ridged cap and wide hands placed on her knees.

"Our Lady of the Waters," Jack whispered as he approached the edge of the pool. Wooden carvings of beaver and otter perched on a large flat stone together. Symbols were scratched into the rocks, some signs for water he recognized, and one large peace sign in rainbow chalk. He gazed at the serene face of a goddess in a lotus position, one hand pointing down to the ground, the other up to the sky.

"These waters are the source, feeding the creek that becomes the river. A long time ago, this spring was a place of prayer, of contemplation, of connection to the water deity. If one is connected to the divine, one is connected to oneself, to the water within."

"And stardust," he murmured, moving his gaze from the lotus goddess to his own reflection in the water. "Everything is made of stardust. Even water. I read that." Jack knelt at the pool's edge and grazed his fingertips along the shimmering surface. It was shockingly cold. This is what it would feel like to touch time, he thought. A constant celestial flow.

The regret of wasting his time in a place he didn't belong welled up inside him and opened the floodgates in his chest, releasing all the words and emotions that had been held stagnant inside him for so long.

"I grew up in this city, and I hate it," Jack said. "I didn't even want to go to this university, but my parents pressured me. Dad is an alumnus. But I don't want to be a company CEO like him. I don't want to wear suits and be stuck in an office building all day and bully people for a living. I don't care about making tons of money. I'd rather research, do fieldwork, maybe teach. I'd rather be somewhere more... green. Quieter. Somewhere you can see the stars, really see them." He thought about the painting and swallowed hard. "And I guess to add insult to injury... my feelings about others are different than what my parents think they should be. So, they disowned me."

His words ran out into a silence that stretched as he stared into the water. Eventually he looked back at Sarah. The light was dancing over her face too. She looked sad. Behind her on the wall was a painted mural, a replica of the painting that had drawn him in. But in this version a maiden emerged from the creek, her long hair trailing behind her into the water. Or was it the other way around, Jack wondered. Was the water becoming her hair?

The painted goddess had Sarah's features, but the eyes were a clear blue-green. With another flash of insight, Jack knew who Sarah really was, even though — or perhaps because — her eyes were muddy and tearful.

"The city no longer serves you," he said to her. "I'm sorry."

She laughed a little and wiped her eyes. "Don't worry about me, Jack. I do what I can with what power I still have. Remember, my job is to move people in the right direction, whatever that may be. It has always been. More importantly," she countered, "this city, and its inhabitants, no longer serve you."

There was a broken water pitcher on the ground under the mural. *I was right about the companion piece*, he thought. Out loud he admitted, "I don't belong here, but I don't know where to go. So, I'm stuck."

"Make a wish."

"What?"

Sarah pantomimed tossing something into the water. "Make a wish, with the coin. You know, like a fountain or a wishing well. That's what the coin is for: an offering for the water goddess. It's not easy, what you've done, Jack — looking beneath your own surface, acknowledging painful truths to yourself. But you have to keep going. Connect to the water. And yourself."

Jack held his breath for a moment, then flicked the coin into the air. It gleamed and spun as it fell, breaking the surface with a deep plunk. He could see it, and others, at the bottom of the pool.

"There is so much left to be found," Sarah whispered, "if only one knows the right places to look."

I know those places, the spring murmured, with Sarah's voice as a whispering undercurrent. *I know you, Jack.*

The pool rippled, circles spreading from the center, and when the water calmed, Jack could see an image, as if looking through a window, of a stream meandering down a natural staircase of wide, flat rocks, until it cascaded over a shelf into a lake below. People, young and old, walked barefoot in the water, or sat and watched the waterfall. Hikers, Jack assumed from their backpacks and the boots they carried or had next to them, stuffed with thick socks.

A bone-weary ache spread through Jack, and he was certain he would feel better if he could just touch the water, feel it running over his hands and feet. He knelt down and plunged his hand beneath the surface, but the pool rippled again, and the perspective panned out until he was standing on a street, shops to either side of him, many flying rainbow flags. A mountain range edged the horizon in front of him, sunset painting the sky above it in bright paths of color. He walked down to the edge of the street where there was a small bridge over a river, beyond which fields stretched alongside the road that led up to the mountain. Hawks circled high above the fields, above the quiet river, and Jack could feel a peaceful, steady flow start inside him, beginning the process of washing away his hurt and confusion.

My sister is shallow and slow, bearing fish and herons and the occasional kayaker. This is an old town, hundreds of years old, but it has new ideas. You will thrive here.

With a jolt of recognition, Jack knew this place.

The candles in the grotto guttered out. He turned, a question on his lips, but Sarah was gone. On the ground where she had stood was a pamphlet for a university, its name imprinted across a picture of a mountain range. It had been one of his college choices before he gave in to his parents.

Taking the lantern, he went back upstairs. He had a lot to do: apply for a transfer, find housing and a job, maybe in one of the stores on Main Street. Maybe he could save up enough money to buy a kayak, or at least rent one on a regular basis. And hiking gear. He took one last look around the silent museum and whispered a prayer of gratitude.

Jack rode back along the riverbank to his dorm, and it didn't bother him when the crickets and water became drowned out by city noise again. He'd be able to hear everything he wanted to hear clearly once he caught the right current.

The Museum of the High Street

Vaughan Stanger

Milena stared at the flashing sign hovering above the exhibition's entrance, then glanced over her shoulder.

"Mum, why is it called moths?"

"M-O-T-H-S stands for the Museum of the High Street. I did say that's where we're going."

"What's a high street?"

"You've heard of Amazon?"

Milena nodded.

"Well, a high street was like a mini-Amazon arranged on either side of a road."

The double doors swept open to reveal a long, gritty-floored hallway, with lots of signs and doors and tall windows. Fluffy holo-clouds floated beneath the pale blue ceiling.

"So, are those shops?"

Her mum chuckled. "That's right. Your gran worked in one selling cosmetics and medicines."

Milena's gran joined them, having successfully exchanged crypto for something called 'hard cash' outside. She pointed towards a blue sign with curvy white lettering.

"Boots was the last shop to close where I lived."

She sounded sad.

A weird-looking robot made of metal rods wobbled up to them. One of its wheels was spinning like an app that had crashed. Its cyber-eyes blinked a greeting.

"Can I help you?"

Its cheerful voice made Milena smile.

"No, thanks," said her mum. "We don't need a guide."

"It's not too late to change your —"

"No thanks!"

The robot wobbled away, searching for other visitors. Milena had counted five so far — all adults.

"What was that thing?"

"A shopping trolley," said her mum. "We won't need it."

"Too pushy," her gran said.

Milena's mum groaned. "How about we do some window shopping?"

Whatever that was.

"Okay."

After they'd walked past several shopfronts, Milena pointed to one topped by a bright green sign.

"What did Oxfam sell?"

Her gran sighed. "Second-hand clothes and books, mostly."

"What's second-hand?"

"Stuff people donated because they didn't need it anymore."

Milena wrinkled her nose. "Who would buy that?"

"Other people."

Her frown deepened. "But why?"

The two adults exchanged glances.

Her mum said, "Oxfam helped poor people."

"Oh, I see."

At least Milena thought she did. She knew poor people were extinct. A bit like moths and tigers and *both* Amazons.

"Can we go in?"

"I'm not sure—"

"Nonsense," said Milena's gran. "We're here to shop!"

Milena followed her inside. Ignoring the rails of holo-clothes, she headed straight for the tall shelves at the back.

Eyes wide, she said, "Are those *real* books?"

Her gran shook her head. "I shouldn't think so."

Milena reached up for one with a statue of a tiger on its cover.

Her mum snapped, "Don't touch!"

The book disappeared. Her gran laughed.

"Too late!"

Milena's mum sighed. "I *knew* that would happen."

Outside the shop, the wonky-wheeled trolley waited for them, its cyber-eyes still blinking. The holo-book floated within its metal frame.

"Please pay for your shopping after you leave this exhibition."

Both adults chuckled.

Her gran said, "Exit via..."

"... gift shop!"

Milena didn't understand what was so funny, but it didn't matter. She had been shopping. That's what counted.

🏛

The gift shop contained lots of shelves and clothes rails, all empty. An Ubi hummed in the corner. Milena frowned because their trolley was now empty.

"Where's my book?"

Her gran smiled. "We have to pay for it first."

"You know, I could still grab the code so we could ubi it at home," her mum said. "That wouldn't cost anything."

Milena crossed her arms. "But it wouldn't be shopping!"

Her gran nodded vigorously. "Milena's right! Don't worry dear, I'll pay."

"Are you sure?"

"It would be my pleasure."

Milena's mum sighed. "Okay, just this once."

When her gran fed a plastic note into the indicated slot, the Ubi purred like Milena's virtual cat.

Her mum frowned as though she now regretted the visit.

"No wonder this place is closing next month. No one *really* misses shopping."

"I do," said her gran.

"Ha! You just miss eating *out*."

"Well yes, that too!"

Milena frowned. "What's eating out?"

Her gran replied: "After the shops disappeared, people still went to the high street to eat. But the Great Pandemic of '31 ended that. Soon afterwards, the government gave every household an Ubi, so there wasn't any reason to eat out anymore."

"But your gran loves a touch of nostalgia," Milena's mum said. "She thought you might enjoy this exhibition."

Her gran gave Milena a serious look. "You did enjoy it, didn't you?"

Milena nodded but her attention was now on the delivery tray. The Ubi had stopped purring. Her book slid out. She snatched it up before *it* disappeared too.

Every page delivered magic. She gazed in wonder at the statues of lions and elephants and other extinct things.

Her mum tapped the book's cover. "Our Ubi could make any of those."

Milena shook her head. "I've got a *much* better idea!"

She didn't want something made for her. She wanted to make something for *herself*. For that, she'd need some modelling clay. Their Ubi could provide it but only if she recycled other stuff first. Unless her gran topped up her feedstock allowance. And once she'd made her animals, she would need somewhere to display them.

Happily, she had an idea about that.

🏛

The elderly man accompanying the boy frowned.

"Are you *sure* you want it?"

The boy nodded.

"Why?"

"Cos it wasn't made by an Ubi. Jamie's got two already!"

The man muttered something about a 'fad'.

"Please!"

The boy didn't seem to mind that the unicorn wasn't one of Milena's better efforts. Keeping up with demand was difficult. The supply of clay was no longer a problem, now that the Ubi which owned the MOTHS building had approved her business plan, but she could only skip so much school.

The man turned to Milena. "Is this thing *really* an Ubinot?"

She smiled at him. "Yes, it is."

He sighed while placing his money on the counter. Milena wrapped the unicorn in paper and handed it to the boy.

Once they'd gone, she waved at her gran, who was standing on the opposite side of the 'road' but too busy to respond while welcoming families into the café.

The High Street was booming again.

During their journey home, Milena asked her gran about fads.

Within a week, she'd opened a new shop selling second-hand Ubinots.

"The Museum of the High Street" was originally published as "The Little Shop That Could" in *Tales of the Cybersalon: A New High Street* in May 2021.

THE MUSEUM OF UNPOPULAR ART

Mark Keane

The receptionist told him he was two hours early for his meeting.

"If you're looking for something to do while you're waiting," she added, "I can recommend a museum that's nearby."

Donal half-listened, too busy thinking about the message on his voicemail. His name had been suggested for a new ad campaign. They liked what they'd seen of his work, and wanted to meet him. He'd gotten the address right, but must have misheard the time.

Donal Lysaght: freelance copywriter, author of promotional bumf, leaflets and brochures. Tedious stuff that paid the bills. Speculative fiction was his true calling — where the familiar intersected the strange, and the incredible could be found in the ordinary. Instead of exploring his imagination, he churned out banal sales pap.

He had two hours to kill in a part of town he didn't know. He left the building, and stopped, his neck muscles tensed. Someone was watching him. He had had the same sense earlier, but now it was much stronger. He turned around. There was nobody there, or no one he could see. A sign on a lamp-post read: *Art Museum Next Left*. The receptionist had mentioned something about a museum.

A second sign directed him to a three-storey building, the paintwork cracked and peeling. There was no name above the door or anything else to suggest it was an art museum. The entrance led into a small foyer dominated by a painting of a bearded man in a tweed suit, two wolfhounds at his feet. Donal read the inscription: *Sir Hugo Drouet, founder of the museum, and his beloved hunting dogs.*

A thin woman with grey, spiky hair stood behind a counter. She handed him a visitor's guide.

"The exhibits are through there," she said, pointing to Donal's left.

He entered the first room. Smallish squares hung on the walls, non-figurative panels. A philistine might have said a four-year-old could do better, but Donal was no philistine. He appreciated the artistic vision in all its forms.

Here were recognised artists, their creativity chosen for display. What had he to show? Three stories in obscure e-zines that garnered faint praise from a few editors and nothing from readers. Who read these e-zines? Donal certainly didn't. Then there were the rejections. *We're going to pass on this. It's not the right fit. While we enjoyed reading your story, it's not for us. It's not quite what we're looking for.* No matter the response, he was compelled to express life as seen through his lens.

He stopped at one of the abstractions, smudged grey with a thin red diagonal line. The entry in the guide read: *View from the Bridge: CG, 1951-2008.* How strange, he thought — only the artist's initials were given.

The adjoining room contained work by a single painter. He paused to read the guide.

The artist, WV, was a troubled soul who hanged himself, aged thirty-four. WV tried to capture the effect produced by pinching both eyes between thumb and index finger. The light that is seen though no light enters the eye, what WV termed the memory of light. He represented this as an excess of black cut through with daubs and dribbles of white. From repeatedly squeezing his eyes, WV damaged his sight. His condition worsened, an extreme blepharospasm that forced his eyes permanently shut so he could no longer see to paint. This brought to an end his depiction of light without light. WV put a noose around his neck and shut out the light for good.

Donal inspected the monochrome paintings, searching for meaning and puzzled by the dismissive commentary in the guide. He continued, entering other rooms, taking his time over portraits with lollipop heads, misshapen and angular bodies, smeared and fragmented images. Larger rooms housed installations. Papier-mâché cubes and oblongs, murals with strobe lighting and dialogue playing on tape recorders, interspersed with cries and screams. Hanging breezeblocks, mounds of grass and ugly weeds, a child's paddling pool filled with razor blades. The few visitors he passed looked away. It was a strange collection, off-kilter in a way that appealed to Donal.

Another room contained work by an artist whose name was given in full — Max Plunkett, born in 1949. A single painting commanded one wall: *Picture of Winifred.* A striking portrait of a young woman: alluring smile, jet-black hair lying in ringlets on her shoulders. Close up, every blemish, every pore in her skin was revealed in magnified photographic detail. Donal moved closer to examine the crusty mucus in the corner of one eye, each flake of rheum painstakingly rendered.

Two smaller canvases, layers of sombre colours with grainy splotches, were titled *Picture of Gwyneth* and *Picture of Isobel.* Donal checked the guide.

Portraits by the young Plunkett were lauded for their attention to detail. The artist renounced this work as mere copying, with no creative merit. Instead, he paid more attention to the background than the sitter. In subsequent work, the figure was absent, painted over with background. Plunkett claimed he imbued the background with the spirit of the subject. Gwyneth and Isobel were understandably outraged when they saw themselves represented by muddy greys and browns. Plunkett soon returned to realism, producing portraits that flattered the subject.

At the end of a corridor, Donal came to a digital sign with scrolling text: *New Acquisition Straight Ahead.* A table under the sign was piled with envelopes and a notice that read: *Please take one.* Donal put an envelope in his pocket, intending to check what it contained once he'd viewed the 'new acquisition'. He followed a sequence of arrows on the floor, through an archway and into a room illuminated by light from a screen. He sat on a bench.

A black-and-white film was playing. A man appeared — clean-cut, hair short and parted on one side. He wore a pale suit, thin dark tie, trousers tight at the ankles. Looking left and right, he walked down a street with houses on both sides. There was the sound of footsteps. The camera lost focus, then picked out arbitrary views. The gable end of a factory. A closeup of the underside of a bridge. An Indian take-away with an ambulance parked outside. A laundromat, someone seated at the window. Another street with different houses. In the distance, a figure approaching. Coming closer, footsteps louder. Closer, right up to the screen. The man in the pale suit.

A change of view, the camera trained on a house with a small garden. The man in the pale suit unlocked the front door. A shift to the interior. He placed a briefcase on a table, opened it with a loud click and took out some pages. He left the room and returned with an envelope, folded one of the pages and put it in the envelope.

The screen went cloudy. The noise of traffic, tyre on tarmac. Then, the view of a street corner. The man in the pale suit appeared and walked towards a building. Donal recognised the front of the museum. Black screen, white letters appearing, one by one: *The Message, a film by Sidney Katz.*

The screen turned bright again. The same man with his neat haircut and pale suit going down a street. The sound of footsteps. The film ran in a loop. Donal stood up and searched for the exit. How long had he been there? He would be late for his meeting.

He arrived, sweating and out of breath. The client apologised profusely, but the meeting had to be postponed. Some confusion over missing documents and conflicting deadlines. They agreed to reschedule it for the following week. Before Donal left, the client handed him a business card.

Out on the street, he watched the traffic *whoosh* past and brooded. Another wasted day, chasing unfulfilling work to eke out a living. How he longed for the freedom and peace of mind to write, and release his imagination. Some evenings, he would open one of his stories on the computer and read passages. A sentence or phrase brought a rush of enthusiasm, the words singing in his ear.

The sky clouded over and an easterly wind nipped his cheeks. He buttoned his coat and felt something in his pocket — the envelope he had taken from that room. In his panic to make the meeting, he had forgotten about it. He opened the envelope and removed a page bearing a single typed sentence.

Leave this message behind The Collected Stories of Jorge Luis Borges on the second floor of the George Street Public Library.

He folded the page and put it back in the envelope. The library was on his way home. He would do it — out of frustration, the need to do something, however irrational. He didn't want to be rational. But it was also the name, Borges, an author Donal admired, a writer of fantastical tales.

Two kids playing with their phones blocked the entrance to the library. Donal glared at them, but they took no notice. He went up the stairs to the second floor, then along the bookcases, past Joyce and Grabiński, past Dostoevsky and Bradbury. He spotted the Borges book, pulled it out and placed the envelope against the back wall. Before returning the book, he leafed through the pages and wondered what it would be like seeing his work in a library or a bookshop. *The Collected Stories of Donal Lysaght.* He scanned the books on the shelves, and imagined his book among them.

The following day, he worked on advertising copy for water filters. It was a referral from an earlier job, promoting photocopiers and office supplies. He drafted and redrafted slogans to best convey the client's mission to personalise customers' needs and sell filters. *Water that tastes the way water should taste. Don't you deserve purity?*

He thought about the film. The man in the suit, putting a page in an envelope, then going to the museum. It bothered Donal, the way he'd followed the instruction so blindly. Perhaps there had been something on the page that he missed, a possible explanation.

He returned to the library. The envelope wasn't there. He pulled out other books but there was no sign of the envelope. He tried the *Information* desk.

"I left it behind the Borges short stories," he said.

The librarian, red-cheeked and spectacles hanging from a chain, had no idea what he was talking about. Donal didn't want to create a scene, and left. He decided to go back to the museum — a quick visit before the rescheduled meeting.

Sir Hugo Drouet and his dogs were there to greet him. The spiky-haired woman handed him the visitor's guide. He walked past the abstract panels without a second look and through the room with the blind suicide's paintings. Rushing past one installation, he almost knocked over some bowls of rice arranged in a row. He slowed down and looked around. It was then he realised the museum didn't have any guards. He checked the guide; the commentary read as he remembered, critical and disparaging. Paintings were lifeless. Installations lacked structure. One artist had no discipline or feeling for line or form, another had some ability but was misguided.

The digital sign still directed visitors to a new acquisition but there was no table with envelopes. In the screening room he watched images flick on and off, not the same sequence as the week before. A view down a street with parked cars. Then, the front of the museum. The sound of footsteps, growing louder. A figure came into view. The camera zoomed in. Donal's face filled the screen.

A shift in perspective, Donal walking away from the camera. Two kids standing in the entrance to the library. Then, a view of bookshelves framing a narrow walkway. Donal bending down, taking a book from the shelf. *The Collected Stories of Jorge Luis Borges.* A close-up of his face, his yearning to see his own book on those shelves captured on the screen. White words against a black background: *The Message, a film by Sidney Katz.* The room hummed in the eerie light.

He returned to the foyer. The spiky-haired woman waited behind the counter.

"What do you think you're playing at?"

She looked up from her display of guides. "How can I help you?"

"What's the meaning of that film? Who is responsible?"

She frowned and handed him a guide, which he pushed away.

"Who made that film? Who is Sidney Katz?"

"Everything is explained in the guide," she said.

Outside, he checked the entrance and adjoining buildings, lamp-posts and the buildings across the street. Nothing anywhere that looked like a camera. Surely it was against the law, an infringement of his privacy. Somehow Donal had known, his instinct had told him he was being watched. He walked away from the museum, in no particular direction. The feeling of being watched wouldn't go away. He crossed a street and went under a bridge, passing shops and parked cars, his thoughts chaotic, one ambiguity after another unravelling in his brain. He sidestepped shoppers and tripped on loose paving. A man in a suit inspected the menu outside a restaurant. The meeting — it had slipped his mind, and it was too late to show up now.

Donal lay awake that night, replaying scenes from the film. In the morning, his face appeared gaunt in the bathroom mirror. Not able to write another word about water filters, he googled the name, Sidney Katz. The first entry was a *Wikipedia* page for Sid Katz. Born in Philadelphia, son of Ukrainian immigrants, educated at Temple University. An actor, typecast as a heavy in TV westerns. A history of depression. Katz had died in 1962 after jumping from a bridge in San Diego. That ruled him out.

Another entry, Sidney B. Katz, Cook County, Illinois, designer of hoods worn by prisoners in solitary confinement. The page included sinister images of calico headcovers with square eye-holes. Donal clicked on different links. *Katz Deli, the best kielbasa sausage in Brooklyn. Katz Plumbing, call the best and flush the rest. Katz Music in Marylebone for rare classical recordings.* Hundreds of other entries, an impossible search, but Donal needed answers.

That afternoon, he watched the museum from across the street. He couldn't face going inside. No one entered or left. Ten minutes, thirty minutes, an hour passed. Finally, a heavyset man in a sheepskin coat came out and made his way to a car parked near the entrance. Donal crossed the road in a running walk to intercept him.

"Excuse me," he called, "can I ask what you were doing in there?"

The man fumbled with his keys, almost dropping them in his rush to open the car door. He kept his face averted, lunged into the seat, and started the engine. Donal watched the car speed away.

Over the next hour, he accosted a younger man and an elderly couple leaving the building, but they refused to answer his questions. This wasn't getting him anywhere. He found a pub nearby where he could plan his next move. Four o'clock, the bar was empty. Was he being filmed at this moment? The barman paid him no heed as he stacked glasses on the shelves. Searching his pockets for a pen and paper, Donal pulled out a card. It had an embossed logo, a quill and inkpot with the words, *Realising your Ambition*. In the corner, a name: *Sidney Katz*.

The client had given him the card when they rescheduled the meeting. Why hadn't he noticed the name before? Donal tried to remember what the client looked like. He'd worn a suit, but all the clients wore suits. Hair, yes, he had hair, short and parted at one side. Tallish, no glasses. That described the man from the first film. Was that whom he'd met? Donal turned over the card. Printed on the back was a telephone number.

He made the call when he got home. The telephone was answered on the first ring.

"Who is Sidney Katz?" Donal asked.

His question was met with silence.

"Why did you make that film?"

"It's better we discuss this in person," came the reply. "We will contact you."

Donal started to give his number.

"We have your details."

A week passed. Donal stayed in his flat, only going out for food. He put in some desultory work on the water filter brochure. At last, he received a text, setting up a meeting at an address in the business district.

He arrived on time and recognised the receptionist as the attendant from the museum. Gone were the grey spikes, her hair now coiffed and hennaed. She acted as though she had never seen him before, and took his name. In the waiting room, Donal checked for anything that might be a camera.

What was he doing there? What did he hope to achieve? He had no answers — helpless, not deciding his own actions, like a character in a story following a script. He had crossed an invisible line, watching events unfold and being watched.

The receptionist brought him into an office with bare white walls. A man sat behind a desk: pale suit, narrow lapels, and thin dark tie. His hair was parted on one side.

"What can I do for you, Mr. Lysaght?"

"You seem to know a lot about me, but I know nothing about you."

"I serve the interests of the Drouet Organisation."

Donal knew that name. Sir Hugo, the painting with the wolfhounds.

"Are you Sidney Katz?"

"If that's what you want."

"I don't want any of this, and I don't want to be part of that film."

"You mean *The Message*?"

"I want to be removed from it."

"It's not quite that simple." Katz leaned back in his chair.

"You've done this without my approval. It's unacceptable. It has to be illegal. I demand the film be destroyed."

"There are cameras everywhere," Katz said. "Video surveillance is part of modern life. Why does it bother you so much?"

"I refuse to be used like this."

Katz pursed his lips.

"What do you want from me?" Donal asked, dismayed by how pathetic he sounded.

"You shouldn't upset yourself. Let's forget the film for now. The important thing is that we have your attention."

"What do you want?"

"You feel undermined and undervalued. We understand your plight." Katz brushed some fluff from his sleeve. "You wish to be a writer and have your writing acknowledged as unique, compelling, and thought-provoking. Your work has come to our attention and we see a great deal of promise." Katz paused. "We can provide you with an admiring readership. Work with us and realise your ambition. A mutually beneficial collaboration. All that's required is your cooperation. Only then can the film be removed and no others shown." Katz leaned forward, his elbows resting on the desk. "We are here to help you, Mr. Lysaght. Rest assured, you're not alone."

Donal took the lift to the ground floor, and dawdled at the entrance, going over everything Katz had said. An admiring readership. Collaboration and cooperation. The film, and not just one film — Katz had implied there were more. He didn't notice the woman until she stood in front of him. Middle-aged, tousled black hair flecked with grey, her face seemed familiar but he couldn't place it.

"I must speak to you." She turned abruptly as though hearing an unexpected sound. "But not here, follow me."

She crossed the road and went down a side street, Donal two steps behind her. They entered a park and continued along a path, past a fountain and play area with swings. She sat on a bench by a pond, hands plunged deep in the pockets of her raincoat. Donal sat beside her.

"Whom did you meet in that building?" she asked.

"A man named Sidney Katz."

"Did he mention my husband?"

Her questions had an urgency that didn't give Donal time to think.

"I don't know your husband."

"He's an artist, Max Plunkett."

Now Donal recognised her; when Plunkett had painted her she was much younger.

"You're Winifred."

She turned to face him. "Have we met before?"

"Your portrait is in the art museum."

She looked away, a nervous tic causing her mouth to twitch. "What do you know about the museum?"

"Absolutely nothing."

"It's a vile purgatory. Don't do what my husband did. They destroyed him." She shifted in her seat. "They killed Willie Vine."

"What do you mean, killed?"

"The poor man took his own life but they were responsible. He went blind because of them."

Donal recalled the painting, *the memory of light.* "Willie Vine, you mean WV."

"The artists who refuse to compromise are reduced to initials. They're only given the skeleton of an identity, and their work is mocked. The museum is a punishment and a warning to others. The ones who cooperate are rewarded with success. Their work doesn't appear there." She took her hand from her pocket and squeezed his arm. "You must have nothing to do with them."

Confused and moved by Winifred's earnest warning, all Donal had were questions. "Why me? How did they find me?"

"Are you an artist?"

The question made him uncomfortable, but Katz must have read his e-zine stories. "I write."

"My husband surrendered and it wasn't enough. They gave him back his name but he's still paying the price."

Donal remembered the room dedicated to Plunkett's work. "His paintings are on display."

"It's not an art gallery. I told you, the museum is a punishment. They own everything and control the artists. It's too difficult to explain here."

"Who's behind this?" He moved closer, their legs touching. "What are they looking for?"

"They pander to popular taste, exploiting talented artists to give the public what it wants." She raised her hand to brush away some stray hair. "They abort art that is difficult and uncomfortable. The public doesn't want to be threatened or feel insecure. They punish any defiance. The artists who don't compromise are destroyed."

Donal struggled for a response, not wanting to appear incredulous. She turned, suddenly, and he followed her gaze. A man stood on the other side of the pond, dark suit, trousers tight at the ankles.

"I must go," she whispered.

He watched her rush away. The man in the suit followed her out of the park.

Donal remained sitting. Everything Winifred had said seemed far-fetched, but he wanted to believe her. All that effort, the film, the meetings, and the message just to get his attention. It meant someone saw something in what he wrote. There was Katz' threat, but was it really a ploy rather than a threat? Part of the negotiation — unconventional, but so much the better.

Katz had offered him readers. What was the good of writing that went unread? Every writer wanted a reader. If you wanted one, why not ten or a hundred or a thousand? A collaboration, Katz had said. Donal came to a decision. No more brochures selling water filters and no more excuses. He would write a story about an unfulfilled protagonist, his visit to an art museum and what he found there. A story to disturb and disorientate. He would give it to Katz to read. A test, not a compromise. Donal refused to compromise.

Three months later, he sat across from Katz in his office.

"Much more work is required to knock this into shape."

Katz shook his head at the pages, which were covered in red ink with comments and question marks. Words, lines, entire paragraphs crossed out. The sixth draft, and Katz still demanded wholesale changes.

"The reader doesn't like being told everything. Show more and tell less."

He leafed through the pages before pushing them across the table to Donal.

"One more iteration." Katz smiled.

Donal straightened the pages. Katz had given him the space to write and provided an advance to cover his bills. He had a dedicated reader now, but Katz was never satisfied. Days spent writing, deleting, revising, weighing each word, striving to convey an authentic sense of alienation. In return, inflexible criticism. Katz saw everything in the simplest terms, with no appreciation of contradiction or absurdity or nuance. He seemed to take pleasure in finding fault.

"Have you visited the Drouet Collection recently?"

Katz was referring to the latest acquisition. The film showing Donal walking down different streets, past shops and houses and under bridges. Donal sitting at a computer, his words on the screen, the cursor stationary. Then, a view of Katz from behind, reading pages of text, crossing out lines, shaking his head and sighing loudly. In the final scene, the camera panned from shelves lined with books to Donal, staring at the pages.

"Are the films necessary?"

"I'm afraid so, but we still recognise your potential." Katz examined his fingernails, in no apparent hurry. Normally he ended the meeting once he returned his corrections.

"Potential based on three e-zine pieces?" It was the first time Donal had mentioned his stories.

"Not those." Katz waved his hand. "What really impressed us was your commercial work. Anyone who can bring to life something as lifeless as photocopiers and stationery has talent worth investing in."

Donal felt his guts shrivel at this casual disregard — his stories had meant nothing to Katz.

"What you call speculative fiction is just reporting life as it is. All that business about disquiet and hidden threats. It's indulgent. What's more, it's lazy. Those brochures, now there we could see your powers of imagination." Katz tapped the desk for emphasis. "Where's the creativity in your stories? There's nothing to grip the reader and raise him from the humdrum of his daily routine. No, it certainly wasn't those e-zine pieces."

Katz laughed. Donal had never heard him laugh before.

"Getting people to buy paperclips requires true creativity. Why waste your talent writing about what is? Write about what could be. Utilise your imagination. Don't limit yourself to drab brown and grey. Turn to fantasy. The sky's the limit with fantasy, a bigger palette to explore greater themes." Katz brought his fingertips together in a steeple. "What's more, the potential in terms of readership is enormous. Feed the readers' hunger for exotic worlds, heroes and villains, good overcoming evil. Do that and you'll find an appreciative readership."

Katz opened a notebook and began writing.

"I believe we've made real progress today. Do you know what I suggest?" Katz didn't wait for a reply. "A deadline for your first novel — nothing too pressing, say six months. You now know what's needed. Less indulgence and more adventure. I will look into preparing a contract. One that protects both our interests. How does that sound?"

Donal looked down at the pages covered in red ink. He thought of Willie Vine and Max Plunkett and Winifred.

"It's time to unleash your creativity. Your audience is out there, waiting for you. All we ask is your cooperation. If you choose not to cooperate, *The Message* must continue."

Donal was driven to write even if no one wanted to read his words. He did not see himself as a martyr, but there was integrity in standing alone and facing down rejection.

"*The Message.*" Donal looked up, and held Katz' questioning gaze. "Why did you choose that title?"

"Various reasons — take your pick. We reached out to you, sent you a message." Katz paused. "Then, of course, there is the 'message' in the sense of meaning. What exactly is the message?" Katz smiled. "Achieve success and bring pleasure and entertainment to others. Or wallow in failure and feed your selfish indulgence."

The Museum of Forsaken Things

Joanna Horrocks

"All right, all right, I'm coming! Hold your zebras!"

Cursing and puffing, the Curator shuffled down the long marble hall, a small black cat and a murmuration of lightning bugs by his side. A polite but insistent rapping sounded through the heavy door.

"Bloody tourists. Pounding on the door at all hours of the day and night. Really, Bastet, you'd think they'd have something better to do than waste their time in silly museums. When I went on vacation, I did things! Saw things! Why, that time in Rome with Marc and Cleo —"

He reached the door and opened it just wide enough to peer out.

"Museums! Why are you people always bothering the bloody museums, when — oh! It's you — Alexandra, was it? Back again already?"

His deeply lined face softened as he recognized the sad-eyed young woman standing silently in the bright morning sunlight, sharply dressed in a crisp white shirt, black trousers, and brogues.

"Well, come in, come in. Don't stand there gabbing all day." The Curator opened the door wide and the suddenly flustered young woman stepped inside.

"I'm sorry," the woman stammered. "I know I've been here quite a lot lately. I don't know why; it's not exactly the happiest place on Earth, is it? All these things that people have abandoned or lost." She choked back something that might have been a sardonic laugh, and the Curator let her ramble on. "It's just that this place is so — I mean, it's not like anything — sorry. I always feel like the next time I come by, I'll find that it's not really here."

"Now, Alexandra," the curator chided, "where else would we be? And once you've found us, you're always welcome here." He opened the door wider and stepped back as a few bewildered tourists hesitantly entered, clearly wondering how they'd gotten there and just where it was they'd gotten to.

"I still don't understand how I did that in the first place. Found this place, I mean," the woman said. "I mean, I turned down that alley off of Dean Street to take my usual shortcut home, and then —"

"Oh, we're always here, when the time is right and what we have to offer needs to be found." The Curator laughed sharply, frightening the fireflies. They flashed a rude gesture and swarmed off.

"Where are they going?" Alex asked.

"Who knows? Wherever it is fireflies go when the sun is up." The Curator had a stray thought. Unfortunately, he caught it before it got away.

"Hmm. Fireflies. Sun. Vampires. You don't suppose — no, no, everyone knows it's buzzards that turn into vampires, not fireflies. Or is it beetles? Bandicoots? Badgers? Something with a B..."

Alex's attention was diverted by a new visitor, another young woman with bronze skin, jet-black hair, and rounded features, who brushed past her with a mask of intense concentration. Despite her purposeful air, she moved with fluid grace as she walked down the hall and turned a corner into another room.

The Curator caught Alex watching her and smiled.

"Ah."

"I'm sorry?" Alex turned back to the Curator.

"I see you've spied Ms. Mehra — Rani. Another regular visitor. She —"

A particularly confused-looking couple approached the pair.

"Excuse me?" said one of the men. "Where are we? What even is this place?"

The Curator turned to assist them. "Good morning! And welcome, welcome to the Museum. Allow me to be your guide."

He smiled apologetically at Alex as he ushered the couple down the hall.

Something in Rani Mehra's look — a desire? a need? — had captured Alex's attention, and she turned and followed where the other woman had gone. She passed the Hall of Broken Vows and Promises; she passed the sign pointing to the Sacrificial Well of Chichen Itza and the Widows' Leap. She came around a corner just in time to see the woman drawing back a velvet rope from a stanchion at the top of a staircase. Ms. Mehra hooked the rope back in place before descending the stairs.

A sign at the top of the stairs read, 'Special Collections and Exchanges — Donors Only'. Alex looked around to be certain no one was watching, then unhooked the velvet rope and followed Rani down the staircase.

🏛

Alex watched quietly from behind a pillar while Rani Mehra stood alone and calm in the lower level of the Museum's large, cloistered courtyard, holding her hands in front of her and looking around and up, as if searching for a hidden bird. Alex startled when she felt something brush against her ankle. Looking down, she found a small, black cat looking up.

"You know, we really would prefer it if visitors didn't disregard our signs."

Alex nearly jumped out of her skin. She turned to find the Curator looming over her shoulder.

"I... no, I'm sorry. I just..."

The Curator took a step to the left and beckoned to Alex. "Well, come on. You'll get a better view from over here."

"I don't think I've seen this part of the museum before," Alex said, joining the Curator at his side. "What's down here? What's she looking for?"

"Ms. Mehra's first visit to the Museum was last spring," the Curator continued without really answering.

"She was quite surprised to find us, as she'd walked down this street nearly every day for several months. Her statement that she would have noticed a building the size of Clarence House sandwiched between a mobile phone store and a curry takeaway was very vehement. And rather loud."

"I can relate to that," Alex replied.

"That first time, she did the same thing you do — just 'looked around'. Like you, she acknowledged and accepted the nature of our collection remarkably quickly, although there was an austerity to her judgment that was initially hard to understand. She spent hours examining the manuscript for *Love's Labour's Won*, painstakingly pieced together from the ashes in Shakespeare's fireplace where the Immortal Bard had meticulously incinerated his only draft, and all she had to say about it afterwards was that Christopher Marlowe might have done a better job."

Alex turned back to watch the other young woman. "With glowing reviews like that, I'm surprised she returned."

The Curator glanced at Alex. "Hm. You know, there was a girl, once, whose beloved kitten died. Her father dug a hole and threw it unceremoniously in the ground, so that all that remained was a little mound of dirt. The girl smirked and called the grave 'pathetic', but that didn't keep her from visiting it every day. She'd sometimes bring a little book to read, along with one of her kitten's favourite toys."

Alex blanched. "How do you know about —"

"Alexandra, lass. We are the Museum of Forsaken Things. It's our job to know the sort of things our customers have lost."

Alex could hardly breathe. She thought about a little mound of dirt, about a house and a family and everything else she'd left behind, and she looked across at Rani Mehra and wondered what it was the woman looking for something in the courtyard had lost.

The Curator turned back toward Rani as well.

"Eventually, Ms. Mehra made her way here to our Hall of Special Collections and Exchanges, where we preserve only those invaluable things our visitors have left in trade."

"What kinds of trades?"

"It varies. One person may wish that the past year of their life had never happened, because it was such a dreadful or traumatic year. Another may have a collection of painful memories they wish they could abandon, another still may desire to be rid of a particularly irksome or inconvenient emotion — an unrequited love, or a yearning for their best friend's partner, uncontrollable anger toward a sibling, that sort of thing. Some of our most exciting and powerful pieces are things for which we've facilitated an exchange.

"Finally, after several months of exploration, Ms. Mehra approached me and said she'd like to make a trade. I asked her what it was she wanted, and she said she really didn't care. In the end, she left with just some trinket from our storeroom. It was really more a matter of something she wanted to leave behind."

In the courtyard, Rani had started whistling, like calling to a very small bird. She faced away from the Curator and Alex as she continued searching for something amongst the exhibits and displays.

Bastet pawed at the Curator's leg and softly meowed, then led him and Alex over to a nearby potted fern, where a faint red light pulsed from under a frond.

"Ah, there you are." He bent down closer to the light and whispered, "Wakey-wakey. She's here."

He turned back to Alex. "We give it free rein of the courtyard, and sometimes it naps in the most obscure places."

Alex and the Curator stepped back as a pinpoint of light rose from beneath the fern, and a soft warmth began to effuse around it.

The Curator held out his hand, and the glowing red point of light floated up out of the case and perched gently on his hand.

"What is that?" she asked.

The Curator said something to the light, which rose and hovered in front of Alex. Now she felt a warmth like the heat of the summer sun wash over her, bathing her in the most intense feeling of peacefulness and optimism she'd ever known.

"Hope. Her hope. All she ever had, and all she ever will."

Alex looked at the Curator, stunned.

"But... A person can't live without hope. Why in the world would she give up something like that?"

"When Ms. Mehra was studying art in college, she made the acquaintance of a classmate, a young American woman named Sarah, and they became close friends. As they spent more and more time together, Ms. Mehra's feelings deepened beyond friendship."

"She fell in love?"

"They both did. They moved back here together and had a wonderful life until a year ago, when Sarah died. It wasn't long after when Ms. Mehra found our museum for the first time.

"When she told me what she wanted to leave behind, I asked if she was certain. She said she had no need of hope any longer, as her lover's death had left her with nothing in life to hope for, and that she'd no longer have to waste her time hoping for things that could never be."

The red light softly pulsed. Alex found it hard to turn away.

"But she was grieving! You could have told her no, that she was wrong."

"It's not our place to judge. She assured me that, after the procedure, we'd never see her again. We came to an agreement, and we made the trade."

The Curator raised his hand, and the point of light flew off unsteadily toward the woman, as if wafted on a breeze.

"It was less than a week before she returned. Since then, she hasn't missed a day."

Alex glanced at the watch on her wrist. "Does she always come at the same time?"

"Hm? Oh, yes. We could set our clocks by her midday visits, if any of our clocks kept proper time."

Alex and the Curator watched as Rani's hope came up behind her, hovering there for a moment, bouncing up and down in what seemed to Alex like nothing less than childlike delight. Then it flitted out in front of her as if to say 'Surprise!'

Rani's eyes lit up, and she bobbed her head from side to side, the light following her every move. She held out her hand, and after a moment of shyness, the light landed on her fingertip. She brought it close to her face and said something to it, and the light bobbed and weaved in response.

"It looks like they're having a conversation," Alex said.

"They are," the Curator replied. "Oh, I can't hear them, either, but you know how it is — walls have ears, and sometimes they talk."

"What are they saying?"

"Oh, you know. The same things one might ask on encountering a former spouse outside the market, or talking with a child who's grown up and left home. She asks it if it's doing well, and if it's happy here in its new home."

Alex paused a moment to watch the woman and the light of her hope in their peculiar dance.

"And is it?" she finally asked.

"Well. Certainly, it misses her, too. I think, perhaps, there are times when it feels sad for her, at least to the extent it's capable of feeling sad. But it's hard to get over being abandoned, and it's made friends here. It has a sense of purpose and it's protected. On top of that, on Friday nights, Bastet organizes what I understand is a cracking game of whist."

"But I don't understand," Alex said. "She looks happy here, to see it."

"Well, of course," said the Curator, "when she's here, in the company of hope. Hope is a joyous thing."

"Why doesn't she simply ask for it back?"

"Ah, lass. There's one thing you must always remember. The Museum never, ever, ever goes back on a trade."

Alex watched Rani Mehra playing with the light. Without noticing what she was doing, she used her sleeve to wipe the dust off the top of the display case where the other woman's hope would return to rest.

🏛

The next time Alex visited the Museum, she descended the staircase to the lower floor and the courtyard, where she pretended to be interested in the seemingly endless exhibits that filled the cloisters and ringed the yard. The real objects of her attention, though, were Rani and her little light of hope.

Had anyone asked just why Rani Mehra had captured her interest so, she might have shrugged and mumbled something about intense brunettes, but there was more to it than that. Alex was a woman who had nearly given up on life, and who now held on tightly to every shred of hope that blessed her because, at times, it felt like the only thing she had left. Rani Mehra was a woman who had abandoned even that. Alex wasn't sure if she meant to somehow rescue Rani, if she was basking in the feeling that her own little shred of hope meant something after all, or if she simply felt the need to bear witness to Rani's loss, but she circled the courtyard each day like a moon caught in a planet's gravity. Whether she was drawn to Rani because she could imagine what that depth of devastation must be like or because she couldn't, the force of the attraction was the same.

Alex wasn't the sort of bold soul who would go up to Rani and start a conversation. She came at the same time every day, she made her rounds of the lower hall, and she observed. If she happened to catch the other woman's eye, she would simply smile and politely nod. She was so cautious and respectful in her demeanour and behaviour that Rani soon came to accept her being there, as if she were no more threatening than the butterflies that descended on the courtyard's potted dame's-rocket and periwinkles each day at noon.

One day, after several weeks, after the visit between the woman and the light had concluded and Rani's hope had flown back to its new home, Rani surprised Alex by walking up to her as she studied a knitted cuckoo in a gilded cage. Alex turned to Rani with a welcoming smile, pleased to see her gentle approach had borne fruit. Stone-faced, the other woman slapped her across her cheek and walked off without a word.

The following day, when Alex encountered Rani in the courtyard, Rani once again smiled at her and blushed. Confused but encouraged, Alex once again waited for Rani's visit with her glowing friend to end. Once again, as Rani was leaving the courtyard, she came up to Alex without any hint of a smile, slapped her, and walked off, once again without a word.

The next time Alex dared to be there, she saw Rani walking toward her with the same stony look and retreated up the grand marble staircase before she could deliver her blow.

Although she was tough around the edges, Alex was, at heart, a gentle soul. She did not go where she was not wanted, and thus it was that a week went by before she got the courage to try to win Rani Mehra's favor with her smile one last time. She was more surprised than ever when Rani motioned to her to join her while she was still visiting with the little red light. When Rani smiled as she approached, she flinched, expecting the slap that was sure to follow, but relaxed a little when none did.

"I'm Alex," she said by way of introduction.

"I know," Rani replied. "You're my stalker. I asked the Curator about you. I found it curious that you were always hanging around."

"It could be I'm just very interested in the exhibits," Alex said.

Rani tilted her head toward the case Alex had been standing by when she waved her over. "You've just spent the last half hour studying an empty case labeled 'Waiting For A Trade'. Alex's mouth opened, then closed again, and her face got red. "Busted," Rani said. When she smiled, her eyes twinkled, and the light perched on her hand glowed a little brighter.

"I don't get it," Alex said. "Right now, you're smiling."

"Well, why not?" Rani said. "It's always nice to know that someone likes you."

"Then why do you slap me every time?"

Rani's smile grew a little sad around the corners of her mouth. She held up her hand with the little red light.

"Because when I'm here, with this little guy, I'm hopeful. I see you noticing me and I think, well, maybe I could let myself meet someone again. But then, when my visit is over and my hope flies off as it always does, seeing you only makes me feel how hopeless everything is."

"I'm sorry," Alex said, and she truly was.

Rani shrugged. "It's okay. It's always hard to leave, but by the time I walk myself home, I'm over it."

Alex thought for a moment. She had an idea, but she wasn't at all sure it was a good one. Still, in for a penny, in for a pound.

"May I walk you home?" she asked.

"Yes," Rani replied, as the light glowed red.

"Promise?"

"Promise."

She said goodbye to the light, which flitted up and touched her cheek before flying off toward its display case. The moment it was gone, the smile left her face and she stared flatly at Alex, all pleasure gone. She turned and started to walk away. Alex watched her for a moment, then called after her.

"A promise is a promise."

Rani stopped and turned back around. She stared at Alex, expecting her to give up and go away, then finally shook her head when she didn't. "All right," she said with a sigh of resignation. "Let's go."

As Alex and Rani left the Museum, the Curator wished them both goodnight. Neither one replied.

On the way to Rani's flat, Alex did most of the talking. Making small talk seemed the thing to do at first, but it was a long walk, and slowly the women opened up to each other, at least a little. Finally. as they reached Rani's building, Rani asked, "Why me?"

Alex began to deflect Rani's question with a shrug and something frivolous, as she might usually have done, but then stopped herself.

"I don't know what it's like to live entirely without hope. But I know what it's like to live with only the faintest sliver. I know I'm not the only person who's ever had a bad family or a bad childhood, but there have been too many days when that faint sliver of hope — hope for something better, or even for something not better, but different — has been the only thing keeping me alive. When the Curator told me what you'd done, I tried to imagine myself doing the same, and failed. I felt I had to try to get to know you, not because there was anything I could do about it, but because

I just couldn't imagine how empty it could feel to live without any hope at all."

"You'd better hope you never know," Rani said. "Goodnight." She went inside without looking back and closed the door. Alex waited until she saw a light go on on the top floor, then walked to the tube station and got herself home.

🏛

The next day, both Rani and Alex were at the Museum once again. This time, after Rani called Alex over, hope dancing merrily between her fingertips, Alex asked Rani to tell her all the things she'd ever felt hopeful about. Rani had to think for a moment, but it all came back to her readily enough. To travel; to continue painting and make a living with her art; and most of all, to find someone and fall in love again. Simple things, really, but standing there, in the courtyard, talking about them in the presence of that tiny, glowing point of light, Rani's eyes and heart and soul fairly shone.

Once again, Rani agreed to let Alex walk her home. Once again, when her visit was over and her hope was gone, she regretted her promise, but she kept it just the same.

Over time, as they got used to each other, Rani confided more and more to Alex while they were at the Museum, and eventually, she even began to talk a little more on their walks home. She shared stories about her job, her family, the myriad aspects of her life, the myriad aspects of her lover's death. Having no hope wasn't the same as having nothing to talk about.

Of course, Alex had no delusion that the hope Rani showed in the presence of the light at the Museum had anything to do with her; she just happened to be there when the light was on. And if neither Alex nor Rani noticed that the light of Rani's hope seemed to glow a little stronger and a little brighter when they were together, surely they could be forgiven for failing to see what was occurring right before their eyes.

One day, when Alex went to the Museum at the usual time, Rani wasn't there. Alex watched with rising apprehension as the little red light that was Rani's hope flitted more and more desperately around the courtyard, looking for her without success, swooping up to Alex and flying anguished, frantic circles around and around her head before careening off. Rani without hope was miserable; without Rani, Rani's hope was lost.

When the red light, quaking, dimmed and hid itself behind a pot of periwinkles, Alex turned and bolted up the stairs.

🏛

It wasn't until Alex resorted to leaning on her door buzzer without letting up that Rani finally leaned out her window and called down, yelling at her to go away. Alex responded by leaning on her buzzer some more. Finally Rani came downstairs and opened the door, stepping outside and closing it behind her instead of letting Alex in.

"What do you want?" she asked, her voice more hollow than Alex had ever heard.

"What do you think I want?" she replied. "I want to know if you're all right."

Rani glared at her for what seemed like forever; then she started to cry. Alex rushed forward to hold her, but she held up her hands and Alex practically screeched to a halt.

Rani wiped her eyes with her sleeve.

"Why did you have to interfere?" she asked. Alex didn't know what to say, so she didn't say anything. Eventually, Rani went on.

"Before you showed up, when I'd go to the Museum, I'd get to spend an hour or so being hopeful, but I didn't have to be hopeful about anything in particular. It was just a beautiful, peaceful feeling, like a warm fizzy bath or a sunny day. And when I left, I could live with losing that. Then you came, and since then we've been talking and I've been remembering all the things I used to hope for."

She looked pointedly at Alex.

"*All* the things. Do you understand?"

Alex started to say something, but Rani stopped her with a look.

"And now when I'm there at the Museum, all those things I used to hope for come rushing back, and I start to hope for them again, and I start to believe that maybe they're even possible, that maybe the life I once wanted for myself would be possible. Then I leave, and we talk, and what comes rushing in is nothing but hopelessness, and in that hopelessness, I know — I absolutely *know* — I'll never have any of that again.

"Knowing that you've lost *something*, knowing that you can't ever even hope for *something*, feels like shite, yeah, but it doesn't feel half as bad if you're not always having to remember exactly what it is you've lost."

"I'm sorry," Alex said.

"Me, too," Rani said. After a moment, she went back inside and closed the door.

For the next week, Rani was a recluse. She called in sick to work and begged off her cousin Leela's party, saying she'd come down with some horrible flu, then set her phone to 'Do not disturb' and threw it in a drawer. She knew she'd have to go back into the world eventually, and she would; just not yet.

When she finally turned her phone back on, her 'missed calls' list was nearly overflowing with call after call from the Museum. She was deciding whether to return them when her phone rang, and she answered it without thinking. It was the Curator. Could she come in to the Museum, he asked? No, no, it wasn't an emergency, not really. It was just that her hope hadn't returned to its case after her last visit. No one had seen it since she left, and he was afraid it might be lost.

She was at the Museum in record time.

The Curator walked with her to the courtyard, the last place her hope had been seen, then left her alone. Finding something so personal, he explained, was like talking to oneself; anyone else would only be in the way.

Rani stood in the middle of the courtyard, looking around and up, as if looking for a lost and injured bird. When Bastet the cat walked in and started weaving figure-eights around her legs, Rani shooed her away. With no idea of how to find the thing that was so precious to her — the tiny, insignificant, immeasurably valuable thing she had given away — she sat down cross-legged on the ground, wrapped her arms around herself and tried her hardest not to cry. When it came to describing her chances of finding her lost hope, *hopeless* was the perfect word.

Bastet meowed, and Rani glanced over at her. The cat had found something to play with, probably a bug. Whatever it was had taken refuge in a pot of periwinkles. Immensely grateful for any distraction, Rani got up and walked over to see what it was the cat had found.

As she got closer to the pot, something hidden in the leaves began to glow. The closer Rani got, the brighter it glowed, and the more it glowed, the more excited and hopeful Rani became. She reached down into the foliage and felt something like a spark settle on her fingertip. When she withdrew her hand, perched on her finger was a glowing, red point of light.

From an alcove, the Curator watched with something that might almost have been a smile.

🏛

When Rani Mehra left the Museum that day, her hope went along with her. When the Curator offered to let her take it back, assuring her that yes, it shared her wish to be reunited, she told him the Museum could have anything she had — *anything* — in return. The Curator told her that it was strictly against policy, as she well knew, but perhaps... well, *perhaps*, he might be able to consider that her contribution hadn't been a gift, really, so much as it had been a loan. He arranged for the proper department to put the little light back in its proper place inside her, and after kissing the curator on the cheek, Rani left the Museum with a smile on her face and hope in her heart.

"When you see Alex," she said, "tell her to come see me, won't you, please? Tell her I'd really like — no, I really *hope* to see her."

Rani practically bounded out the door.

But of course, the Curator hadn't told Rani the truth. As the Curator had said to Alex, the Museum never, ever, ever goes back on a trade... and as far as the Museum is concerned, there's no such thing as a loan.

🏛

"I must say, Alex," the Curator said, "it's very rare that someone offers us something in return for something for someone else, rather than herself. Are you certain there was nothing you would have wanted from us for yourself in exchange?"

"I'm sure," Alex replied, watching Rani from a window until she turned the corner at the end of the street, then letting the heavy curtain drop. "Besides, you said this was the only way."

"Well, yes, I'm afraid that's so. Who knows what the consequences might be if word got out that we let someone go back on a trade? I trust myself not to talk, but you and Ms. Mehra — well, you're only human, after all.

"I appreciate that our negotiation wasn't easy, but I'm glad we were able to come to terms on an exchange."

"Will I remember anything at all of the last year?"

"I'm afraid not. After all, once you've consummated your donation, your past year won't belong to you anymore. Of course, it will always be here for you to visit, should you ever find us again. Although I doubt you will."

"I don't understand. You said that once I'd found you, I'd always be welcome here."

"Ah, yes, but when did you find us?"

"About... three months ago." Understanding dawned in Alex's eyes. "So once I give up the history of my past year, I won't remember ever finding this place, will I?"

The Curator gave Alex a small, sad shrug.

"What about her?" She glanced toward the curtained window. "Will she remember me?"

"How could she? After all, your year will no longer exist in history, so you were never here."

Alex sighed, resigned to the deal she'd made.

"Why did you?" the Curator asked. "Make the trade, that is. Besides the obvious fact of your growing feelings for each other."

Alex blushed just for a moment. Then she became more serious. "I almost gave up all hope myself, once upon a time. Oh, not like this" — she indicated the Museum — "but I know something of what it's like. And I couldn't bear to see how happy she was when she was here, where her hope was, and how utterly defeated she was when she was where it wasn't. I hope it makes her happy now."

The Curator held out his hand to guide Alex through the lobby and down the hall. "Ah, lass," he said. "Being bereft of hope is a terrible, empty thing. But bearing and enduring hope — whether it's the tragic, desperate hope that a dead lover will return, or the aching, burning hope that one might someday find love again — that takes courage. You helped Ms. Mehra want to find the courage to endure hope once again, and perhaps that has been your greatest gift to her after all."

They approached a set of unmarked double doors, and the Curator held one open, gesturing for Alex to go on through. Alex paused.

"I was just thinking," she said. "I know you said neither of us will remember this place or each other. But before we found this place, we'd both walked down this street many times before. That means we might both walk down it again, doesn't it? Maybe even at the same time. Even if we don't remember each other, we might see each other again, and — well, who knows?"

The Curator smiled. "One can always hope," he whispered, as he ushered Alex through the double doors.

THE MUSEUM OF PERPETUAL SERVICE

Laurel Beckley

"Retreat? Hell, we just landed!"

Cassandra walked faster, the soles of her felt-lined slippers soundless against the slick marble of the museum floor. She hated the military museum in general, and *abhorred* the exhibit for the siege of Liden in particular. Liden had happened decades ago, but for her it was like yesterday. The rest of the museum was just garish propaganda for Hecubate nationalism.

Unfortunately, the Liden exhibit's entrances and exits were located next to the staff entrance, and the exhibits were all activated by motion sensors in the floor. Each time she arrived in the morning, and every time she left the staff spaces, Cassandra set off Colonel Daeda's famous refusal to return his forces to the destroyer *Priam*. He'd continued to the siege in spite of the overwhelming odds, and had triumphed, but not without a staggering loss of life on both sides of the conflict.

Humming to drown out the sound of sonic grenades and spacecraft and battle behind her as she neared the exit to the Liden exhibit and the staff door, Cassandra fumbled in her pocket for her badge. She would *not* look to her left, which depicted the fall of Biodome 5. There was a plaque before that particular portion she'd read once, on accident.

"Hey! You!" A middle-aged man stood at the entrance to the exhibit. Two teenagers sulked behind him, their faces washed with the red and blue of light from the simulation. "You a docent?"

Cassandra found her badge, held it up for inspection even though he was too far to read the fine print. "Intern." Before he could inform her that she was far too old to be an intern of anything outside of a crematorium, she added, "How can I help you?"

She braced herself for the question, but he only wanted directions to the nearest bathroom. She explained, trying to drown out the artistic screams of the dying — a mix of professional actors and real recordings pulled straight from the helmet cams of the soldiers — and did not look to the right, where the life casts engaged in pretend battle, their pre-programmed movements jerky and precise. She couldn't stop her hopeless scouring of each one, hoping to see a familiar face.

Movement at her peripheral — fuck. She was looking right at the life cast of Corporal Tolus, back arched, simulated intestines spilling from a ragged tear in their combat armor, right after they deciphered the code that brought down the biodome's life support system and murdered one thousand twenty-eight civilians.

Bile rose in Cassandra's throat as names and numbers swarmed in her mind. She turned, not bothering to check if the family was gone, and swiped her badge across the door.

In the safety of the staff area, she paused to collect herself. For a second, she'd imagined those tortured eyes were looking right at her. It was *not* actually Corporal Tolus, since Corporal Tolus had survived the battle, and she could not see their eyes through the helmet, but the truth was hardly better.

The Museum of the Hecubate Fleet was a small museum. Its main draw was not the meticulous rendering of wars past, but the life casts, which weren't mannequins but active duty service members frozen in stasis in their exhibits. It was a centuries-long practice, since the foundation of the Federation of Hecuba, after the first War of Manifest Destiny brought three moons together. Combat armor came equipped with cryogenic technology that triggered upon catastrophic injury, placing soldiers in stasis to preserve their lives until adequate treatment was available.

The simple solution had been to put those who couldn't be healed in storage, but war endured, cryogenics technology outpaced medical capacity, space was at a premium, and all of a sudden the military was stuck with a bunch of cryogenically frozen people on the verge of death with no means to treat them and nowhere to put them. Then someone had had the bright idea to use the soldiers in museums. It would offer authenticity, and the soldiers would still serve their nation.

There had been some hedging on consent, then, but now it was all very straightforward and humane, if a person read the museum's website documenting the practice. After medical assessment, soldiers were shipped in to the museum as they were and rendered anonymous: their faces hidden behind their opaque helmet shields, their identities listed by number only. Keeping them in stasis meant they did not die. They felt nothing. They continued to serve. Even more: the soldiers had *agreed* to serve. They'd all checked that box upon enlistment.

It was a simple box, offering up their service into perpetuity if the needs required. A box added when a parent complained about consent one too many times. A nothing box, one that a young adult convinced of their own immortality would never think twice over. So easily overlooked, among all the other things that needed to be signed and sworn.

Cassandra hadn't checked that box. But her cousin Anaïs had.

🏛

Work soothed her. Lines of code, numbers and letters that marched across her screen. Cassandra had always been a wizard at coding, at finding the tangles and missed punctuation and logic irregularities. Once, she had not considered the consequences of exploiting those tangles and creating backdoors for herself. Now, though. Now she thought *too* hard about consequences. Consequences were everything.

Cassandra's computer blinked an alert. High-priority meeting in five minutes.

A flash of fear froze her to her spot. This meeting hadn't been on her calendar. Had they found out? No. No, she had been careful. Very careful. It had been nothing to erase her data profile and create a new one tailormade for an internship in museum database management, but she could have missed something. She wasn't as sharp as she used to be.

"Andra, come on, we'll be late."

Cassandra jumped, but it was just another intern, one whose name Cassandra could never remember and who was a good thirty years younger than her. She relaxed. If the museum administration had found her secret, they wouldn't be having a meeting with another intern present.

"Right behind you," she said, clearing her screen. Her knees creaked as she rose, the grinding in the left needing three steps to smooth away.

She followed the other intern — Yael? Yeava? Something with a Y — out of the staff area and onto the main floor.

"Retreat? Hell, we just landed!" boomed after her. She'd gone straight into panic mode before reading the message's contents, and was surprised when they went straight into the main theatre instead of up the lift to the administrative staff offices and the larger conference room. They joined a queue of staff and interns, along with a cluster of docents and hospitality ambassadors, distinct in their uniforms of khaki and green coveralls.

Cassandra scanned the theatre as she took a seat among the interns, feeling like a gray-haired weed among youthful blossoms. Everyone was here, including the President of the Board of Trustees *and* the Foundation Chair, who couldn't stand being in the same room together.

The museum director clomped up onto the stage. His face was grim. Cassandra's blood boiled at the sight of her old commanding officer.

"I wish I could say good morning to you all," Director Aiden Daeda said, unable to stay still. His prosthetic leg hit the floor with every other step, punctuating his words. He liked to remind everyone of his sacrifice to the Federation. His heroism, which would have been described as something decidedly less positive had the Hecubates lost.

Cassandra wondered, not for the first time, how he lived with the guilt of having survived when so many had died.

"But despite lobbying and meetings and letters from constituents, I'm sorry to tell you that the Hecubate President —" The director did not say the current president's name, no one in this room had voted for him, "— decided that the museum is part of the budget cuts, along with a large portion of our endowment. We're funded through the start of the next fiscal year, which will give us time to reallocate the collection —"

A hand shot into the air. The head curator. "What about the life casts?"

Cassandra leaned forward.

The director cleared his throat. "A select few will be redistributed to other military museums within the system. Others have been assigned to the Hecubate Museum of History. The majority, however, will belong to private collections."

Cassandra gasped — the sound drowned out by similar noises of protest. A historian jolted from their seat, fists clenched. "They can't go to private collections!"

"The terms of their contract —"

"They're *people*, dammit!" the historian snapped.

Both the Foundation Chair and the Board of Trustees President stepped onto the stage, flanking the director and signaling that in this, at least, they were unified. The Chair stated, her voice silky smooth and broaching no further debate, "They are service members who signed a contract allowing for their continued, honorable service."

The historian wasn't having it. "You're selling *people*."

"They are continuing to serve their nation," the chair said.

"Conditions will be established to ensure their dignity is preserved," Daeda added, his eyes darting to the man and woman on his left and right.

Cassandra thought of the person playing Corporal Tolus in the exhibit — and wondered just what dignities that person had remaining. The life casts came to the museum in the condition they were in, although their bodies were often gently manipulated to produce a desired effect. Most were stationary, particularly those service members from the Federation's earliest wars. More recent additions — like Corporal Tolus — had limited movement, which was pre-programmed into their cryogenic combat armor.

"How long?" the historian demanded.

"How long, what?" Daeda asked.

"How long until you sell these people to the highest bidder?"

From the glares coming from the head curator and the three people on the stage, this historian would no longer be employed with the museum after this meeting, but it didn't matter. Cassandra needed to know this answer, too.

"The museum will close in six months." Daeda paused. "If asked, you tell our visitors that the museum is part of a strategic reallocation of resources, and that all artifacts will be ethically redistributed between public and private institutions."

🏛

The life cast of Corporal Tolus seized as they were struck by a rifle-cannon blast. Simulated blood boiled out of their body, heading in a separation direction from their intestines. It was not factually accurate, Cassandra thought, staring at the scene. For one, Liden had gravity. And two, the suit hadn't severed in half. Not even close.

"Who *are* you?" Cassandra whispered, staring into the opaque face shield of the person in the cast. They did not answer her question, but she imagined, as she always did, that Anaïs stared unknowingly back at her. In her imagination, Anaïs twisted her head, whispered, *I can't live in the dark.*

"Andra, want to get drinks tonight?" One of the interns had materialized beside her, the one who had asked her about the meeting. Their name was Yael.

In the background, Colonel Daeda shouted his famous phrase. Cassandra shuddered. She could still feel Anaïs' eyes on her, even though it was silly to think that the life cast was her cousin.

"Andra?" Yael asked.

Cassandra came back to herself. "Right. Sure, that sounds great. Let me grab my purse." The work day was effectively over, anyhow. All anyone could talk about was the museum's pending closure. All she could think about was the fact that she was running out of time.

🏛

Going to a bar for drinks had been a mistake. She had no desire to chat with children who saw the museum as ancient history instead of lived memory. But she also couldn't face her empty apartment. So much of her life was empty, so much driven away by what her ex-wife called her obsession, what her children told her was delusion, what her extended family declared extended post-traumatic grief. And she couldn't stay at the museum and stare at the person playing Corporal Tolus.

"They can't sell *people*," Yael said, drawing Cassandra's attention to the group at large.

"They certainly plan to." This from an intern from admin. She still wore her badge. Her name was Maia.

"They're not really people, though." This from another admin intern, who flinched from the glares directed at him but stoically doubled down. He'd taken off his badge. "They're corpsicles —"

"They're not dead!" Yael yelled.

"What I *mean* is that, what *else* would they be?" the second admin intern said. "They can't feel anything. Besides, they're all service members who were so horribly injured that it was either let them die or stick them in suspension until science advanced enough to heal them. If it weren't for the museum, they'd be actually dead."

"Instead, they're worse than dead," Yael said.

"We have to remember that *they* signed up for this. It was all a *choice*. No one was forced into it." Cassandra snorted, but no one heard her. "The museum has been around for centuries — anyone who signed up for post-life service knew it was a possibility. So *what* is the big deal?"

Maia leaned forward in her chair. Her pale skin was turning red, even in the blue ambient lights of the bar. "So you have no problem whatsoever that the museum's leadership is literally going to be selling *people* into private collections?"

"It's not like they'll know anything's different," the second intern snapped.

"What if they die in these private collections?" Yael asked.

"They'll die if you release them, if that's what you're going for," the second admin intern said. "The medical expenses alone... can you imagine it? The museum must have over a hundred life casts!"

"Three hundred twenty-seven," Cassandra murmured. Again, no one heard her, but she didn't care. There were one hundred sixty-three scattered about in exhibits — she knew the exact breakdown for each — one hundred thirty-five in storage, and twenty-nine in processing for a new exhibit that was now clearly scuttled. She'd thought through all the implications already, and this argument was giving her a headache. She'd found a solution to this problem within her first month at the museum, and then spent the next three months trying to find something better. She hadn't.

"The museum should contact the families so that they know what is happening," Maia said.

"Some of them have been in stasis as long as the Federation has existed!" the second admin intern scoffed. "That is literally *centuries* ago. Their families are either long gone or don't want them. Get serious."

"It doesn't matter, anyway. The life casts are anonymous," Yael said. Their shoulders slumped. "I checked. There's no way to tell who is who."

"The head curator maintains the list in his private database. It's encrypted so even he can't tell who's who without a cypher — and there are three: one each maintained by the director, the president of the board, and the foundation chair. They need to be activated at the same time to decrypt the database," Cassandra said, to no one.

She eyed her drink, regretting her decision to join these children at this bar. With a shrug, she drained the dregs, coughing at the bitter aftertaste. When she thunked the glass onto the table — why was everything in this place *sticky?* — she noticed the silence. All four interns stared at her. "What?" she asked.

"How do you know that?" Maia asked.

Cassandra's head spun, just from that one beer. Everything inside her screamed to run to the bar, order drinks until her credit maxed, and spend the rest of her life puking into a recycler. She took a deep breath. Then another. The interns still stared at her, expectant. Fuck it. The museum was closing anyway.

"My cousin checked the post-life box when she enlisted. She was at Liden. She... didn't make it. I'm trying to find her." Her throat closed up, preventing her from saying more.

"Liden was... that was sixty-five years ago," Maia said, eyes wide.

Cassandra nodded, accepting the hit. Twenty-three thousand, nine hundred seventy-one days ago. "She was on the destroyer *Priam.*" These were military historians, even the admin interns; Cassandra didn't need to explain what had happened to the *Priam.* "I was on the *Priam,* too, but I was infantry. We'd already deployed when the hit came."

"How do you know she wasn't..." Even the second admin intern couldn't say it.

Cassandra could. She had faced all the possibilities, had dedicated her life to Liden and its aftermath. "There were one hundred forty-three deaths aboard the *Priam,*" she said. "I've tracked the locations of all of the bodies but six. I think the six missing are here."

Not said, because she didn't have to: she was certain Anaïs was one of the six.

Not said, because they would never know: she had promised Anaïs she wouldn't let her spend eternity in stasis.

"If she checked the box, then she agreed to this," the second admin intern said.

Cassandra wondered, not for the first time tonight, if the kid had skipped empathy training somewhere in his development. Fuck, her brain hurt. Her bones ached. "Yes, but it's more nuanced than that. Do you read every terms of service agreement before you sign? There were a lot of boxes, and we never thought anything about it because when you're young, you don't think you're going to die. But then Liden happened."

"How come it took you sixty-five years?" the second intern asked.

Dammit, she was going to blast this kid.

"Okay." Yael snapped their fingers, drawing everyone's attention back to them before Cassandra could wring the little bastard's neck. "So we have a mission now. Save Andra's cousin." They pulled up their pad, preparing to take notes like the good student they were. "Right. We've got six months. Six months to get access to the curator's database, and copy the cypher keys from the —" they paused, looking at Cassandra as if for confirmation. Their smile faltered at the amused look on her face.

"We do not have six months," Cassandra said, not bothering to correct them about her cousin. "We do not have tomorrow. There are one hundred sixty-four people trapped in life casts who are not on display in an exhibit. They will be sold first."

"Not sent to a museum?" Maia asked.

Cassandra shook her head. "Not when there is money to be made."

The second admin intern raised his hands. "I *cannot* be a part of this," he said. "I can't go to jail — I have *plans* for my life, *thanks*."

"If you tell anyone..." Maia hissed, but he was already gone, headed to the bar to close down his account and regain whatever culpable deniability he could.

As the other interns argued, a plan formed in Cassandra's mind. A plan that wasn't her first plan, or her second, or even her third, but the one she'd come up with in her first month at the museum and rejected with every fiber of her being. Yet, when faced with reality, it was still the only solution she could think of. She took another drink, trying to convince herself it was the right one.

She left them arguing at the bar, too wrapped up in their own brilliance to realize she was gone.

She arrived at the delivery entrance instead of the staff door. Security nodded at her when she flashed her fake employee badge — she'd copied the credentials over from one of the night-shift historians who'd been on sabbatical for three months — and entered the building. She was a little wobbly, but hoped security wouldn't think anything of an old lady late to the night shift.

There were six shipping pods in delivery. The sight of them, silver and round, made Cassandra's stomach churn. So. The museum was fast-tracking their plans. She examined them, but there was no way to see inside to the contents, not that she'd be able to see who was who.

Cassandra took the stairs to her next stop, her left knee creaking.

The tech inside life cast storage stood when she entered. "Hey, this is a restricted area."

Cassandra smiled, gave him her best *I'm just someone's little lost grandmother*, and clocked him across the head with her purse when he came close. She shifted his body — still breathing, just unconscious and going to have a hell of a headache when he woke, along with minor brain trauma — aside with a grunt, and settled into the tech's chair.

She logged him out and logged back in as her faked credentials, then flicked on the lights to the warehouse, illuminating row after row after row of pods, all one hundred twenty-nine of them. She assumed the six pods had been removed from storage, and she needed to *see* what she was about to do. She hadn't seen the damage she'd caused when she'd deactivated Biodome 5.

Cassandra had been counter cyber-intelligence attached to the infantry, able to encrypt and decrypt codes on the ground to access various installations and biodomes. After the war, she'd changed her name to regain some anonymity. In recent years, she'd learned quite a bit about cryogenics, and during her time at the museum, she'd discovered quite a few irregularities within the network.

The museum's network and cryogenic support was a patchwork of systems built over each other. Redundancies and logical fallacies sprawled everywhere. All she had to do was change some parameters, convince the rudimentary system AI that no was yes and wrong was right, and she'd trigger the shutdown of every single life cast pod. It was very similar to how she'd terminated the life support in Biodome 5.

And now she was sentencing another three hundred twenty-seven people to death.

Her fingers shook as she changed the coding to engage the life support shutdown.

She'd known somewhere, deep down in a part of her she'd tried to bury with alcohol and exercise, that this solution had always been the only solution.

Cassandra wasn't saving Anaïs, or anyone else. There was no salvation here, merely a promise kept: that no one else would endure perpetual military service by accidentally checking one overlooked box out of hundreds. That no one else would spend eternity in the dark, trapped in a liminal space between life and death. There was saving, and there was *saving*.

It was done very quickly. Odd how mass murder could come with just a few strokes on a keyboard. Cassandra stood, wiped her hands on the front of her pants. In a moment, the life support keeping the soldiers in stasis would fail, and the failure would generate a series of alarms that would bring help too late to do much more than prepare the bodies for long-overdue funerals.

Cassandra found that she could not stay in the warehouse and listen to the alarms and imagine the gasps and screams of people waking and dying inside their metal prisons. She walked up the stairs to the main floor in a daze, although she was not surprised to find herself back at the Liden exhibit. In a way, she had never left Liden.

The recording of Colonel Daeda screamed over and over and over, activated by her presence, but Cassandra ignored him. She eased into the exhibit's exit, her hip popping as she stepped over the barrier, and stood before the person who had been cast as Corporal Cassandra Tolus. Tomorrow, after security arrested her and the technicians cleared all the bodies, this person would no longer be anonymous. All the people trapped as life casts would at last be known. Just as she would be known, too.

Cassandra stared into the opaque helmet, and for the first time, her reflection stared back.

THE MUSEUM OF FINE REGRETS

Chloe Smith

The Hindsight Museum of Fine Regrets is open to the public. Anyone can walk through its pillared entrance, wander the wide, dark-paneled galleries.

There's a sign in the marble atrium, reminding visitors that the cost of admission is assessed only after the fact: they will have to pay as they exit. The museum curators lurk beyond the final door, trawling for gems of bitterness among the exiting crowds. The curators know that not all regrets are created equal; they recognize the most fervent and personal, the ones that can stand representative of human experience, if given shape and form worthy of the museum's pedestals.

The curators are selective, but it doesn't matter. Whether they claim your deepest regret or not, all visitors must pay. You may be one of the few who wander through the doors out of idle curiosity, drawn in only by prurience and schadenfreude. You may be a supporting member of the museum, someone who recognizes in one of the regrets on display an echo of your own discomforts. It doesn't even matter if you are a museum donor already. The museum accepts all forms of currency, raw energy, and spirit. Everyone pays.

Tristan doesn't plan on paying for this last visit, though.

He's followed the Hindsight Museum rules during each previous visit. Six times in the last three months he's made careful, unremarkable tours through the different wings, loitering in front of the burnished specimens with their protective glass and soft-focused lights. Research visits are harder without Cymera. A partner would have halved the time it all took, reduced the chance he'd catch someone's eye or stick in their memory. It's alright, though — he can handle the challenge. He pretended to the vicarious nostalgia that moves visitors to study every display. He thanked the ticket takers at the end when they relieved him of a shred of hope, the feeling of a good night's sleep, or whatever they feel like demanding that day. He smiled acknowledgement when they reminded him that he got the donor rates.

He hated every minute of it.

Tristan has never had any use for regrets. That's not who he is. The fact that he's even here, that something of his ended up under glass in this museum — that's Cymera's fault. He can't let that stand.

He knows, though, that the regret museum exerts an addictive pull on many people. Membership numbers are high, and repeat visitors so common that there is a division of membership services specifically tasked with approaching the highfliers and delicately suggesting they scale back their visiting hours, or step out and get some sunlight, or 'Don't you have someone you can call to come get you now?'

Tristan sees those people, caught up in their fascination with the dioramas of the Roads Not Taken or the portrait hall of the Ones That Got Away. Many of them have the look of donors, come to stand and stare for hours at the regrets they created. Tristan feels bad for them, but also, what are they thinking?

He'd never let himself get caught like that.

If he focused on the past that much, he'd have become a museum donor a dozen times already. The curators could have crafted a *What was I thinking?* miniature for each occasion that he lent money to his drunkard cousin or failed to get up from the gambling table when he was ahead. Looking back to his youth, he could have fashioned any number of memories — the things he said to his father, the decision to leave school, the first time he got caught — into a gleaming shrine of *What opportunities did I squander?* But no, it just didn't seem worth the energy to hold onto anything that long. Incubating regrets only weighed you down, made you an easier mark.

Easier to focus on the present, really. Or better yet, the future. That's where his strengths lie: Making real what *could be, might be, shouldn't be*. Tristan changes things. He breaks bonds and lets them slip into new shapes.

It's a very good ability for a thief to have.

Tristan is a good planner, especially now that he's working alone. He's never yet used his power while within the museum's walls. He wants no one to see anything more than one unremarkable visitor among many. He's memorized the layout of the different wings, from the gallery of Buyer's Remorse to the exhibit of Things that Could Have Made You Happy, both filled with glittering, oppressive objects, promises of a satisfaction that never comes. He knows the faces of the different security guards, although he's made sure they don't remember him. That part was easy; they have to stay focused on those patrons too enamored of the display pieces, the ones who try to step close enough to touch, to feel the reality of regret like a breath against the skin.

Tristan walks now at a carefully unassuming pace, neither hurried nor dragging. It's an hour before closing. The staff will have started targeting the most obsessed, those who sit or stand, entrapped, before one beloved memory-piece. It's always hardest to get them to leave. Tristan is counting on it.

He turns his steps towards the gallery of Perfect Replies. It's not a place the obsessives tend to settle, so it empties out later in the day. The gallery is organized chronologically, from comebacks thought of hours after the inciting insult, to those perfected months or years after the point when they could land. The regrets in this room are low-stakes, but after walking its full length, hearing zinger after zinger, anyone present will feel their ears ringing.

Although Tristan has run this gauntlet before, he's not immune to the cocktail of laughter and frustration that batters him by the time he's halfway through. The lone attendant loitering at the low-stakes end of the hall watches him from a distance as he halts, wheezing, halfway along it. The sound of quips and barbed compliments fills the air, so

Tristan can't hear the woman. He can tell she's not eager to leave her post, come farther into the room to check on him. It's almost closing, after all, and she must have heard variations on, 'I wouldn't expect more from someone who—' many times already today. He bends over, hands on his knees, takes a quieting breath, and then makes a show of looking back at her. *Can I really make it through all these feelings?* Sometimes it's too much, and the museum is set up to anticipate that. The attendant points to an exit sign a few feet farther along. Visitors who are overcome can retreat through the side staircases. It's not unusual. Tristan nods his thanks and hobbles to the door, which snicks closed behind him.

There is no knob or latch on the other side. These stairs are for quick exits only. They descend through all the museum's levels, and end at the gift shop, which sells only things you can't take with you. Tristan doesn't head down, though. Instead, he climbs up, to the higher floors, those holding the most profound and heartfelt regrets. Regrets like the one Cymera left him with.

Tristan pauses on the fourth-floor landing, waits for time to pass, for the museum's doors to lock and the day shift to leave. He faces the blank surface of the closed door. Regrets should be forever untouchable, and so the museum has invested in all available security features — human, electronic, structural. Overnight guards stalk the periphery. The walls, even the doors and window frames are reinforced, the locks coded and pick-proof. It is the museum of hindsight, though, and Tristan is counting on that. It is an edifice designed and safeguarded by those obsessed with learning from the past, not preparing for the unexpected.

It's time for Tristan to exercise his skillset. He steps in close, bends down, and whispers to the invisible mechanism within the door. He tells the lock that it doesn't have to be cold metal holding electromagnets in place. That in the infinite progression of possible realities, its atoms could be at the exploding heart of a star, in the delicate structure of a katydid's leg, among the fine grains of ash settling after a fire. The door quivers in its frame as the lock heats and fractures, its component parts succumbing to a sudden attack of entropy.

Tristan pulls out a fine metal tool and pries the now-unlocked door open.

The room within is not his destination, but it is a necessary stop along the way.

It is also the most dangerous space within the museum. Security guards routinely steer away repeat visitors. Tristan himself has only made it through once. He knows how dangerous it is. He also knows this is the only way to get the job done.

There are some regrets so visceral, so toxic, that they are born in suffering and must be expelled with prejudice, lest they eat their bearers away from within. In this room, each enshrined in crystal frames to showcase their dark self-abnegation, are regrets at survival.

Tristan feels their weight as soon as he steps inside. There are no glass barriers between viewer and regret here. Signs warn visitors to stay back and mind their extremities, but those seem superfluous in the face of the repulsive forces the regrets exert.

Tristan chooses one of the most toxic regrets in the museum collection, the Wish to Never Have Been Born. It hangs within a gilt frame, grim and shadowy and exuding self-abnegation. The placard on the wall beside it identifies the creator and donor as an adolescent with untreated depression. Tristan must weather the regret's pain, the desire to disappear, for everything to *just go away*. Each footstep closer is a battle, a stifling blanket of emotions. He is lucky he never carried his own such regret. How could the donor have survived? How could they have let this regret continue to exist, to hang in a museum, tormenting others? One step closer. Another.

He reaches closer, fighting the repulsion and the urge to look away from suffering. This regret takes the form of a crumpled spot of darkness, traced with uncomfortable, brain-coral folds. It looks like nausea feels, and he has to force his hand out to touch it.

The regret slides from its crystal frame. Its shadow flickers and metastasizes, grows monstrous tentacles that wrap around him, as if to swallow him whole.

His vision darkens as the shadow-regret slides over his head like a hood, down over his shoulders, torso, and legs. It swaddles him in a cocoon of darkness. But then, once it has him in his maw, the sense of alien darkness begins to fade. The regret's physical manifestation grows pale, almost invisible. He no longer feels repulsed by the regret. It has made its feeling his own, and that feeling is... nothing. There is numb emptiness where Tristan once stood. It would be the easiest thing in the world to forget everything but the regret's impulse towards invisibility and non-existence.

But no. Tristan holds his plan, this job, tight in the forefront of his mind. He lets the regret whisper its poisons at the edges of his thoughts, but it will not ride or master him.

He looks down at his limbs. They are barely there, ghostly within the shadow-cloak of the poisonous regret. It will be enough to let him move silent and weightless through the rest of the fourth floor, into and through the galleries protected by laser eyes and weight-sensitive floors.

He repeats his purpose over and over, sotto voce, keeping himself focused and resistant to despair as he walks through the fourth-floor rooms. He passes the cases filled with secrets that should never have been shared. He comes to the room housing the museum's finest treasures.

Focused on resisting his disguise's poison, he cannot pay attention to externalities, but he knows he has reached the hall of Broken Relationships. Most of these are jewel-like, multifaceted emotions built from layers of blame and culpability, unexpressed love and infatuation overindulged. Some are complex and formless, almost impossible to define. These regrets do not emerge from a single action, and they defy the clarity of counterfactual questions. Others are painfully simple: *Why didn't I tell her I loved her?* Or *Why wasn't our timing better? Why didn't I say yes?* Or *Why didn't I say no?*

They are all messy and poignant, individually detailed and universally compelling.

Tristan crosses the last floor. He shakes away the stolen regret. The shadow desire for non-existence drops to the floor and crawls away into darkness, leaving his mind free to take in more than the gross shapes of his surroundings.

Tristan had the path memorized. He counted his steps. He knew he would uncloak an arm's reach from his target. He did everything right, anticipated every challenge.

But he finds the case empty.

Tristan stares at the space, uncomprehending.

He knows this is where it rested. His lovely, excruciating, ultimate regret. The jewel-like, crystalline moment of *I should have told her not to leave*. He passed its resting place multiple times, snuck glimpses from the corner of his eye. He allowed himself one full, careful observation, standing at a moderate distance, letting his eyes run over its vibrant colors and intricate surface, letting himself feel the gravitational strength of its pull. He let the memories it holds wash over him, the way Cymera's eyes glittered with tears even as her voice stayed steady. The sound of the door closing behind her. The ache of tension in his back and shoulders, the stiffness of resolve knotted into his muscles.

He came back to the regret because he was casing the joint. Not because he was stuck on it. Never that. He had to learn from it. He couldn't leave the regret here, part of this terrible museum. His first visit had been a mistake, of course. That, he will admit. It was weakness to ever enter this monument to failure, weakness to bow before the cold-eyed curator whose laser eye had identified what he carried, even as he'd denied it to himself.

Tristan was weak then, but he planned to redeem that weakness with this theft. Once the regret was back in his possession, he would be able to destroy it and let himself forget.

Or you could change your story. Win back Cymera, so this isn't even a regret anymore, a part of him whispered. It's the part that always believes in his power to reconfigure and recreate. Tristan doesn't want to admit that part, even to himself. Hope has no place in the Museum of Fine Regrets.

But now the regret is gone. The velvet stand that held it is empty, although the protective glass panel remains pristine, untouched.

Tristan can't help himself. He curses, looks from one case to another, as if he could have forgotten the shape and placement of his own regret. As if his failures are easily confused with any other's.

Someone speaks in the museum's silence. "You." Tristan freezes. He knows that voice. He turns.

Someone walks towards him, threading her way among the cases without tripping the floor or disturbing a single sensor. It is the attendant from earlier, the one in the comeback hall who waved him to the nearest exit. He remembers her navy blazer and comfortable shoes, the mane of red-brown hair that framed her face.

All those details shift as she approaches. Her appearance blurs and refocuses, becoming someone painfully familiar. Freckled skin, wide-set eyes, curling black hair pinned into a tight and practical knot. He knows she is letting him see the face he knew.

That is her talent, after all, to be whoever an observer needs or expects to see. It's what allowed her to pass through so many forbidden doorways, to fleece so many unsuspecting marks. It's the skill that made her such a good thief, that made her such a key part of his team.

It's why he could never trust her. It's why he let her leave, didn't believe her tears, refused to call her back.

He steels himself now. "Cymera. You just couldn't resist making me look a fool one last time, could you?"

She stops. Her lovely, mobile face twists. "Is that what you think? Truly? Of all the possibilities you are capable of, you can only see the one where I'm here out of spite?"

He feels his talent for entropy pulse through him, tingling along all his nerves. The desire to change, unmake, reform is always strongest around her. It's that unpredictability, she said once, that fascinated her.

He finds he has no patience for this conversation. There's nothing new in it, just recycled bits of tired arguments and painful memories.

"Why are you here, then?" he demands. "You stole my regret for some proof? You need some evidence to show that I cared more, that you won and I'm still haunted?"

"*Your* regret?" she asks.

"Yes," he insists. "My regret. See —" he points to the card on the wall. The one that should read *The End of*

Tristan and Cymera, with the description of his mistake, his silence, his inaction.

The card is blank, as empty as the case. He turns back to her, confused. "Did you destroy it, then?"

It's possible she could have come here out of altruism, to free him from the hold of the past. She could have learned some new, destructive magic, something capable of snuffing out his regret completely. If that's what happened, though, why does he still feel this way? If the regret is gone, why does it still hurt to look at her?

He thought that he could take the regret in his hand, whisper a new possibility, and it would wither and unmake itself, leaving him free.

"Come on, Cymera," he says. "Cut the crap. Tell me the truth."

She raises one eyebrow, professional mask back in place. "The truth? You'd really accept the truth from me? Let me show you..." She reaches into an inner pocket of her museum blazer, pulls out an object and shoves it at him. He sees it glitter, feels the words he should have spoken rise, choking, but then, in a flash, her hand is empty.

"Where did it go?" She stares at him across her extended palm. "I still feel it. What did you do?"

"*You* still feel it?" he demands. "*You* took *my* regret. Those were my feelings."

"It wasn't *your* regret," she tells him, voice rising to match. "It was mine. I felt the curators scissor it out of my chest."

He doesn't understand. "Yours? What do you regret?"

"I shouldn't have left." And then, with matching confusion layered over the pain in her tone, "How could it be your regret, when all the giving up, the leaving, was on my side?"

"You don't get to own that regret," he tells her. "It's my fault for letting you go."

Pressure builds behind his eyes, in the roiling spot beneath his breastbone. He feels a tug there, as sharp and as profound as when the curator first drew out his regret.

Something flares once again in the air between them, light and bright and gone too quickly for him to see. The regret carved out of his heartache, the one he spent months stalking, examining from every angle through the glass of its case, that one had nothing of Cymera in its makeup. It was all him, in the end, all his perspective and his reality.

A glimmer of understanding begins to surface. He looks into her face. He's always seen her as masked, even when she showed him her undisguised features — but there has to be sorrow and pain hidden behind the set of her mouth and narrowed eyes. Her regret, he realizes, matched his own in weight and measure.

He takes a breath. "You really don't think I could have done things differently?"

"Well, maybe a bit." She half smiles, and the familiar, quicksilver gesture shakes him again, makes him remember a past not made solely of rue. "I didn't see your feelings when I looked in the case. Your pain isn't what I held in my hand."

He knows the messy uncertainty of possibility. He's always known it. He just didn't think about how that multiplicity extends into the past, as well as the future.

"Cymera," he says, "You've seen me with doors..."

She snorts. "Yes, you don't need to remind me of your talents."

"Yes, yes." He brushes past her impatience. "But you know it's not just doors. It's about paradoxes — different contradicting realities. I pick one that works best for my moment. But what if, what if there were two realities, *equally* strong and powerful and apt?"

"They couldn't *both* be right," she says.

"Not completely right," he agrees, "but not completely wrong, either."

She looks like she is examining the idea from all angles. "The regret was yours *and* mine both."

"And the truth is larger than either one." He feels the old thrill of building something — a plan, an explanation, anything — together with her. "There was nothing in this place that matched both our memories."

She nods. "So the paradox resolved itself."

"But —" He stops, then forces himself to admit the truth. "I still hurt. Now that it's gone, shouldn't we both be older and wiser? Lesson learned and on to the next?"

She gives him a look. "Oh, Tristan. That's not how this works. Our story isn't a romantic comedy or a bildungsroman. Why do you think we saw the regret so differently? There's no single, linear lesson to learn here. I wasn't a plot device for you. And you weren't one for me. We were just two people entangled together until we weren't anymore."

He wants to fight her, to disagree. He wants there to be a clear trajectory, anything besides the lingering feelings he can no longer see. But he knows she's right.

"So what do we do now?" he asks her. "Burn this place to the ground on our way out?" That was always the second part of his plan. No regrets left behind.

She considers. "We could... But maybe some of these regrets have uses. Not as museum pieces, sitting here and collecting dust, but somewhere, to someone. We can't be the only creators who needed to see our regret again. We could... not close the door on our way out? Maybe leave a couple of holes in the walls while we're at it?"

He smiles. "I like your thinking."

Her face begins to change again, and with it her body, remodeling itself to fit the moment, gaining the strength it needs to rip doors from hinges and punch windows out of frames.

He imagines the regrets that will be buried in the rubble after they go. Maybe some will fade, oxidize into nothing when confronted with the elements. Others may lie in the ruins of the Hindsight Museum, waiting for their creators to return and repossess them. Some may be scavenged by strangers, repurposed to something new and useful. Who knows?

He steps forward, lays his hand against the case that once held their regret. He flexes his fingers and the cases shatter into glittering shards.

The alarm blares, shrill and too late. She's already running for the far wall, past cases that crumble as he follows her.

"I was also thinking," he yells, "maybe we should consider working together again?"

"Maybe," she says. "We'll see what happens." Even above the din all around them, he thinks he can hear possibility in her voice, something beyond the wreck of the museum they'll leave behind.

About the Curators

Arlen Feldman, The Museum of Lost Dreams

As well as writing fiction, Arlen Feldman is a software engineer, entrepreneur, maker, and computer book author — useful if you are in the market for some industrial-strength doorstops. He is a common haunter of museums, the stranger the better. He lives in Colorado Springs, Colorado. His website is cowthulu.com. Twitter: @arlenfeldman, Mastodon: @cowthulu@mastodon.social

Dominick Cancilla, The Museum of the Evolucalypse

Dominick Cancilla lives in Santa Monica, California, and has memberships with multiple local museums and botanical gardens. He particularly recommends the Museum of Jurassic Technology, which was the original inspiration for the story included here.

John Joseph Ryan, The Museum of Smells

John Joseph Ryan's work has appeared in *River Styx, McSweeney's,* and *Suspense Magazine* (U.S.), and in international publications such as *Mystery Magazine (Canada), Channel Magazine* (Ireland), *Grievous Bodily Harm* (Australia), and *A-Z of Horror: 'L' is for Lycans* (U.K.). John's collaborative noir short, "Hothouse by the River", was published by the University of Iowa Center for the Book. He is also the author of a bestselling crime novel, *A Bullet Apiece* (Amphorae Publishing Group, 2015), and he contributed a chapter on Walt Whitman and Abraham Lincoln's relationship to the textbook *Teaching Lincoln: Legacies and Classroom Strategies* (Peter Lang, 2014). John lives in St. Louis, Missouri, home to world-class fine-art and history museums free to the visiting public.

Marilee Dahlman, The Museum of Space Exploration

Marilee grew up in the Midwest and now lives in Washington, DC. Her other stories have appeared in *Apparition Lit, The Bitter Oleander, Cleaver, Molotov Cocktail, Mystery Weekly, Orca Literary, Saturday Evening Post,* and elsewhere.

Abhijato Sensarma, The Museum of Identity

Abhijato Sensarma is currently an undergraduate student at Ashoka University, India. His short fiction has been published in *Metaphorosis, The Mark Literary Review, Verse of Silence, Havok Publishing,* and *Samjoko Magazine,* among other publications. He can be followed on Twitter @ob_jato.

Pauline Yates, The Museum of Inspiration

Pauline Yates lives in Queensland, Australia, and writes horror and dark speculative fiction. She's an Australian Shadows Awards short fiction finalist, and her AHWA-winning short story, "The Best Medicine", was translated for the *Mondi Incantati* series produced by Riflessi di Luce Lunare (RiLL), Italy. Her short stories appear or are forthcoming in numerous anthologies and magazines, and her debut YA sci-fi novel is due for release in 2023. When not writing, which rarely happens because thinking about her stories is the same thing, she enjoys connecting with nature and taking photos of the sunrise. Links to her website and publications can be found here: https://linktr.ee/paulineyates.

Ryan Cole, The Museum of Living Color

Ryan Cole is a speculative fiction writer who lives in Virginia with his husband and snuggly pug child. He is a winner of the 2021 Writers of the Future contest, and his work has appeared in *Writers of the Future, Vol. 37, Ember Journal*, and the anthology *Mother: Tales of Love & Terror* by Weird Little Worlds Press. Find out more at www.ryancolewrites.com.

Alexander Danner, The Museum of Fog

Alexander Danner is a writer in various media, including prose fiction and comics, and two textbooks about comics, but these days primarily writes audio drama. He is co-creator of the serial audio drama *Greater Boston* (www.GreaterBostonShow.com), and is a script writer on the forthcoming audio adaptation of the classic indie comic series *ElfQuest*, by Wendy and Richard Pini. His fiction has appeared in various literary magazines, as well as in the science fiction anthologies *Machine of Death* and *The Girl at the End of the World*. He teaches at Emerson College.

He is also the sound designer of the serial audio drama What's the Frequency?, and a contributing sound designer on *Unwell: A Midwestern Gothic Mystery*.

Alexander vaguely recalls a brief middle-school stint volunteering at the Long Island Museum of Natural History. Very vaguely. What did he do while he was there? Unknown. It is a mystery.

Eve Morton, The Museum Nihilo

Eve Morton is an author writing from Waterloo, Ontario, Canada. She has two sons, a partner, a lot of coffee, and a PhD in English Literature. When not chasing kids around, she's reading audiobooks and trying to write something. Her latest novel is the LGBTQ thriller *The Serenity Nearby*.

Marisca Pichette, The Museum of Glass

Once a museum educator, Marisca Pichette now spends her time collecting interesting pieces of glass, bones, and other fragments. More of her work can be found in *Strange Horizons, Fireside Magazine, Fusion Fragment, Apparition Lit, PseudoPod*, and *PodCastle*, among others. Her speculative poetry collection, *Rivers in Your Skin, Sirens in Your Hair*, is out now from Android Press. Find her on Twitter as @MariscaPichette and Instagram as @marisca_write.

Nathan Milner, The Museum of Shifting Histories

Nathan Milner has pursued writing for decades as a journalist, copywriter, marketer, and novelist. His middle-grade novels include the *Dinosorcerers* series. Nathan lives with his wife and two daughters in rural Northeastern Pennsylvania.

Lori J. Torone, The Museum of Hydrological Phenomena

Lori J. Torone is a fantasy writer whose work has appeared or is forthcoming in *Metaphorosis, Podcastle*, and *99 Fleeting Fantasies*. Her independently published work, including the collection *Through the Oak Door*, can be found on Amazon under Lori Fitzgerald. She is an adjunct professor in her alma mater, St. Joseph's University, Brooklyn, in the English and Speech departments. She lives in New York with her two teenagers and small rescue dog. Her favorite museum is The Met Cloisters in Fort Tryon Park. Connect with Lori on Twitter @MedievalLit.

Vaughan Stanger, The Museum of the High Street

After a brief stint as an astronomer and then a much longer one as research project manager in a defence and aerospace engineering company, Vaughan Stanger now writes science fiction and fantasy full-time. Having wandered around many museums in his time, he is now shocked to discover that he is old enough to be an exhibit. Vaughan's stories have appeared in *Daily Science Fiction, Abyss & Apex, Nature Futures,* and *Interzone*, amongst others. His most recent collection is *The Last Moonshot and Other Stories*. Several of his stories have been translated into foreign languages. Follow Vaughan's writing adventures at www.vaughanstanger.com or @VaughanStanger.

Mark Keane, The Museum of Unpopular Art

Mark Keane has taught for many years in universities in the UK and North America. Recent short-story fiction has appeared in *Granfalloon, Terror House, upstreet, A Thin Slice of Anxiety, Liquid Imagination, Superpresent, Night Picnic, Firewords, Into the Void, the Dark Lane,* and *What Monsters Do for Love* anthologies, and *Best Indie Speculative Fiction 2021*. He lives in Edinburgh (Scotland).

Joanna Horrocks, The Museum of Forsaken Things

Joanna Horrocks is a writer, a photographer/digital artist, and a clinical psychologist. Her work has appeared in speculative fiction and literary mags and journals, anthologies, and on television (as Joanna Pashdag). Some of her favorite childhood memories are of getting lost in multiple museums up and down the East Coast. Today, she can be found on Twitter and on Post @JoannaHorrocks, on Mastodon as @JoannaHorrocks@zirk.us, and at home in Honolulu with an almost alarming number of free-range geckos and the occasional semi-feral cat.

Laurel Beckley, The Museum of Perpetual Service

Laurel Beckley is a writer, Marine Corps veteran, and librarian. She is from Oregon, and currently lives in northern Virginia with her wife, fur creatures, and a collection of gently neglected houseplants. Once upon a time, she was a docent at a military museum that uses life casts instead of mannequins, but the life casts are a little different than in this story.

Chloe Smith, The Museum of Fine Regrets

Chloe Smith has degrees in both history and library science, so thinking about museums was really only the next logical step. Despite her training, she works as a middle school teacher, moonlights as a proofreader for *Fantasy Magazine*, and writes science fiction and fantasy stories whenever she can make the time. Her fiction has appeared in *Metaphorosis* and *Daily Science Fiction*, among other places, and her debut novella, *Virgin Land*, is coming out from Luna Press

Publishing in 2023. She lives in the San Francisco Bay Area, which is also home to her favorite museum, the Oakland Museum of California.

Kring Demetrio, cover art

Kring Demetrio is a self-taught illustrator based in Cebu, Philippines. She draws inspiration from reading folkloric stories and popular myths. Deeply embedded in her drawings are etchings made from empty ballpoint pens and wooden skewers; usually depicting lines and other decorative images. Her work can be found in magazines, tabletop games, children's books, album covers, and gallery shows. She lives with her partner and their cats.

See more of her work at www.thedrawerkring.com

COPYRIGHT

Publisher

Joyful Heave is an imprint of
Metaphorosis Publishing
Neskowin, OR, USA

www.metaphorosis.com

"Metaphorosis" is a registered trademark.

Discounts available

Substantial discounts are available for educational institutions, including writing workshops. Discounts are also available for quantity purchases. For details, contact Metaphorosis at metaphorosis.com/about

METAPHOROSIS PUBLISHING

Metaphorosis offers beautifully written science fiction and fantasy. Our imprints include:

Metaphorosis Magazine

Plant Based Press

Verdage

Vestige

Joyful Heave

You can also find us:
@Metaphorosis@writing.exchange (Mastodon)
@Metaphorosis (Twitter)
www.facebook.com/metaphorosis

Help keep Metaphorosis running at
Patreon.com/metaphorosis

See more about some of our books on the following pages.

Metaphorosis
a magazine of speculative fiction

Metaphorosis is an online speculative fiction magazine dedicated to quality writing. We publish an original story every week, along with author bios, interviews, and notes on story origins.

We also publish monthly print and e-book issues, as well as yearly Best of and Complete anthologies.

See us online at magazine.Metaphorosis.com.

Vegan-friendly science fiction and fantasy, including anthologies of the year's best SFF stories, from 2016-2020.

Chambers of the Heart
speculative stories
by
B. Morris Allen

A heart that's a building, a dog that's a program, a woman sinking irretrievably — stories about love, loss, and movement.

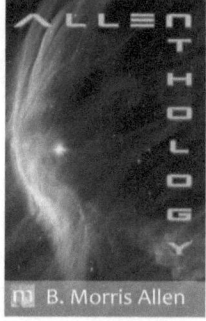

Susurrus

A darkly romantic story of magic, love, and suffering.

Allenthology: Volume I

Including three full collections of SFF stories.

Science fiction and fantasy books for writers – full of great stories, often with an additional focus on the craft of speculative fiction writing.

Reading 5X5 x3

Changes

How do stories move from 'maybe' to published?

Here are 15 case studies of stories published in *Metaphorosis* magazine.

Reading 5X5 x2

Duets

How do authors' voices change when they collaborate?

A round-robin of five talented science fiction and fantasy authors collaborating with each other and writing solo.

Including stories by Evan Marcroft, David Gallay, J. Tynan Burke, L'Erin Ogle, and Douglas Anstruther.

Score

an SFF symphony

An anthology with an emotional score from the heights of joy to the depths of despair – but always with a little hope shining through.

Reading 5X5

Five stories, five times

See how different writers take on the same material.

Reading 5X5

Writers' Edition

Two extra stories, the story seed, and authors' notes on writing.

Vestige

Novelettes, novellas, and novels by Metaphorosis authors.

The Nocturnals
Mariah Montoya

Night is Dangerous. Day is deadly.
Where day and night last thirty years, humans move constantly stay ahead of the night and cruel Nocturnals that call it home. But a boy is lost out there.